I0552855

Under The Gun

Hellhounds Series: Book 1

Theo Mann

The Invisible Publishing Company

Hellhounds Series

Contents

Chapter 1

C aptain Owen LeMaine leaned in close and bellowed into his SIC's ear to make himself heard over the deafening wind. "The drop zone should be all clear, but don't take any chances. Cover your ass even before you get on the ground. Understand?"

Lieutenant Eliot Polasek gave LeMaine a thumbs-up, but he didn't waste his breath trying to answer. A thick, pressurized glass mask covered his face and welded to the helmet encasing his skull. It attached seamlessly to a black suit enclosing the rest of his body.

LeMaine turned his attention to the rest of his squad. The Hellhounds crouched in a row behind Polasek and LeMaine mentally checked and rechecked their drop gear, too.

He went down the row doing a quick head count—his fiftieth for this hour alone. Polasek. Heckler. Kellogg. Lemon. Nunn. O'Hara. Peterman. LeMaine trusted each of them not to make a mistake with their equipment or their orders, but LeMaine couldn't help checking anyway.

As soon as he got to the end of the line, they moved forward to the spacecraft *Renown's* rear hatch. The hatch stood open to the atmosphere and the pounding wind tore at their suits. Only their safety anchors stopped the wind from ripping the squad out into orbit.

LeMaine held onto the railing running the length of the ship's hull and climbed his way to the cockpit. Corporal Kent Monk wrestled the stick while dozens of screens displayed the ship's location on the dashboard.

LeMaine read their position on Monk's instruments. One navigation panel showed a chart of the planet Ziea spread out below them, but LeMaine couldn't see anything in the darkness outside the cockpit window. Night and cloud obscured the surface far below.

Another chart displayed the layout of this solar system all the way back to Elia itself. Dozens of planets, moons, stations, satellites, and outposts dotted the system between here and home, but to LeMaine and every other Elian, Elia would always be the center of the universe.

Two other systems flanked this one on either side. Elia enjoyed a friendly diplomatic relationship with the Axichis. The Imoliv...not so much, but at least a buffer zone separated the Elian system from the Imoliv's hostility.

None of that concerned LeMaine. He wasn't here to solve the galaxy's problems. He swatted Monk's shoulder and waved the hulking pilot toward the back. Monk activated the autopilot and unclipped his safety harness.

He climbed out of his seat and the autopilot took over. The *Renown* adjusted her attitude and then held steady.

Monk pulled his helmet over his scruffy spiked hair and it locked into his suit collar. He had to stoop to get out of the cockpit that was way too small for him.

He followed LeMaine back to the hatch where Monk took his place at the end of the line. Now all the Hellhounds were in one place. LeMaine made one more check of all their equipment before he fought his way hand over hand to the front of the line.

He pulled down his own helmet and turned back to his squad. Each of his people gave him a thumbs up and he gave it back. This was it. He checked a digital read-out on the wrist of his suit sleeve. It was time. No more messing around.

He turned to the open hatch, took a running leap, and dove out into open space. He resisted the urge to look back and make sure the rest of the Hellhounds copied him. He didn't need to check, but he still found himself questioning if they all got away all right.

The next instant, he struck the atmosphere with colossal force. The wind pounded his suit and gravity dragged him toward the planet at terminal velocity.

He instinctively curled into a ball and tucked his face mask against his shoulder. He'd executed more of these drops in his career than he could count. He didn't even think about them anymore.

The next instant, delicious heat spread over his arms, back, and thighs, but he didn't dare to uncurl enough to look out. His suit took the punishing heat of falling through the atmosphere. One wrong move would either incinerate him on entry or the impact would tear his limbs off.

He held that position as the noise and bombardment reached an epic pitch. Just when he couldn't stand it a second longer, a vibrating alarm buzzed on his wrist.

He flung out his arms and legs with all his strength. Webbing extended from his suit and the high-tensile fabric caught the atmosphere. It slowed him and he started to soar through the high clouds.

He still couldn't see anything beyond his mask. He had no way of knowing if he was even over the right continent to make the drop zone.

The moment he extended his suit, a grid blinked on inside his mask. It displayed the same navigation chart from the *Renown* with himself and his eight subordinates zooming toward the drop zone.

LeMaine adjusted the wings of his suit and steered toward the drop zone while he checked the altimeter on his wrist. He was only a thousand feet above the ground.

True to his word, he extended both wrists toward the ground and clenched his fists. Twin weapons locked outward from hidden slots in his suit and he swept them across the blackness beneath him.

He adjusted the display on his mask with a quick shake of his head. No life signs showed up down there, but that could be a mistake.

All kinds of alien life inhabited the planets in the Elia solar system. Some were friendly and some not. Elian scientists kept discovering new species every day.

Ziea might be home to any number of dangerous creatures that the Elians' technology couldn't detect yet. If anyone was down there, he wouldn't know it until after they had already shot him out of the sky.

That thought made him steer faster toward the ground. He had to get down there and get this damn suit off quickly. He wouldn't feel safe until he checked the area with his own eyes.

His helmet's internal instruments revealed a dense forest concealing the drop zone. He measured his descent, but he still wound up crashing through the canopy and snapping off several branches on his landing.

He plummeted the last hundred feet, braked with his wings, and with one last scan of the ground, he dropped between tall trees. His feet hit the sod and he ran the last little way to slow his momentum.

As soon as he stopped running, he stripped off his helmet and wheeled in all directions. He passed his weapons back and forth over the surroundings, but nothing sprang out to attack him. He listened. Nothing.

He finally let himself relax, but only a little bit. He had to rendezvous with the squad.

He slotted his weapons back inside his sleeves, grabbed the zipper pull open his suit, and peeled it off to reveal his combat fatigues underneath. A loaded backpack hugged his spine with two large Crossfire carbines strapped to its sides.

He squatted down, crammed his suit into his pack, and unbuckled his weapons keeping a close watch on the surroundings all the time. He couldn't take any chances on this planet.

Ziea was the last stop on the way out into open space. Colonization efforts from Elia didn't always make it out this far. The planet only had one human colony at the last census. Even that might be misleading considering how long it took information to travel this distance.

The native alien inhabitants operated under their own rules. Intelligence on exactly what those rules were did NOT make it back to Elia. The Hellhounds were going in blind, deaf, and dumb with no clue what might be waiting for them.

Only one piece of useful information made it back to Elian Military Command. Some of the aliens on the planet had organized themselves into a criminal syndicate amassing weapons and supplies.

They openly stated their aim to overrun the local colony outpost, take control of the planet for themselves, and turn it into their own private little kingdom.

How far they'd gotten in accomplishing that goal was anybody's guess. The Elian Military had gotten tied up in other operations around the system, so the Hellhounds got called in to straighten out the mess.

The Hellhounds always got called in to straighten out the mess in one way or another. That was the Hellhounds' job. The elite squad of commandos could go in where the regular Elian Military feared to tread.

Then the Hellhounds did what they did best. They rained fire and brimstone on whoever needed fire and brimstone rained on them.

LeMaine double-checked the cartridges of Crossfire gel that provided power to his carbines. He satisfied himself that his weapons were ready to fire at a moment's notice.

He slung on his backpack, hung one carbine over his shoulder, and grasped the other. He also took a moment to check his sidearms and to pat the cuff of his pants leg where he kept his survival knife.

He glanced down at his wrist. A remote panel in his jacket sleeve showed him another navigation display. Eight life signs appeared on it—all human.

He set off toward the nearest cluster where Monk, Nunn, and Polasek had already gathered. The others converged on that location, too.

LeMaine strained to see anything else in the dark. He passed his weapon from right to left and cursed Elian technology for leaving him blind on this planet. Was anything out there? Was anything dangerous stalking him right now?

He kept checking his position in between sweeps until he spotted the three squad members ahead. He heard Corporal Molly Nunn laughing. The sound annoyed LeMaine until he finally got close enough to see them.

LeMaine relaxed when he discovered Monk, Nunn, and Polasek standing back to back in a tight circle. They aimed their weapons outward into the darkness while they migrated down a long hill toward the gully at the bottom.

Monk spun around and aimed his weapon at LeMaine in the dark. Monk's deep-chested bellow rang through the forest. "Stop right there! Don't come any closer! Elian Special Forces! Identify yourself!"

"Stand down, Corporal," LeMaine replied. "It's only me."

Monk jerked his gun upward to aim at the sky. "Jesus, Sir! You scared the shit out of me."

"And there's a lot of shit to scare out of a barge like you, isn't there?" Nunn quipped over her shoulder. "Did you see anything out there, Sir?"

LeMaine turned his back to the group and squinted into the darkness. "Nothing. I guess it really is deserted."

"What do you want to do next?" Polasek checked his remote and nodded toward the gully. "I don't like the look of *that*. We'd be sitting ducks down there."

"I agree," LeMaine replied. "Stand fast here until the others catch up."

The four soldiers stopped walking, but none of them let their guard down or lower their weapons. LeMaine took advantage of his squad's cover to check his remote more closely.

Polasek was right about the gully. It turned out to be a lot steeper than the charts led LeMaine to believe. He didn't want to go down there even if it did offer the most direct route to the squad's destination.

His remote identified two more squad members coming closer them, and in a minute, Lieutenant Stuart Peterman and Corporal Brien O'Hara appeared out of the shadows.

O'Hara's brilliant blue eyes and white-blonde hair showed up even in this darkness. He posed such a stark contrast to Peterman's slighter, darker outline.

"Stop right there! Don't come any closer!" Monk bellowed. "Elian Special Forces! Identify......"

Nunn slapped his shoulder. "Will you knock that off? You can see on your remote who they are. Shit, Monk! Dust the cobwebs out of your brain."

"He's got a permanent cobweb-generating factory in there," O'Hara chimed in. "The minute he dusts out one batch, his internal silkworms start spinning a new...."

"Bag it, Sergeant," LeMaine cut in. "Pay attention, all of you. We're on assignment here." He checked the last three readings on his remote. "What's keeping those three?"

"They aren't moving," Peterman observed. "Something might be wrong."

"Maybe Lemon fell down a rabbit hole," O'Hara blurted out and then fell silent when LeMaine glared at him.

"Kellogg is with them," Polasek added. "Maybe one of them is hurt."

"You want me to go check, Sir?" Nunn asked.

"No. We all need to stay together from now on. Come on. They aren't that far away."

LeMaine set off into the dark and the squad arranged themselves behind him. O'Hara and Peterman fell in on either side and slightly behind LeMaine followed by Nunn and Monk. Polasek brought up the rear.

The squad took an arrow formation with LeMaine at the point. He alternately strained his eyes to see into the dark and to check his people's position. The three remaining squad members still hadn't moved.

He was starting to fear the worst when he found them. Sure enough, tiny Corporal Krista Lemon sat on the ground with her legs stretched out in front of her. She still hadn't taken off her suit and she kept her weapons extended while she checked the surroundings.

The squad's medic, Sergeant Mason Kellogg, bent over her lower left leg and she grimaced in pain every time he touched her. Corporal Glenn Heckler stood guard over the pair and aimed his weapon outward to scan the dark forest.

Heckler swung his carbine to aim at the sky when LeMaine and the others pulled up. "What's the problem, Sergeant?" LeMaine asked.

"No problem, Sir," Kellogg replied over his shoulder. "Just a broken ankle. I can have her on her feet in a sec."

"I told you she fell down a rabbit hole," O'Hara muttered in the background.

"I didn't fall down a goddamn rabbit hole, you jackass!" Lemon spat. "If you don't cut the snappy jokes, I swear to Christ, I'll...."

"How did it happen?" LeMaine interrupted.

Lemon shrugged and lowered her sharp black eyes. She winced when Kellogg did something to her leg. "I couldn't see a goddamn thing coming in to the drop zone. I checked the chart, but there must have been something there it didn't pick up. I hit a branch or something on the way in. That's all."

LeMaine squeezed her shoulder. "No harm done. It could have happened to any of us. Sit tight and let Kellogg work it out for you." He walked over to Heckler. "Any sign out there?"

"Nope." The big, burly Marine moved his tongue around in his mouth like he was chewing something. "I didn't exactly do a scientific survey of the place, though. I landed a few hundred yards over there and heard Lemon cursing, so I came over here to check it out. I've been here ever since."

"You'd likely hear Lemon cursing even if she didn't break her ankle," Nunn told him.

"Suck it, bitch!" Lemon snarled and Nunn burst out laughing.

Polasek and Peterman wandered over to LeMaine's side. "What about it, Sir?" Polasek asked. "Any ideas on our route?"

All three men consulted their remotes. "The sun will be up in a few hours," LeMaine remarked. "Let's follow this ridge along the gully. We'll at least be heading in the right direction and visibility will be better up here."

A high-pitched whine drew everyone's attention back to Kellogg and Lemon. The medic attached an electronic device to Lemon's leg and, with one extra loud crackling buzz, it injected a powerful jolt into her shin.

She gritted her teeth and convulsed in rapid spasms. Her eyes rolled back in their sockets and she jerked backward to flop on the ground. Her head lolled and she went limp.

Nunn puffed out her cheeks. "Phew! I will never understand how she does that without screaming."

"She's tougher than she looks." Kellogg removed the bone electrolyzer from Lemon's shin and pulled a high-powered pressure syringe from his pack. "Now for the antidote."

He pressed it to Lemon's shoulder and it hissed when it injected the antidote into her muscle. She lay still for a second and then, without warning, she shot upright like a rocket. "Holy fucking shit! Son of a bitch, you fucking cocksuckers!"

Nunn turned away. "And she's back."

LeMaine squeezed Lemon's shoulder again. "On your feet, Sergeant. We're moving out."

Heckler spun around and extended his hand to Lemon. She grasped his wrist and he hoisted her to her feet while Kellogg packed up his gear.

Lemon tested her ankle and then started stripping off her suit in a hurry. She barely came up to Heckler's chest and most of the squad towered over her, but no one ever doubted Lemon's toughness. She could take nearly anyone in the squad in a fight except maybe Monk.

The rest of the squad stood around and waited while she finished organizing her gear. She finally locked her carbine into position. "Ready, Sir."

"Let's move it out," LeMaine ordered and he led the way down the ridge.

Chapter 2

Polasek hustled up to LeMaine's side. "So.... where are we supposed to meet this supposed diplomat?"

"Your guess is as good as mine. She's running around somewhere on this damn planet."

Polasek snorted. "That narrows it down. Do we even know what the hell she looks like?"

"Nope," LeMaine replied over his shoulder. "We don't even know what species she is."

"Oh, joy," Polasek sneered. "That should make her super easy to identify. How do we know she isn't working for the other side?"

"There is no other side here, Lieutenant. They're all our enemies."

"Even the colonists?"

LeMaine shrugged. "Just because they're human doesn't make them our friends. These colonists have been living outside Elian society for generations and we don't know anything about their culture. They could have gone even farther off the rails than the aliens."

"Whoever the aliens turn out to be," Polasek muttered.

Just then, a shout went up behind them. O'Hara stood at the far end of their formation and pointed down the ridge over the terrain the squad had just covered.

LeMaine and the other Hellhounds assembled around O'Hara and followed his gaze. Broad daylight lit up the whole landscape, but no matter how often they searched their surroundings, the squad still didn't see anyone. They didn't even see anything moving—no animals, no insects—nothing.

"Holy f-in' crap!" Heckler snarled. "They're heading straight for us!'

Nunn furrowed her brow at a cluster of figures winding through the forest where the squad just dropped. "What the hell is that? Are they even human?"

Peterman consulted his remote. "They aren't human. They're Maczhi."

"Speak English for once in your life," Lemon snapped.

"We don't care what species they are," Kellogg chimed in. "Just tell us if they're dangerous."

"They're listed in the Academy of Sciences database," Peterman explained. "The colonists mentioned them and the Elian Assembly granted the Maczhi citizenship seventy years ago, but that's all we know about them. The Academy doesn't even have a description of them."

Heckler rolled his eyes to Heaven and groaned. "Could this damn mission be any more of a fiasco? How the holy hell are we supposed to deal with them if we don't know if they're hostile or not?"

"They don't seem to be speeding up to intercept us," Polasek remarked. "Maybe they just want to talk to us."

"Keep wishing that, genius," O'Hara chimed in. "Let me ask you this. If a bunch of armed alien strangers plunged through the atmosphere to land on your planet, would you just stroll up to them in the middle of nowhere to talk to them? Excuse me if I don't believe that."

"You're right, champ. We need a sniper." LeMaine swatted O'Hara's shoulder. "Go get into position....and take Nunn and Monk with you. Flank us and get a bead on them. Stand ready to return fire if they get hostile."

"What are *you* gonna do, Sir?" Kellogg asked. "Don't tell me you're gonna stand out here and wait to be shot."

Nunn snorted. "That would definitely alert us to their intentions, wouldn't it?"

"I told you to go get into position," LeMaine repeated. "Lemon, you take Heckler and Kellogg over there. Stay in sight, but be ready to counterattack if anything goes wrong. Peterman, you stay here with me and Polasek."

Polasek and Peterman flanked LeMaine facing the strangers who got closer by the minute. The group of bodies flashed between the trees and became more visible as they got nearer.

They stood erect and walked bipedally, but their arms were too long to be human and their large heads bobbed from side to side when they walked.

A second later, they emerged from the undergrowth at the base of the ridge. They started climbing it on a direct intercept route for the squad and LeMaine saw instantly that they were all armed. Some carried Elian carbines, but most sported smaller weapons of some make he didn't recognize.

LeMaine tightened his grip on his gun, but he fought down the urge to raise it. He still didn't know if these aliens meant him and his squad any harm.

Like O'Hara said, these aliens would be stupid to confront strangers without protecting themselves. Them carrying weapons didn't mean they were enemies. At least, LeMaine hoped not.

Peterman cleared his throat and murmured in LeMaine's ear. "They're malnourished, Sir. See their eyes?"

LeMaine scrambled to figure out what Peterman meant. Then he saw it. Some milky, greenish-tinged substance oozed from their eyes and some of the creatures had difficulty walking up the hill.

The Maczhi reached the ridge and turned down it to meet the squad. The Maczhi lowered their weapons as they got nearer and LeMaine matched them, but he didn't relax his stance.

A few Maczhi fell even farther behind as they got nearer. They must be really weak. The whole group seemed far more concerned with casting furtive looks at the countryside than making sure the squad didn't harm them.

The tallest, strongest Maczhi halted in front of LeMaine, Peterman, and Polasek. The creature turned its milky eyes from one man to the next and then nodded. "Elian?"

"That's right," Peterman replied. "This is Captain Owen LeMaine of the Elian Military Command. This is Lieutenant Eliot Polasek and I'm Lieutenant Stuart Peterman. What's your name?"

The creature let out a shaky sigh and the arm holding its weapon drooped at its side as though it just couldn't hold the thing up a second longer. "My name.... issss...."

The alien buckled without getting the words out. It collapsed on the ground at LeMaine's feet. LeMaine inhaled a breath to call out for Kellogg when, at that moment, a rocket whistled overhead and smashed into the ridge behind the aliens.

LeMaine and his men jerked up their weapons ready to blow somebody away, but the shot didn't come from the Maczhi. It came from the far end of the ridge in the direction the Hellhounds had been walking to begin with.

LeMaine spun around fast as five more rockets screamed out of the sky. They came from miles away, arced high in the sky, and plastered the ridge crawling closer to the party all the time.

"Get off the ridge!" LeMaine bellowed. "Get down into the gully!"

Monk, Nunn, and O'Hara charged out of their hiding place. Monk leveled his carbine at the slumped Maczhi, half of whom didn't move when the bombardment started.

Peterman caught Monk's arms just in time. "Don't shoot! Can't you see they're helpless?"

Polasek waved the three down the hill toward the gully. "They were a distraction!"

"No!" LeMaine grabbed Lemon, Kellogg, and Heckler, who raced forward to follow LeMaine's orders. "Help me! Come on! Pick them up!"

Lemon hesitated, but when LeMaine got under the big Maczhi's shoulder and heaved him to his feet, the rest of the squad copied him.

Monk slung his carbine across his big barrel chest and picked up another two Maczhi, one in each arm. Heckler also picked up one of the stricken aliens and the rest of the squad dove in to help.

Missiles shrieked down on them and erupted in the sod. LeMaine dodged explosions, tripped under the Maczhi's weight, and staggered onward to get off the ridge as fast as possible.

He finally stumbled into the gully, but the rocket blasts only followed the squad there. "Come on! This way!" He took off at a run in the direction they had been following the ridge to begin with.

"Captain!" Kellogg called from behind.

LeMaine craned his head around to see Kellogg squatting next to one of the Maczhi. The creature wasn't moving and LeMaine didn't see it breathing, either.

LeMaine hesitated. How did he know these Maczhi weren't the ones he was supposed to make contact with? That dying creature might be the diplomat LeMaine was ordered to rendezvous with to complete this mission.

He opened his mouth to order Kellogg to leave the alien behind when a devastating smash blasted the gully apart right in front of Kellogg. The impact ripped the medic away from the Maczhi's body and Kellogg went flying backward.

He smacked into Heckler. The big Marine spun around, dropped his Maczhi, seized Kellogg by the collar, and yanked Kellogg out of range of another explosion.

Kellogg toppled off his feet and slammed down on the ground next to Heckler. Heckler slung his alien over his shoulder before he grabbed another fistful on Kellogg's fatigues. He wrestled Kellogg to his feet and they both took off running down the gully to catch up with LeMaine and the others.

LeMaine scanned the area in front of him for any sign of danger. The Maczhi he was helping turned out to be a lot heavier than he looked and LeMaine couldn't exactly defend himself with his hands full.

The next time he raced around one of the gully's many corners, he lowered the alien to the ground. "Put them down over here," he told his people. "Get into position and stand ready to defend each other."

Monk sealed his carbine to his cheek and jerked the barrel from side to side and up at the ridgetop. "Where are they, Sir?" he panted. "I didn't see them."

"Neither did I, but we can't leave ourselves exposed for these people."

The rest of the squad deposited their new friends in a pile and then the Hellhounds surrounded them with their weapons aimed outward.

LeMaine pulled Peterman over to the big Maczhi who first addressed them. "Who attacked us?" Peterman called down into the creature's face. "Where is the bombardment coming from?"

The creature's damp eyes swam open and he struggled to make himself heard. Blasts kept hammering the ridge walls and raining dirt and clods on the Hellhounds' heads.

"Did they attack us or you?" Peterman yelled over the noise. "Who is shooting at us? Where are they?"

The creature pointed up the gully. "Colonists.... Coming from the colony."

LeMaine froze and Peterman spun around to stare at him. The colonists! Did the human Elian colonists attack a squad of the Elian Military? If they did, the situation on this planet must have deteriorated much farther than anyone realized.

"Cezian......" the Maczhi husked. "Cezian coming.... from...." He pointed down the gully where the squad and the Maczhi first arrived.

Peterman swallowed hard and straightened up. He pursed his lips, took a fresh grip on his carbine, and turned away to take his place between Heckler and Lemon.

LeMaine took one more desperate look around. He didn't want anyone to know how much this information disturbed him. He secretly sent up a prayer of gratitude to the Gods of Combat that only Peterman had heard what the Maczhi said.

The Hellhounds couldn't possibly mistake the Cezians for friendlies. They had infiltrated Elia from the Cezian system and the Cezians had caused no end of trouble on every planet they infested. Now they were here.

More rocket blasts devastated the gully, but when LeMaine shook his head clear, he noticed that the explosions didn't come near the squad. The shots started to inch farther up the gully toward the squad's drop zone. Whoever was shooting off these rockets must be trying to hit the Cezians.

LeMaine squatted down and got his face right near the big Maczhi. "We have to go! You can come with us if you can walk, but we can't carry you anymore. We can defend you, but you have to walk! Understand?"

The creature opened and closed its eyes with impossible slowness. LeMaine couldn't wait any longer. He straightened up, checked his carbine, and batted Heckler's elbow. "Move it out! This way!"

He charged down the gully putting as much distance between himself and the Cezians as he could. How far away were they?

He glanced over his shoulder to check on his squad and saw seven Maczhi loping along behind them.

The colonists must have been bombarding the Cezians and LeMaine didn't blame them, so he headed in the direction from which the rockets were launching. Monk and Kellogg brought up the rear and kept swiveling backward to guard the squad, but no Cezians appeared. Where were they?

The gully ended where the ridge met another rise. LeMaine charged up it and saw that he was right. Rockets soared over the squad to detonate in the forests. Dust and dirt shot out of the trees every time a rocket struck its target. With any luck, the Cezians would be back there somewhere.

LeMaine checked his people and then the Maczhi before he pushed forward at a fast walk. Kellogg changed his position to keep pace with the Maczhi. He took a medical scanner out of his pack and scanned the aliens on the march.

Peterman dropped back to the big Maczhi's side. "You didn't tell me your name."

"Zadae," the creature rasped. "My name is Zadae."

"Where do you come from?" Peterman asked.

The creature pointed behind him. "The mountains. Our people...."

An ear-splitting screech cut him off. LeMaine whipped around with every hair on end and his blood ran cold as a swarm of Cezians charged over the nearest rise.

The first wave planted themselves on the hilltop and unloaded fusion rifles down on the squad. Lemon dropped to her knee and jammed her carbine into her shoulder.

She spat a fountain of shots up the hill and cut down half the aliens, but at the same time, another mob flooded over the peak and descended on the squad en masse.

The Cezians' horrible scaly faces, horned skulls, and many eyes set off an instinctive reaction in LeMaine. He lunged for Lemon and dragged her away. The first assault cut down five Maczhi, but LeMaine didn't turn back. He couldn't let his squad fall to these cutthroats.

He shouldered his carbine and passed it back and forth to clear a path for the retreating squad. He mowed down every Cezian he could see and herded his people farther into this endless wilderness.

His only hope for survival was to find the colonists. If they had rockets, maybe they had enough weaponry to hold the Cezians at bay.

Monk, Heckler, and Nunn appeared at LeMaine's sides and added their fire to his. The Cezians dropped back before the squad's assault, but only for a second.

A moment later, another colossal wave of Cezians charged out of nowhere. They completely ignored the danger and ran straight into the Hellhounds' fire.

Monk backed up another step and bumped into Lemon. Lemon, Kellogg, and O'Hara stood in a line at a right angle to Nunn, Monk, LeMaine, and Heckler. The other three Hellhounds had to fight to their utmost just to stop the enemy from surrounding them.

Peterman and Polasek defended the other side, but it was all useless against so many Cezians. The aliens flooded the squads' position and then, impossibly, the Cezians rushed around the squad.

The Cezians let out a blood-curdling war cry and abandoned the squad entirely. LeMaine spun around following them with his weapon, but the Cezians paid no attention to him and his squad.

The Cezians flooded down another gully all running the same direction. LeMaine's stomach dropped when he spotted a large walled village constructed into the gully itself. Two enormous stone walls four feet thick blocked it off in front and behind. The gully walls formed the other two sides of the broad square.

Rooves and houses squatted behind the walls and ten enormous thermal cannons perched on top. Strange creatures manned the guns. Each one wore a hideous mask with giant black eye circles. LeMaine took a second to realize they were human beings wearing protective gear. These must be the colonists.

The Cezians attacked the walls and started clambering up the stones to reach the cannons. LeMaine reacted in an instant, jerked up his weapon, and unloaded on the Cezians from behind.

The colonists swiveled their cannons downward and opened fire on the Cezians, too. Thermal blasts scorched the ground cutting the Cezians off the walls. The colonists cleared dozens of attackers, but more Cezians materialized out of nowhere.

They climbed on top of their comrades' dismembered bodies and started to gain the top.

"Advance!" LeMaine yelled to his squad. "Open fire!"

His people lined up on both sides and the Hellhounds stalked down the hill toward the compound. LeMaine took aim and plastered Cezians off the stack. The wall left them totally exposed and they tumbled down, dead.

Chapter 3

The gunners on the compound walls swung their thermal cannons up and trained the weapons on the Hellhounds. LeMaine held his carbine ready to shoot down any Cezians that dared to move. His brain lurched when he realized he was aiming directly at the colonists.

He lowered his carbine and called down the line. "Lower your weapons! Show your hands."

He let his gun drop onto its strap and raised his hands where the gunners could see them. "Elian Special Forces! We're here from the Elian Military Command! We're here to help you!"

The gunners didn't move. Their masks made them look like aliens themselves.

"What do you know?" O'Hara muttered. "I signed on to the Special Forces to travel to distant planets and get my head shot off by Elian citizens."

LeMaine raised his arms higher above his head. "I'm Captain Owen LeMaine of the Elian Military Command! We're responding to your distress call."

"Show us some ID!" one of the gunners called back in a gruff, deep-chested voice.

"Oh, no damn way!" Lemon snarled. "He did NOT just ask the captain for ID."

LeMaine kept his arms and hands extended where the gunners could see every move he made. He stripped back the left sleeve and held up his arm so the gunners could see the smooth white skin of his inner wrist.

The familiar flood of prickly heat burned his skin when the tattoo started to glow brightly enough for the gunners to see.

LeMaine couldn't read their expressions through their masks. They kept their weapons trained on him as steadily as ever.

LeMaine's mind started to shift gears. How could he get his people out of here before the gunners opened fire?

All at once, the guy who demanded to see his ID let go of his cannon, ripped off his mask, jerked sideways, and called down to someone on the ground. "Open the gate!"

Lemon started to raise her carbine to aim at the man, but Polasek stopped her and pushed her barrel down.

A deep rumble trembled the soil and the vibration went up LeMaine's legs as a giant section of the stone wall scraped back out of the way. It left a wide passage into the compound.

"Uh-uh," Lemon hissed. "We are NOT going in there, not after these dipshits demanded the captain's ID."

"Quiet!" LeMaine whispered. "Do you want to wait out here for the Cezians to come back? Get inside, all of you, and don't show any hostility to these people."

"Until you say so, right?" Heckler snarled under his breath.

"You said it, not me." LeMaine turned away and extended his hand to the tall man who hopped down from the wall to meet him.

"Thank you for helping us," the man began. "We've been waiting for reinforcements for over a year and a half."

LeMaine frowned. "Reinforcements? We aren't here to reinforce anything. We're here on a diplomatic mission."

"You said you were here to help us," the man countered. "You can only help us by helping us win the civil war."

LeMaine glanced over at Peterman, but the lieutenant only shrugged. "I don't know anything about any civil war," Peterman replied.

The tall man frowned, too, but at that moment, a scuffle broke out behind them. LeMaine turned to see a bunch of colonists trying to force the surviving Maczhi out of the compound.

The Maczhi put up a struggle and the colonists attacked them with venomous ferocity. One of the armed defenders started clubbing Zadae with a rifle. More colonists moved in to kick the Maczhi back outside the gate.

LeMaine strode over and forced himself between them. "Hold it! What are you doing?"

"This village is human only," the tall man cut in. "No aliens allowed." He turned to his people. "Throw them out. Quit messing around. Shoot them if you have to."

"Stop!" LeMaine snapped. "You can't just throw them out. They would be dead in seconds if the Cezians came back."

The tall man waved that away. "Not our problem. We have laws. We built this colony to keep the human bloodline pure. We don't allow any aliens inside our compound. That's our highest law."

"Humans and Maczhi aren't genetically compatible," Peterman interjected. "They can't interbreed with you and these Maczhi are on the verge of starvation. You have nothing to fear from them."

"We have laws for a reason." The tall man sliced his finger at his people. "You heard me. Get rid of them."

"No!" LeMaine lunged to intervene. He got between the Maczhi and the colonists, but a different group of colonists standing around watching pulled out weapons faster than any of the Hellhounds could react.

Three quick cracks rang out and the last Maczhi hit the dirt. LeMaine flung up his hands. "What the hell! You didn't have to do that!"

"I told you we did. Now, are you going to stand around all day or are you going to finish your mission by helping us?"

LeMaine narrowed his eyes at the man. LeMaine was already developed a powerful dislike for this scumbag. The man being another human and an Elian citizen meant exactly shit to LeMaine if the guy was going to act like this.

The tall man turned back to his people and started snapping orders at everyone. "Break down the camp. Pack up and get ready to move. Now that the Elian Military is here, it's time to prepare our offensive."

"What offensive?" LeMaine hesitated to ask. He didn't really want to know.

"Our offensive against the Cezians. Now that you're here, you can help us drive them out completely. We can finally win this war and claim Ziea for humans."

"I told you we aren't here to engage in any war," LeMaine cut in. "There are only nine of us. We wouldn't do you much good and we have a diplomatic mission to fulfill instead."

The tall man whirled around and glared at him. "What diplomatic mission? Don't tell me the Elian Command wants to negotiate with the Cezians. They're vermin."

Peterman came to LeMaine's side. "Excuse me, but it seems like we all got off on the wrong foot here. I'm Lieutenant Stuart Peterman and I'm the Command negotiator on this squad. I didn't catch your name."

The tall man scowled at Peterman and jerked his chin at LeMaine. "How can you be the negotiator when *he's* the one in charge?"

"That's just one of the crazy ways Command organizes our squad." Peterman stuck out his hand. "It's good to meet you."

The guy sneered at Peterman's hand and then indulged Peterman by shaking it. "Nelson Macon. Good to meet you."

Peterman's eyes snapped wide open and he gasped in such obvious surprise and delight that LeMaine could swear Peterman must be putting on an act. "*The* Nelson Macon? No way! I've read all about you. I read the whole database about your colony on Evilia. You're legendary!"

Macon brightened up instantly. "You know about that?"

"Sure! The whole diplomatic corps knows about that colony. I had no idea you were rebuilding out here." Peterman scanned the village with exaggerated amazement. "This place is incredible! You really pulled it out of the hat, didn't you?"

Macon swelled out his chest and his expression changed to one of pompous arrogance. "I make it my business to promote the human race's interests wherever I go. As soon as we rid this planet of all the alien scum, we can turn Ziea into a thriving hub to rival Elia itself."

Peterman beamed up at him. "That's wonderful. I really hope you succeed."

Macon glanced over at LeMaine and his expression hardened again. "If you aren't here to help us win the war, what *are* you doing here? If you try to negotiate with the Cezians, I'll have no choice but to treat you as our enemies."

"We aren't here to negotiate with the Cezians," Peterman told him. "We didn't even know the Cezians were on this planet."

"Who are you here to negotiate with, then?" Macon asked.

Peterman glanced over at LeMaine and a charge of understanding passed between the two men. Neither of them trusted this idiot further than they could throw him.

"We're here to rendezvous with an Elian diplomat," LeMaine replied. "She came here six months ago to finalize a citizenship agreement between the Elian Assembly and one of the alien groups on this planet."

Macon frowned. "The Elian Assembly can't extend citizenship to aliens. That's ridiculous."

LeMaine opened his mouth to argue back. He almost reminded this jackass that the Elian Assembly already included more than fifty alien species scattered all over the system, but Peterman cut him off.

"Who knows what the Elian Assembly is up to, right? Besides, this diplomat hasn't even met with the aliens in question yet, so it doesn't matter. All we have to do is find her. We don't have anything to say about what she does."

"What species is she offering citizenship?" Macon demanded. "It can't be the Maczhi."

"The Maczhi are already citizens, Einstein," Heckler growled from behind.

"The Maczhi are scum," Macon fired back. "They're too stupid and useless to be Elian citizens."

LeMaine bit back a powerful urge to slap this shithead's empty skull. "Like the lieutenant just said, we aren't here to negotiate with anyone. We're here to protect this diplomat and get her off the planet in one piece. Command lost contact with her and we have to find her."

Macon rubbed his chin thinking it over. "I know all the colonists here and I never heard of any diplomat."

"Maybe she isn't human," Lemon blurted out. "Did you ever think of that?"

LeMaine cringed, but at least Lemon didn't follow up the remark with a string of expletives like she usually did.

Macon thought it over and then shrugged again. "Well, you're here and you'll be falling back with us, so you can help us with the offensive. You might as well come inside and we can brief you on the situation."

He led the way deeper into the village. A few of the colonists eyed the Hellhounds, but most people were far too busy packing up their stuff. They even dismantled the houses and took the rooves apart piece by piece.

"I'll assign you quarters until we leave," Macon told LeMaine. "We can also fit you out with weapons better suited to the environment than those carbines. They don't really work in this atmosphere."

"They were working just fine a few minutes ago," LeMaine muttered.

He wasn't surprised when Macon ignored him. LeMaine made a mental note to pick Peterman's brain for everything the lieutenant could tell him about Macon, but LeMaine thought he already knew.

Macon was a fanatic, a human supremacist. He shot those Maczhi rather than give them a chance to leave the village alive.

So Macon built another colony on Evilia and now he was here. LeMaine could only think of two possible reasons why a guy like Macon would leave a thriving metropolis like Evilia to come to a backwater rock like this.

Either the Evilians drove him out for his obnoxious attitudes or Macon was so viru-lently anti-alien that he left of his own free will. He set up a colony here, on the outskirts of known space, so he could maintain the purity of the human bloodline.

A man like that wouldn't listen to reason. He'd be too irrational to admit that nine people couldn't make a difference in any war, especially not a war against the Cezians. Not even nine highly trained special forces operatives like the Hellhounds could do the impossible.

Macon would never believe that. He saw only his campaign against the Cezians and now he found himself Hellhounds to help his cause. Macon thought he could butter up LeMaine and hopefully win him over by being nice to him. Little did Macon know.

Macon confirmed LeMaine's worst fears by rambling on about the civil war as the group made their way between the many houses. "We used to have our own outpost down in the Grara Canyon, but when the Cezians attacked, we had to fall back up here. We built this compound while we regrouped for a counteroffensive."

"Why did the Cezians attack you?" Peterman asked over LeMaine's shoulder.

"Why do the Cezians do anything?" Macon countered. "They attacked. No one cares why they did it."

"The Cezians don't just attack armed outposts for no reason. They're too smart for that."

"Smart!" Macon snorted. "They're brainless. They're violent heathens. They don't care who they kill."

"You're wrong. They have never acted violently on any other planet until the residents attack the Cezians first. They must have had a reason to go after your outpost."

Macon shrugged that off. "We might have interfered with shipments of food and medical supplies coming from Elian Command that were slated for the Cezian colony, but we're the real Elian citizens. Why should Command supply the Cezians instead of us? Now the Cezians are using Command-supplied weapons against us."

LeMaine's jaw dropped. "You...stole.... Command food and medical supplies.... from the Cezians?" He rubbed his temples. "Sweet Jesus!"

"We needed those supplies more than they did. After we moved up here, we were working on a strain of virus we hoped would wipe them all out in one stroke, but some of our lab equipment got damaged so we had to give it up. We've been concentrating most of our efforts on lifting as many arms and ammunition as we can from the Maczhi."

LeMaine froze and gaped at the man in horrified disbelief. "You stole arms and ammunition from the Maczhi?"

"Sure. They weren't using them—not for anything useful."

"Were they using their weapons to defend themselves against the Cezians?" Peterman asked.

LeMaine clamped his eyes shut and swallowed hard. "Let me guess. You stole food and medical supplies from the Maczhi, too."

"Of course we did. They're alien scum. What were we supposed to do—let our own people starve?"

LeMaine pulled himself together and got a sick feeling in his stomach when he surveyed the compound with new eyes. "Do you have somewhere me and my people can sit down for a while? One of my people got injured on the way in and I want to check on her."

"Sure. Come this way."

Macon led the squad between a few more houses. LeMaine caught Peterman glancing at him, but LeMaine said nothing. He didn't want to think about how many intergalactic laws these so-called Elian citizens had broken.... or how many lives their lunacy had already cost.

Macon waved toward a courtyard between two large houses. "You can wait here. I'll organize a place for you to stay until we leave....and I'll have some weapons and supplies brought over for you."

Chapter 4

Nunn, Heckler, and Monk sat down on a bench against the nearest wall. They measured the surroundings and then propped their carbines within reach.

Heckler pulled out a huge hunting knife, picked up a stick from the ground, and started whittling it. He shaved off a splinter, smoothed it out, stuck the makeshift toothpick in his mouth, and started chewing on it.

LeMaine went over to Lemon. "You okay, Sergeant? How's the ankle?"

"It hurts." She squinted at the colonists working on their houses. "Don't tell me we're actually gonna help these cocksuckers."

LeMaine jerked his thumb over his shoulder. "Go get yourself another shot of antidote and tell Kellogg I said to rescan your ankle to make sure the bone electrolyzed completely. We need you ready to march."

"Yes, Sir."

LeMaine made a circuit of the courtyard to check that the rest of the squad was all right. He happened to pass Kellogg as he bent over Lemon's ankle.

LeMaine noticed for the first time that the back of Kellogg's neck had turned purple. A giant bruise disappeared down his jacket collar.

LeMaine waited for Kellogg to finish and then LeMaine held out his hand. "Give me your scanner, Sergeant."

Kellogg cracked a grin when he handed it over. "What's the matter, Sir? You aren't going to start double-checking my work every time someone gets hurt, are you?"

"Keep a civil tone, Sergeant. How I run my squad is my business."

Kellogg bit his lip to stop himself from smirking. "Yes, Sir."

LeMaine pointed the scanner at Kellogg's neck. "You have whiplash, Sergeant."

Kellogg's head shot up. "Sir?"

"That isn't all he has," Lemon grumbled.

LeMaine frowned at the scanner. "You have a hairline fracture to your third cervical vertebra. We need to electrolyze that before we leave."

The color drained from Kellogg's face and his cheeks sagged. "No, Sir! No.... you can't.... please, no."

"I have to, son. If we don't treat it now, you could wind up paralyzed from the neck down. You don't want that and I don't want that and none of us wants that."

Lemon cackled with cruel laughter. "Ha ha! You hear this, Hellhounds? We all get to stand around and watch our buddy Kellogg get zapped instead of the other way around."

"Shut up, Lemon," LeMaine snapped.

Kellogg gulped and his voice cracked. "Please, Sir.... you can't do this to me...."

LeMaine gripped his shoulder and gave him a slight shake. "I have to, son. I'm sorry."

"But.... I feel fine! Can't you at least...."

"No," LeMaine said a little more firmly. "You don't feel it now because you've been in combat. The adrenaline is masking any pain, but you might not feel it even without the adrenaline. Now lie down."

Kellogg didn't move. He stared blankly at LeMaine's face. Kellogg didn't see his commanding officer anymore. He gaped at something beyond sight, something too horrible for him to look away.

LeMaine lowered his voice to a barely audible murmur. "Lie down, Mason."

Kellogg gulped again, shuddered, and turned away looking greyer than ever. He didn't see Lemon vacate the bench so he could lie down.

Kellogg turned his face to the wall and shut his eyes while LeMaine laid the electrolyzer against Kellogg's neck. The reader screen gave LeMaine a perfect view of the cervical bones hidden beneath the skin.

An unusual silence fell over the squad while LeMaine zeroed the electrolyzer onto the fracture. The break was barely visible, but that only made it all the more dangerous.

LeMaine rummaged in Kellogg's pack until he found the syringe. He loaded it with antidote so it would be ready as soon as he fired the electrolyzer.

No one breathed behind LeMaine's back. He rested his other hand on Kellogg's head to steady the young medic and then LeMaine stabbed his finger into the trigger.

Kellogg let out a sickening shriek and his whole body convulsed. He almost rolled off the bench. LeMaine tightened his grip on Kellogg's head to hold him still and he grabbed Kellogg's arm with his other hand to make sure he didn't move.

The next second, Kellogg wilted and went limp. A shaky sigh went through the group. "Damn!" Lemon's voice trembled. "That was bad."

LeMaine concentrated all his attention on the electrolyzer. "The fracture is fused. It didn't touch the spinal cord."

His hands shook when he picked up the antidote syringe. He glanced around to find the whole damn squad watching his every move.

LeMaine nodded at Lemon and Heckler who stood nearby. "Come over here and help me restrain him so he doesn't jump when I inject him."

They crossed to his side without a word. Lemon went to Kellogg's legs, hunched over, and covered them with her weight to hold them down. Heckler leaned over Kellogg's torso and clamped Kellogg's arms down.

LeMaine steadied himself, rechecked the dosage, pressed the syringe to Kellogg's arm, and fired. Kellogg let out another spine-chilling scream and jolted against all three of his comrades holding him down. Then he collapsed again and pitiful whimpering sobs came from him.

LeMaine nodded to Lemon and Heckler. They stood up and returned to their places. LeMaine ruffled Kellogg's hair and then left him alone. "You're all done, son. You did real good. You can get up now."

Kellogg heaved himself off the bench and ran his wrist across his nose. He swung his legs off the bench and sniffed down at his hands.

Lemon reached over, patted his cheek, and then squeezed the back of his neck. The rest of the squad relaxed at that signal and they all started talking as though none of it ever happened.

"What do you want to do about this, Sir?" Polasek asked LeMaine. "We can't let these crooks keep robbing the Cezians and the Maczhi of their goods."

LeMaine dropped onto the bench next to his SIC and started untying his own boot. He'd been walking around with a stone in his shoe for hours. "There's nothing we can do. We aren't here to stop a civil war or to win a civil war or anything else."

"That's the diplomat's job," Peterman added. "Our best bet to work this out is to find her."

"We don't even know where she is," Nunn pointed out.

"I think we can all assume she sure as hell isn't here," Heckler snarled. "She wouldn't be caught dead within a hundred miles of these freaks."

"Makes it a little more challenging that we don't even know which alien group she was supposed to negotiate with," O'Hara chimed in. "She could be running around communing with the damn cockroaches for all we know."

Nunn burst out laughing. "Maybe she is one herself."

"Doubtful," LeMaine told her. "She came from the Assembly. She's a certified Elian diplomat."

"Which means she wasn't scurrying around on the Assembly floor getting stepped on by Tenzorians," Peterman added.

The whole squad exploded in laughter. Peterman didn't often make jokes, but when he did, he surprised the squad so much that his quips sounded so much funnier than anyone else's.

LeMaine laughed with the rest. He genuinely liked and cared about every member of his squad. He valued each one for their unique skills and personality. He spent so much time with them that they had become his second family.

He started to say something when Macon returned with his arms loaded with fusion rifles. He put them down in a pile in the middle of the courtyard. "These should be enough to get you started. I won't put you in a house right now. We're about to move out in a few minutes, so pack your stuff and be ready to leave when I give the word."

He left before anyone could reply. "Son of a bitch!" Lemon hissed. "I am NOT using a goddamn fusion rifle. I don't care if I have to join the damn Cezians."

"We aren't really moving out with *them*, are we, Sir?" Polasek asked.

"Not a chance. We have our own mission that doesn't include killing innocent people."

"The Cezians aren't exactly innocent," Heckler growled. "They've killed plenty."

"Maybe," LeMaine replied, "but if this chump is telling the truth, it sounds like the Cezians had plenty of provocation this time. I couldn't say for certain, but I'd be willing to bet the Cezians were the ones who sent that distress call to Command. They must have wanted someone to rein in these colonists so the supply shipments could get through."

Monk spun around and slammed his beefy hand on LeMaine's shoulder. The blow almost buckled LeMaine off his seat. "That's why you're the boss, Sir. Keep thinking like that and they'll promote you to colonel next."

LeMaine snorted. "Yeah. I'll be a colonel commanding you slackers the same as always. I keep getting promoted, but they never give me that desk job they promised."

The others laughed out loud. "You—a desk jockey?" Nunn made a face. "I'll believe that when I see it."

"Can you blame Command for keeping you down here with us?" Polasek asked. "You're the best. No one else would be able to handle this squad the way you do."

"No one would want to," O'Hara chimed in.

"No one else would put up with your mouth, Sergeant," LeMaine shot back. "How about we find a nice safe place where you, Nunn, and Kellogg can all wise off to each other far away from any combat zone?"

O'Hara turned bright red, but he didn't stop grinning. "Who would bust your ass day and night if you did that?"

"Is that what you're trying to do—bust my ass?"

"Someone has to, right?"

The others laughed again until Kellogg interrupted "Heads up. Incoming."

Everyone spun around to see what he meant. He usually joined in with the back-and-forth jokes and wisecracks, but after what just happened, he surprised everyone into sudden silence.

LeMaine stiffened when Macon came back. The man was empty-handed this time and a long line of colonists marched behind him heading for the compound gate.

They pushed carts loaded with household goods and some even carried the poles from their disassembled rooves. Others wheeled their thermal cannons mounted on chassis and nearly all of the colonists carried weapons.

LeMaine got to his feet at Macon's approach and the rest of the Hellhounds copied him. They picked up their weapons and Heckler spat out his toothpick.

Macon clapped his hands, rubbed them, and grinned around at the squad. "Time to go! You can all go up front and keep an eye out for...."

"We aren't going with you," LeMaine told him. "We're going on with our mission.... which doesn't include fighting your war for you."

Macon blinked and recovered instantly. "It's your war, too. Do you think the Cezians will forget you shooting so many of their people? If you go out there alone, you'll be dead in a few hours."

"Maybe not," Peterman interrupted. "The Cezians respect anyone who fights to defend themselves. That's all we did."

Macon curled his lip in disdain. "You won't last ten minutes out there without our weaponry."

"So far, we've been in more danger from your weaponry than from the Cezians," Nunn chimed in.

Macon rounded on LeMaine. "Don't tell me you plan to go along with this."

"He doesn't go along with anything," Polasek cut in. "He's our commanding officer. Do you think we told him we were all too chickenshit to go with you?"

Some of the others laughed, but LeMaine didn't move. He held Macon's gaze even when Macon kept casting questioning glances at the other Hellhounds.

Just then, Monk stomped over to LeMaine's side. The giant pilot planted himself next to LeMaine and LeMaine could just picture the expression on Monk's face when he crushed his weapon in a death grip.

Macon's countenance changed instantly. He compressed his lips and his eyes flashed. "Fine. Be that way, but just take a word of warning. Whoever isn't with us is against us. If we meet you again, don't expect any special treatment."

"I'll give you *extra* special treatment," Monk boomed. "Ask me nicely and I'll even put a cherry on top for your birthday."

Macon shot the huge pilot one glance and then went back to glaring at LeMaine. "You'll regret this."

"I doubt that," LeMaine murmured.

Macon pinched his lips one more time, turned on his heel, and stalked off. LeMaine turned away, too. He wasn't winning too many friends on this planet.

"Let's get the hell out of this shithole," Lemon hissed. "This place stinks."

"Where are we going, Sir?" Heckler asked. "We'd be taking our lives in our hands contacting the Cezians."

LeMaine returned to the bench, slammed his backpack down, and stripped it open. "What are you doing?" Polasek asked.

"I'm contacting Command. I have to report the colonists interfering with supply shipments. Command will send out a security detail with the next shipment."

O'Hara burst out in loud laughter. "These gutless colonists will get more than they bargained for when they attack a shipment and wind up facing a full security company."

LeMaine pulled out a communications relay, hooked it up to the remote panel in his sleeve, and patched it to the *Renown's* cockpit, but nothing happened. "Shit!"

"What's wrong, Sir?" Monk asked. "Won't they send out the security detail?"

"I can't raise the *Renown*."

Another tense silence fell over the group while LeMaine tried one configuration after another to patch the relay through the *Renown's* communications systems.

He finally gave up and pointed at Polasek. "Get out your equipment, Lieutenant. The rest of you, at ease while we work this out."

Everyone sat back down, but they didn't relax. They started going over their gear, cleaning their weapons, checking Crossfire gel cartridges, and readjusting their packs.

They gathered in a cluster on the opposite side of the courtyard. LeMaine heard Kellogg warming up and talking to the others again.

Polasek unzipped his backpack to reveal a larger array tucked inside. He turned it on and the screen displayed four different images including the navigation charts and life sign readings that appeared in miniature on the squad's remotes.

Polasek set to work over his instruments. First he connected his relay to the communications system, and when that failed, he tuned his array to scan the atmosphere.

"The *Renown* is still in orbit," he told LeMaine. "She's still on autopilot where we left her."

"Can you access the navigation system?"

"There's too much interference." Polasek frowned at the readings. "This planet has some unknown gas suspended in the atmosphere. It's blocking certain frequencies."

"Why doesn't it interfere with communications to Elia?" LeMaine asked. "Whoever sent that distress call didn't have any trouble getting through the atmosphere."

"It looks like the gas lets certain wavelengths through just fine, but I wouldn't like to say for sure."

"That isn't good enough, Lieutenant," LeMaine told him. "All our lives depend on being able to call the *Renown* to retrieve us. If we can't raise the ship now, we have to break off our mission to find a way to contact her."

"I understand, Sir. You do what you gotta do, but I can't access the *Renown* from here. This array is too weak and it's designed to use the frequencies the atmosphere is most likely to deflect. I'm sorry."

LeMaine scowled at his SIC, but arguing with Polasek wouldn't salvage this mess. "What do you recommend? Is there anywhere on this planet where we can get through the interference?"

"Most of the communications between Ziea and Elia came from the colonists' old outpost—the Grara Outpost. That's all I know."

LeMaine turned around to find the whole squad watching him. They pretended not to. Their hands went through the motions of organizing their gear, but they all shot questioning glances at LeMaine and Polasek and eavesdropped on the conversation. Why shouldn't they? The situation put the whole squad at risk.

LeMaine read the same question in all their faces. How the living crap were they supposed to get off this stinking planet without the *Renown*?

The Hellhounds had been in much more dangerous situations than this. They'd been stranded on hostile planets under heavy fire and lost a lot of good people before the survivors made it out.

LeMaine didn't doubt he could get the squad out of here. He just had to figure out how.

"Peterman!" he called out. "What do you know about the communications infrastructure on this planet? Where are communications from this planet coming from?"

"All communications from Ziea come from the Grara Outpost."

LeMaine took a second to understand what Peterman just said. "Are you seriously suggesting that...."

Peterman nodded. "The Cezians must have taken over the outpost after the colonists abandoned it.... or after the Cezians drove them out—one or the other. Now the Cezians are using the communications system to send messages to Elia."

LeMaine rubbed his forehead again. "Shit!"

"I can't wait!" O'Hara chirped. "We might as well move in with the Cezians because...."

LeMaine wasn't listening anymore. He got to his feet. "Locate the outpost, Lieutenant, and patch the coordinates to our remotes. Move out, all of you."

He returned to his own pack and zipped it shut. He wasn't looking forward to seeing the Cezians again and that was putting it mildly.

He had only one option left—find the Grara Outpost and contact either Command or the *Renown*. No diplomat was worth his squad's lives.

If Peterman was right, the Hellhounds would be marching straight into the Cezians' headquarters. The Hellhounds would have to do just that to reach the only communications system that could get them off the planet alive.

Chapter 5

LeMaine glanced behind him and relaxed slightly when he saw Kellogg right behind him and Lemon on her feet. Neither of them showed any signs of their injuries slowing them down.

Monk occupied the far rear position and the giant pilot kept looking over his shoulder, too. Everyone did. The squad stayed much more alert since they left the colonists' walled compound, but they still didn't see anything.

LeMaine checked his remote and adjusted the range to watch Macon and his followers move farther away from the Hellhounds' route. Good. If LeMaine never saw those people again, it would be too soon.

Now he had a much bigger problem. He had to drop everything and concentrate all his resources on contacting the *Renown* or someone at Command who could send out another vessel to pick up the Hellhounds.

He stopped on a ridge overlooking vast canyons, dusty planes, and a few scrubby river bottoms in the distance. The rest of the squad gathered around him and Polasek came to his side. "There's the outpost, Sir."

"Christ, it's crawling with damn Cezians!" Heckler growled.

"Maybe they'll become attracted to you and let us inside to use their array to get into your good graces," O'Hara suggested.

"I'll get into *your* good graces, shithead!" Heckler snarled.

LeMaine bumped Polasek's elbow and nodded to his right. "Take a look at that."

Everyone followed the direction of his nod. Monk hefted his carbine when a bunch of Cezians stuck their heads over another ridge to the north.

"They aren't attacking," Peterman observed. "I wonder why not."

"You said they respect people who defend themselves," Nunn replied. "Maybe they never tried to attack us at all. Maybe they saw humans heading for the compound and thought we were colonists."

"They're keeping us under surveillance," Polasek surmised. "They're watching us get closer to the compound to see what we do."

LeMaine laid his hand on Monk's arm and pushed his carbine muzzle toward the ground. "Don't do anything to threaten them, but stay sharp. We'll keep an eye on them. Don't retaliate until they act first."

He started walking and frowned at his remote. "Polasek!" he called over his shoulder. "Why aren't those Cezians showing up on the chart?"

"Who knows what the hell is going on with this damn atmosphere, Sir? All our gear is going haywire."

"Not helpful," Heckler growled. "Not helpful at all, Lieutenant."

"What the hell am I supposed to do—reconfigure the gaseous composition of the atmosphere? I don't make the damn rules."

"Oh, really?" Kellogg chimed in. "Here we all thought you were the chemistry wizard on the squad."

"That's you, Casanova." O'Hara dodged to his right and jostled Kellogg.

LeMaine fiddled with his remote some more and then gave it up. "If those Cezians aren't showing up on the chart, anyone could be out there sneaking up on us. We would never see them coming."

"Don't say that, Sir!" Nunn called out. "You'll give little old Kellogg nightmares."

"Shut the hell up!" Kellogg fired back.

"No one can talk smack about Kellogg anymore," Lemon announced. "I've decided to adopt him as a pet."

"A pet who electrolyzes all your fractures," Heckler added. "You could make a million with a pet like that back home."

"You two are soul mates after all," O'Hara went on. "You can break all the bones you like and he'll electrolyze them for you."

"It sounds like a new intergalactic fashion trend to me," Monk rumbled and everyone laughed.

"Shhht!" LeMaine hissed and everyone fell instantly silent.

LeMaine stopped dead in his tracks and waved behind him. He beckoned O'Hara forward and LeMaine crawled up the next hill on his stomach.

O'Hara and Polasek stretched out on LeMaine's right and left. The three men peered over the hilltop at the outpost in the distance.

O'Hara pulled his carbine forward, fitted a telescopic scope to it, and sighted through the lens to the building perched between two hills.

"How many?" LeMaine asked.

"Visible ones, you mean?" O'Hara asked without taking his eye away from his scope. "Ten on the roof.... fifteen on the ground......twenty inside."

"What about weapons?"

"Hmmm...." O'Hara swept his barrel the other way. "Cannons on the roof, but they aren't thermals. Might be anti-matter......or EM. I can't tell from here, but my money is on anti-matter."

LeMaine jerked around. "Anti-matter! No one in the Elian system has that kind of technology."

"They do now, Sir. Maybe they brought it with them from their own system."

"If they have that...." LeMaine raised his head a little higher, but he couldn't see as much detail around the outpost as O'Hara could. "What the hell are they doing out *here*? If they have anti-matter weapons, they could conquer the whole system."

O'Hara put his carbine down and his bright blue eyes found LeMaine's. "Maybe they don't want to, Sir. They've been in the Elian system off and on for centuries and they've only ever established isolated colonies."

LeMaine pulled himself together and checked his remote. The second group of Cezians still didn't show up on the chart, but they were still there.

They poked their heads over the northern hills to watch the squad. If these people were in contact with the outpost, they could alert their comrades that the squad was approaching....so why didn't they attack? Anti-matter cannons could hit the squad at this distance.

LeMaine took a calculated risk and stood up. "Let's go.... but keep your guns down. Don't make any of them think we're threatening them."

"We *are* threatening them," Heckler muttered.

LeMaine started down the hill and the Hellhounds closed more tightly around him. Monk and Heckler both made a much more obvious show of turning backward and covering the squad on all sides.

O'Hara eased up to LeMaine's side. "What do you want to hit first if the shit goes down, Sir?"

LeMaine kept his voice low measuring the defenses on top of the outpost. "The cannoneers first......" Then he scanned the area. "I don't see the transmission dish."

O'Hara furrowed his brow. "You're right, Sir. It should be on the roof."

"Did they dismantle it?" LeMaine turned to Peterman. "When was the last time a transmission came through from Ziea?"

"About four weeks ago. That's when Command picked up the distress signal."

LeMaine halted again and consulted his remote. "There it is. It's inside the building."

"That's impossible," Polasek countered. "The building's construction would block transmission."

"One thing I can promise you," LeMaine replied. "We won't be sending any signal if we don't get inside."

His head snapped sideways as a fluid river of movement caught his peripheral vision. He turned around to see the Cezians who followed the squad from the colonists' compound.

The Cezians raced past the squad and charged into the open. They broke across open ground to reach the outpost first.

The gunners on the roof swung their weapons around, and when they saw who it was, they returned to aiming at the squad.

LeMaine sighed. "So much for the element of surprise."

"Were you trying for the element of surprise?" O'Hara chuckled. "You're losing your touch, Sir."

LeMaine came to the last small rise before a broad section of ground right in front of the outpost. "Stay here," he whispered to O'Hara. "Cover me."

"You got it, Sir." O'Hara dropped behind the hill, propped his carbine on the rim, and eyed down his scope at the cannoneers.

LeMaine nodded to Polasek and they strode in front of the rest of the squad. LeMaine let his carbine hang and sighed heavily when he raised his empty hands above his head. He was getting too damn old for this shit.

He halted in the middle of the empty space with his hands raised. He would never have dared to do that without the rest of the squad standing armed and ready behind him.

LeMaine could feel O'Hara's carbine sight tracing back and forth across those gunners up there. The sniper's reflexes would detect the gunners' slightest move. O'Hara would be able to take them out before they blew LeMaine away—at least LeMaine hoped so.

"Elian Special Forces!" he called out to the Cezians on the roof. "We're here responding to your distress call! I'm Captain Owen LeMaine of the Elian Military Command. We're here to enforce intergalactic law and ensure you receive the supply shipments you're entitled to!"

A few of the Cezians exchanged glances and LeMaine's heart leapt. Maybe these people weren't as bloodthirsty and murderous as everyone thought. Could this be the moment when Cezian-Elian relations took a massive one-eighty-degree turn?

The Cezians faced the squad and LeMaine's heart sank all over again when the gunners took fresh grips on their weapons. Their expressions hardened and a charge of tension went through the Hellhounds.

LeMaine gave it one last desperate shot. "The colonists will be punished for stealing your goods! Your future shipments will be escorted by a full security detail and the guilty parties will be tried and imprisoned. The colonists are acting outside intergalactic law and the Elian Military Command will...."

A catastrophic boom shook the ground and the whole squad crouched for cover, but the shot didn't come from the gunners on the outpost roof.

The Hellhounds spun around to see a hundred colonists lining the hills behind the squad's position. The colonists aimed their fusion rifles down at the squad and over the Hellhounds' heads toward the outpost.

LeMaine's stomach turned when the colonists opened fire with a bunch of thermal cannons. One of those shots smashed down right on top of the spot where O'Hara was hiding.

O'Hara sprang to his feet to get away. Two more blasts ruptured the dirt on either side of him. He raised his arms above his head and broke into a run, but a second later, another pounding smash landed right on top of him.

A cloud of dirt hid him for a second, and when a breath of wind blew the dust away, O'Hara wasn't there anymore.

"O'Hara!" Nunn bellowed and she charged up the hill to reach him.

She made it halfway before a bunch of colonists pivoted their rifles downward to shoot at her. The whole squad jerked up their carbines to cover her. The Hellhounds spat shots at the colonists until the cannoneers on the outpost roof opened up.

They bombarded the hillsides where the colonists sheltered and catastrophic blasts blasted out the hillsides. Their fire struck the hill right in front of Nunn and forced her to retreat. Then the Cezians turned their guns on the Hellhounds.

LeMaine sidestepped to get closer to Monk and Kellogg. "Get up there, Sergeant!' he bellowed to Kellogg. "Get O'Hara out of there!"

Kellogg charged forward and Monk advanced to cover him, but at that moment, another cannon blast exploded next to Kellogg's foot. He dodged left and almost ran into another two shots hammering the ground from both sides.

Monk grabbed him, but the Cezians at the outpost and the colonists in the hills left nowhere to hide. "This way!" LeMaine yelled to his people. He grabbed Kellogg and pulled him northward.

Monk, Lemon, and Heckler swiveled together to cover the squad's retreat.

A bunch of Cezians streamed out of the outpost aiming fusion rifles at the fleeing squad. Peterman and Polasek defended their comrades while the squad made a break for the hills.

Nunn tried one more time to fall back with the others, but another volley of explosions cut her off. She had no place left to run, so she tucked her chin and charged up the hill to where O'Hara went down.

She skidded in the dirt and flipped onto her back. Her head, arms, and carbine stuck over the hill and she spat shots at the colonists. She hit enough of them to win herself a moment's reprieve.

She rolled onto her stomach and LeMaine lost sight of her behind the hill. What was she finding up there? Was O'Hara already dead?

LeMaine didn't have time to think about that. He dove behind another hill to the side of the battle and towed the others in behind him.

He pushed Monk, Lemon, and Heckler down behind the hill followed shortly by Kellogg. Heckler cradled his blood-saturated arm and snarled through his teeth. "Cocksuckers! I'll kill you for this."

LeMaine peeked over the hilltop and his throat tightened. Peterman and Polasek inched closer, but at that moment, Polasek took a shot in the hip and went down still shooting.

Peterman sidestepped to straddle him. Peterman yelled something down at Polasek and Polasek hooked his elbow around Peterman's ankle.

Peterman backed away dragging Polasek toward the hills. Polasek gripped his carbine in one hand and swept his weapon across the line of Cezians. The two lieutenants made it ten feet before another shot clipped Peterman's shoulder.

He whipped around to raise his carbine when another rifle blast struck him square in the stomach. He toppled on top of Polasek. Polasek screamed out for his friend, but Polasek couldn't even walk, much less get them both out of there.

Polasek bolted up into a sitting position, snatched Peterman's carbine, and opened up with both weapons. He let out a feral roar mowing down the Cezians without mercy.

LeMaine didn't hesitate. He vaulted over the hilltop yelling, "Stay here....and stay down!"

He raced to Polasek's side, but his SIC didn't even see him. He bared his teeth howling in murderous fury at the last Cezians left alive. He cut them down until a carpet of bodies separated him from the outpost.

"Hold your fire, Lieutenant!" LeMaine bellowed in his ear.

Polasek snapped out of his frenzy just in time for LeMaine to grab his SIC's arm. LeMaine took a fistful of Peterman's collar and started dragging both men off the battlefield.

He bent his head under the load until a shriek made him look up. He caught a fleeting glimpse of five thermal cannons adjusting their aim straight down at Nunn's position, but LeMaine still couldn't see her.

He did see Lemon, though. The tiny sergeant skimmed up the hills to the ridge and she dashed down it so fast the colonists never saw her coming.

She carpeted the gunners with shots until she finished off five of them. The other cannoneers concentrated on the outpost and didn't notice Lemon getting closer.

She sprang down into the hollow, and a second later, she emerged supporting Nunn on one side and carrying O'Hara's limp body over her shoulder.

Nunn held onto her carbine behind Lemon's back. She hit another gunner who noticed their retreat. Lemon staggered over the hilltop and started to descend.

LeMaine gave one last bone-crushing heave and dragged Peterman and Polasek to safety. LeMaine checked for the others and his stomach twisted when four colonists popped over another hill. They had migrated northward to cut off Lemon's retreat and they unloaded on her while she was unarmed and defenseless.

She pitched forward, O'Hara's body went flying, and he hit the deck. Lemon sprawled on her stomach and started crawling through the dirt to reach O'Hara, but the colonists' rifle fire blocked her path.

Nunn flipped over again and distracted the colonists, but only for a second. They split their attack with two returning Nunn's fire and the other two trying to hit Lemon.

Lemon scrambled over to O'Hara's body and started pawing at his pockets. She yelled something to Nunn and Nunn called back. Nunn pulled a block of Plaostine out of her jacket and started working in a frenzy to prime it.

Lemon finally succeeded in freeing a cartridge of Crossfire gel from O'Hara's pockets. She manhandled her carbine to reload it under heavy fire from the colonists.

She finally got the cartridge loaded, but when she spun around to return fire, one of the colonists shot her in the leg. The blast splintered through the ankle she broke when she landed and she screamed out.

LeMaine launched out of his hiding place and would have run into the line of fire, but Monk grabbed his arm and hauled him down. "I'll go, Sir. You stay here."

Monk broke cover before LeMaine could protest. In a second, the big pilot waded out into the open area covering the hills with his carbine. LeMaine almost followed him, but a yell from Kellogg distracted him.

LeMaine squatted down to find Kellogg bending over Peterman. "He's crashing!" Kellogg bellowed. "I have to operate now or we'll lose him."

LeMaine didn't have to look over the hill to know the answer. "We can't do it here." He checked the last remaining squad members. LeMaine, Kellogg, and Monk were the only ones left uninjured.

Heckler leaned in. Blood saturated his jacket and he hugged his limp, useless left arm against his stomach. "Go! Go! Take him—now!"

Kellogg shot to his feet and hastily crammed his scanner back into his pack. He looped Peterman's arm over his shoulder and started hauling Peterman away. The hill behind them connected to another gully. They didn't have to expose themselves to get away from the battle.

Heckler picked up Polasek. Heckler was so big that he lifted Polasek's feet right off the ground. Polasek hollered in pain, but Heckler only gritted his teeth and took off following Kellogg.

LeMaine straightened up to see Monk lugging Lemon under one arm. Monk stalked backward dangling her by one giant hand while he passed his carbine back and forth across the colonists' position.

The colonists saw him getting away with one of their victims. The two gunners attacking Nunn broke off to shoot down Monk, but at that moment, Nunn lobbed her Plaostine block at them.

It bounced at their feet and a deafening explosion blasted the hill apart. All the colonists went down and the noise attracted the other cannoneers.

They swung their cannons around, but Nunn only pitched another block at them. LeMaine ran up to Monk and Monk shoved Lemon into LeMaine's arms. LeMaine stood his ground and added his carbine fire to Monk's. Lemon twisted in his hold and they both unloaded on the colonists.

Monk stalked back to Nunn, picked her up, and grabbed O'Hara by the collar. He pulled O'Hara along the ground while LeMaine and Lemon covered their retreat.

LeMaine inched backward until Monk got behind the hill. LeMaine almost ran for it with the rest of the squad, but right before he turned away, he noticed that no more shots were coming from the outpost.

He glanced over to see the Cezians watching him from the rooftop. They still bombarded the colonists with cannon shots, but they didn't shoot at the Hellhounds anymore.

Their hard eyes followed LeMaine and his people off the battlefield. A few colonists vaulted to their feet to aim at the retreating squad, but the Cezians jerked their cannons sideways and blew the colonists away before they could threaten the squad again.

LeMaine took the hint and dropped behind the hill. He crouched there just long enough to make sure there was nothing he could do for Nunn, Lemon, or O'Hara. They needed Kellogg and fast.

LeMaine pulled Lemon's arm over his left shoulder and Monk slung Nunn across his back. Then, without discussing it first, Monk and LeMaine both got under O'Hara's arms and staggered away into the gully.

Chapter 6

LeMaine ran his forehead across his shoulder, squinted through the lamplight, and struggled to focus his eyes. "Oooo.... kay.... I found the rip.... It's in the splenic vein. The spleen looks all right...."

"Make an incision under the second floating rib," Kellogg barked over his shoulder.

LeMaine looked around on either side of him. "Where's the scalpel?"

"Just a minute," Kellogg panted. "I'm using it."

LeMaine checked Peterman's vital signs. "His blood pressure is bottoming out."

"There's nothing I can do about that right now," Kellogg snapped. "Just hang tight. I'm almost done."

LeMaine dragged his attention away from the scanner hooked up to Peterman's arm. LeMaine didn't want to see the moment when Peterman flatlined because LeMaine didn't have the medical training to save him.

LeMaine got a sick feeling in his stomach when he glanced over at Kellogg. The young medic hunched over O'Hara working fast. Blood saturated Kellogg's arms up to his elbows and he kept cursing under his breath.

LeMaine didn't want to know what Kellogg was doing over there and looking at the rest of the Hellhounds didn't make LeMaine feel any better.

Monk, Heckler, Nunn, and Lemon sat in a line on the floor across the hollow where the Hellhounds took refuge after that disastrous battle. The squad shot LeMaine frightened glances before they looked away at nothing.

Heckler cradled his shredded arm and pressed a wad of gauze to his shoulder. Lemon's foot hung by a scrap of gory flesh with a makeshift tourniquet tied around the stump.

A wicked gash sliced across Nunn's forehead and disappeared in her dark hair. Blood drenched the side of her face. She kept slipping in and out of consciousness and her head fell on Heckler's shoulder.

Polasek had passed out with a gunshot through his pelvis. Monk had gotten away unharmed, but he didn't look any happier than the rest of the squad.

Kellogg passed the scalpel back to LeMaine. "Here. Make the incision and give it back. I need it."

LeMaine bent over Peterman's body, located the floating rib, and ignited the laser to cut into the young lieutenant's flesh. LeMaine cut through the abdominal muscle and black blood poured out all over his hands. It spattered the floor and coated LeMaine's boots.

"Find the tear," Kellogg ordered. "I can't help you seal it right now, so just pinch it off and stop him from bleeding out until I finish with O'Hara."

LeMaine didn't ask how long that would take. He pushed a few loops of intestine out of the way and used the scanner to locate the torn vein. He pinched it off. "I got it. It isn't bleeding anymore."

"Give him a blood transfusion right away."

LeMaine couldn't reach Kellogg's pack from here and he couldn't let go of Peterman. "Here, Sir." Monk swiveled onto his knees and started rummaging in Kellogg's kit.

He handed over a small solid cube wrapped in paper. Monk tore off the cover and slapped the transfusion into LeMaine's free hand.

LeMaine pressed the block to the exposed skin of Peterman's inner arm. The cube contracted and squished in on itself until it squashed flat.

"His pressure is stabilizing, but he's still below 80 systolic," LeMaine told Kellogg.

"Give him another one, but that's it. If it isn't enough, there's nothing we can do. We need the others for O'Hara." Kellogg glanced over at Monk. "Give me the other three, Monk."

Monk got to his feet and started tearing Kellogg's kit apart. He handed LeMaine one more transfusion and took the other three to Kellogg. Monk started to open one of the blocks. "No!" Kellogg snapped. "Not yet!"

"Sorry!" Monk stammered. "I thought...."

Kellogg puffed out his cheeks. "It's all right. Help me, Monk."

Monk swallowed hard and moved over to O'Hara's side. The rest of the conscious squad members watched in breathless silence. Monk's face drained of all color when he looked down at O'Hara.

Kellogg nodded at O'Hara. "Here. Hold this for me."

Monk did as Kellogg said and compressed his lips while Kellogg finished what he was doing. "Give me back the scalpel."

LeMaine handed it over. He didn't mind someone better trained than himself taking over.

Kellogg worked over O'Hara for a long time. He kept barking orders at both Monk and LeMaine until, hours later, Kellogg finally stepped back. "There. It's done. Give him the transfusions now."

Monk injected the three transfusions into O'Hara's arm. Kellogg turned around to face LeMaine and LeMaine barely recognized him.

Blood and gore covered Kellogg's face, uniform, and even caked his hair. His hands and forearms dripped blood and a deranged look gleamed in his normally friendly green eyes.

LeMaine actually suffered a pang of fear when Kellogg approached him. LeMaine hadn't felt that since he was a recruit.

Kellogg glanced down at Peterman and then at the scanner showing Peterman's vital signs. "He's stabilizing. You did good, Sir."

LeMaine ran his free hand across his forehead in pure relief. "Thanks...... How's O'Hara?"

"He'll make it." Kellogg swiveled around Peterman and peered into the man's abdominal cavity. LeMaine had been pinching off the splenic vein all this time. He hadn't dared to move.

Kellogg started working on Peterman next. He didn't joke around. He didn't look away from his work once.

He went into this madness in situations like this. He became something more like a machine or a monster who saw nothing but the job of saving his comrades from their injuries.

He worked for a long time before he finally told LeMaine, "You can let go of the vein now." Kellogg stood back and peered into the incision. "Good. The seal is holding." He checked Peterman's vitals. "I'll close the incision now. Give him a dose of antibiotics, Sir."

LeMaine got the syringe out of Kellogg's pack and injected Peterman with antibiotics while Kellogg checked on Polasek. Kellogg knelt down next to Polasek and aimed his scanner at Polasek's abdomen. "Son of a bitch! God damn it!"

LeMaine's head shot up. "What?"

"Get over here, Sir!" Kellogg snapped. "Hurry. Drop that. Monk—bring my pack over here. Hurry up."

LeMaine knelt down next to Polasek, too, but LeMaine didn't dare to ask what was wrong with him.

Kellogg burst into a blur of movement barking orders in all directions. Lemon, Heckler, and Nunn cringed against the wall not daring to move or speak.

Kellogg pulled a length of tubing out of his pack. "He needs a transfusion. He's been bleeding out all this time. Damn it! It's a miracle he's alive at all. Roll up your sleeve, Sir. Hurry up."

LeMaine ripped up his sleeve and finally sat down next to Polasek. Kellogg inserted a needle into LeMaine's arm and hooked him up to Polasek's vein.

"Bring that scalpel over here, Monk," Kellogg ordered. "Get Polasek's fatigues off. Hurry."

Monk's fingers fumbled stripping off Polasek's clothes to reveal the gunshot tearing through his hip. As soon as he exposed Polasek's skin, LeMaine saw what Kellogg meant.

The shot went through the hip joint itself and blood pooled under the skin in blue-black pouches. Lemon turned her face away. Nunn covered her eyes when Kellogg sliced into the blood pockets and started carving through Polasek's muscle.

Kellogg didn't quit until he found the severed blood vessel. He pinched it off and released the clamp on the transfusion tubing. Blood started flowing from LeMaine into Polasek.

LeMaine watched in numb shock as Kellogg repaired the tear, checked all of Polasek's other vital organs, and finally sealed the incisions.

Kellogg clamped the tubing and removed the needle from LeMaine's arm. "Go sit down over there, Sir," Kellogg ordered. "You're gonna feel weak for a while."

"I have to...."

Kellogg shot him a look that silenced LeMaine instantly. LeMaine might be the commanding officer, but Kellogg was in charge now.

Kellogg turned to the other three and measured their injuries with a glance. "You first, Heckler."

"Thanks, man," Heckler croaked. "I appreciate it."

Kellogg scanned Heckler's arm. "The bone is shattered, but we can reconstruct it. Lie down."

Heckler nodded and stretched out on the floor next to Polasek. Heckler growled through locked teeth while Kellogg rearranged the shredded muscle and skin on Heckler's upper arm, but Kellogg acted like he didn't hear.

He placed the electrolyzer over the wound and, without a word of warning, he fired it. Heckler jerked back with a terrible bellow of pain. His teeth ground so hard the sound carried through the hollow.

He crashed down unconscious, but Kellogg didn't give him the antidote right away. He left Heckler unconscious, got busy sealing the torn flesh, and reattached the tendons dangling off the bone.

When Kellogg finally finished, he injected the antidote and Heckler shot awake with another agonized roar. He thundered in pain, his whole body trembled, and he glared at Kellogg only to collapse back on the ground.

Heckler flung his good arm over his eyes with a groan that ended in a whimper. Kellogg turned toward Lemon. "Is this the thanks I get for fixing this earlier?"

Lemon didn't take the joke. She blinked up at him and her lower lip trembled. "Can you fix it, Kellogg?"

"Sure, sweetie," he murmured. "It's gonna hurt, but it will be all right. You'll see."

She gulped. "I was only joking earlier when I said I was gonna make you my pet. You know that right? I didn't mean anything by it."

He actually smiled for the first time since the squad found this hollow. "I'd be honored to be your pet anytime, sweetie. Now do you want to lie down or do you want to stay there?"

There was nowhere else to lie down. Polasek and Heckler took up all the space on the floor. O'Hara and Peterman lay sprawled on two shelves against the far wall.

"I guess I'll just stay here," Lemon replied.

Kellogg loaded the syringe. "I'm going to give you some painkillers before I put the bones back in place."

She pinched her lips together too hard to speak and she forced herself to nod. He injected her with a dose of painkillers and then bent over her foot. It flopped to one side of her severed ankle and she hissed through her teeth when he pivoted the foot into the right position.

He took a long time to splint it in place before he electrolyzed the bone. He left her unconscious, too, while he repaired all the soft tissue and reattached the ligaments.

LeMaine slumped against the wall while Kellogg sealed the gash on Nunn's face and scalp. Kellogg scanned her head and announced that she only had a concussion.

The transfusion to Polasek was catching up with LeMaine and the exhaustion of the last several hours threatened to drag him under. This was definitely one of the worst outcomes of his career, but at least he didn't lose anybody—yet.

Kellogg put all his gear back in his kit. Heckler sat up when Kellogg zipped his pack closed. "Lie down here, buddy."

Kellogg shook his head. "I need to check on O'Hara."

"Lie down, Sergeant," LeMaine cut in. "You're dead on your feet."

Kellogg looked up at him and the medic's eyes changed. He no longer looked like a wild animal fighting for his life. He was back to being a young man with a soft heart.

Kellogg looked down at the floor. He wasn't in command anymore. He fought harder than anyone else and for longer than anyone else. Only the madness of battle kept him going this long.

He moved over into Heckler's place and stretched out, but his gaze kept darting over to O'Hara. "You'll wake me up if anything happens, right?"

LeMaine did his best to smile, but he didn't feel like it very much. "You'll be the first person I call. Trust me."

Kellogg nodded, but he didn't shut his eyes. He stared up at the ceiling and his eyes glazed over. He went into a stupor beyond fatigue, beyond life and death, beyond blood and smoke and fire.

LeMaine leaned his head against the wall and started to shut his eyes when his remote buzzed against his arm. He barely had time to look down at it and see a dot approaching.

The next instant, someone dropped into the gully right outside the hollow. LeMaine snatched his carbine and the rest of the squad reacted just as fast. Monk whipped around jamming his weapon into his shoulder.

Heckler, Nunn, and Lemon all grabbed their guns, too, but Monk was the only one on his feet. LeMaine rotated onto his knees, but his body felt rubbery and weak. He paused there to let his vision swim back into focus just as the figure stepped into the hollow entrance.

It was another Maczhi, but nothing like the Maczhi the squad met on the ridge. This one surveyed the squad with clear, direct eyes. It stood much more erect than the others. Its posture made its arms seem shorter and its whole aspect much more humanoid.

It wore a strange combination of garments that concealed whatever gender it was, but the square cut of its shoulders and the taper of muscle leading down to its pelvis gave LeMaine a clear impression that this was a male—a strong one.

The alien's smooth, dark eyes snapped to the injured squad members, back to LeMaine kneeling on the floor, and over to O'Hara and Peterman lying unconscious where Kellogg had left them.

The intruder didn't shrink at all from Monk's threats or from any other weapon aimed at him. The stranger took a few slow, deliberate steps into the lamplight. "You're Elian...." His eyes darted to the insignia on the squad's uniforms. "Elian Special Forces."

"How did you find us?" LeMaine demanded. "What are you doing here?"

"You fought the colonists. They're still searching for you."

LeMaine measured the creature and made a gut decision. LeMaine lowered his carbine. "Where did you come from? We met some other Maczhi in the hills. They were starving and on the brink of death."

"Many Maczhi are starving and on the brink of death. They huddle in their encampments and never venture into the mountains. They would do better if they did."

LeMaine checked the creature's clothing again. The stranger carried two fusion rifles across his back, but he made no move to pull them forward. He didn't even try to defend himself, but no one could mistake this alien for being helpless.

LeMaine sat down and the rest of the Hellhounds started to relax—all except Monk.

"We know about the colonists stealing food and medicine from the Maczhi," LeMaine went on. "We'll stop it if we can—as soon as we find a way to contact our Command."

"The colonists will find you long before you do that." The alien strolled over to O'Hara and looked down at him.

Monk lunged for the creature and jammed his gun barrel in the alien's face. "Get your stinking ass away from him."

"Stand down, Monk," LeMaine ordered. "You can see he's unarmed."

Monk lowered his carbine, but he didn't back away.

"I'm Captain Owen LeMaine," LeMaine told the stranger. He really wished he had Peterman with him right now. "What's your name?"

The alien studied O'Hara with special intensity. "Buca."

"You didn't tell me how you found us."

"I followed you from the Grara Outpost....and I wasn't the only one." Buca returned to the hollow entrance and squatted there. He gazed out into the night, and for the first time, he pulled one of his rifles forward.

He rested it on his lap with his finger on the trigger guard, but he aimed the weapon outward into the darkness, not at the Hellhounds.

"Who followed us?" Heckler asked. "Where are they?"

"The Cezians sent scouts to find out where you were," Buca replied. "And the colonists tracked you to this hollow. They set up guard posts to alert their chief of your movements. They'll follow you when you leave here."

"Macon!" Nunn hissed. "That bastard!"

Buca raised his eyebrows at her. "You know him?"

"We had the misfortune of meeting him yesterday," Heckler growled. "That's how we found out the colonists were stealing from the Maczhi...and the Cezians. He didn't even try to hide it from us."

Buca went back to studying the darkness. "The colonists talk in their camp about killing all of you. They want to make sure you don't alert the Elian Command. The colonists want to claim this planet for themselves and drive all the aliens out."

"How do you know they're planning to kill us?" LeMaine asked. "How do you know they posted guards to keep us under surveillance?"

Buca turned around again. His direct, unwavering gaze sent a shiver up LeMaine's spine. "I followed them. I listened outside their camp. It always pays to keep your enemies under your eye."

"We gotta get the hell out of here," Lemon muttered. "This is bad."

"Keep your shorts on, Sergeant. We aren't dead yet." LeMaine turned back to Buca. "If you're right, then we need to contact Command as soon as possible. We lost contact with our ship. That's why we went to the Cezian outpost—to use their communications system."

"I know that," Buca replied. "I saw everything."

"If you know that, then you know we never did anything to the Cezians. It was the colonists who started the fight."

Buca nodded. "I know."

"We can alert Command to what's going on here, but if you're right about the colonists, they'll try to stop us from going near the outpost again."

Buca nodded again. "There is another array, but it's far from here."

"Is it controlled by the Cezians, too?" Kellogg asked.

"It's controlled by no one. No one has used it in years. I'm not even sure if it works anymore."

Heckler groaned. "Wonderful. So we'll trek across open country getting shot at by deranged colonists while we're looking for an array we don't even know we can use. It sounds like my idea of a good time."

"Where is this array?" LeMaine asked.

Buca pointed into the darkness. "It's to the south.... beyond the mountains."

LeMaine pulled up the navigation chart on his remote. "How far is it?"

"Maybe five days' travel through the mountains. I can take you there.... for a price."

LeMaine stiffened. "What price?"

"I will help you contact your Command, but I want you to take me with you when you go. I want to leave this planet and start a new life on Elia. I might even join the Elian Special Forces."

LeMaine had to laugh. "You might want to reconsider that, pal. As you can see, life in the Elian Special Forces isn't all it's cracked up to be."

Buca cast another appraising glance around. "I can see what it's like."

"Anyway, we're stranded here for now. None of us is going anywhere until we get access to that array."

"What about using Polasek's rig to patch into the array?" Kellogg suggested. "He couldn't raise the *Renown*, but his rig might be able to reach another system if it isn't too far away."

"The other system is non-operational, pinhead," Heckler countered. "We don't even know if it has power."

"Buca said he wasn't sure if it works," Kellogg pointed out. "It could be just fine."

"If it is, the colonists will try to stop us from reaching that, too," Nunn added. "They might even take control of it before we get there to defend it from us."

"We'd have better luck with the Cezians," LeMaine replied. "Their array is closer and we already know that one is working."

"Yeah, see, there's just one problem with that," Heckler argued. "There's a whole pack of mangy colonists standing between us and the outpost."

"Actually," Nunn told him, "there's the other slight problem of the fact that three of our guys are barely hanging onto life and the rest of us aren't in sparkling condition, either. We ain't going nowhere for a while, and when we do, we ain't going back into a battle like that."

"Monk, Kellogg, and I are all right," LeMaine pointed out. "If it comes to that, the three of us can go back to the outpost, make contact with the Cezians, and see about using their array."

"Peterman isn't barely hanging onto life," Kellogg told him. "He'll be back on his feet in twenty-four hours and the rest of you should be cleared for active duty by then, too."

"That leaves O'Hara and Polasek," Nunn added. "What are we gonna do—leave them unguarded?"

"If it comes to your safety," LeMaine decided, "you can all stay here while I go to the outpost alone."

A chorus of protests erupted on all sides. "No way, Sir!" Monk boomed.

"I'm going with you," Kellogg fired back.

"You are NOT going back to the outpost alone," Heckler growled.

"Dream on, Sir," Nunn snapped.

Buca looked back and forth between the parties with interest, but he didn't say anything.

"If you know about what happened earlier," LeMaine asked him, "maybe you can answer a question for me. How did the colonists sneak up on us like that? We never saw them coming."

"Polasek said the atmosphere made our remotes malfunction," Nunn suggested.

"Not entirely," LeMaine countered. "Our remotes showed up everything inside the outpost, but not the Cezians who followed us. Then, just a few minutes ago, our remotes detected Buca outside, but our remotes should have picked him up long before he got near us." LeMaine turned back to Buca. "How do you explain that?"

Buca shrugged again. "The colonists use technology to mask their movements. Ever since the Cezians took the Grara Outpost, the Cezians use Elian technology to track the colonists' movements. They do it to ward off the colonists' attacks and the colonists use technology to hide themselves."

"That explains it." Kellogg took one more hesitant look at Buca and swiveled around to stretch out next to Polasek. "If you're gonna shoot me, just make it quick, okay? I don't want to know it's coming."

Buca cocked his head to study the young medic, but Kellogg didn't see him. Kellogg laid out on the floor and shut his eyes.

LeMaine relaxed against the wall, but he didn't stop observing Buca. The Maczhi moved into their hollow and set himself up as a guard at the entrance without asking.

Who was he? LeMaine teemed with more questions, but he held back from asking them.

The rest of the Hellhounds settled down one after the other...except Monk. He planted himself between Buca on one side and O'Hara and Peterman on the other. Monk stayed standing up with his carbine raised, but he stopped short of actually pointing it at Buca.

Buca's unwavering eye measured Monk's body language, but the Maczhi didn't move from his position. He couldn't fail to see Lemon and Heckler both keeping their guns ready to protect Kellogg and Polasek if it came to that, but it never did come to that because Buca didn't move.

LeMaine finally gave it up and set his carbine aside. He was too exhausted and drained to keep his eyes open.

"How do you find food in the mountains?" he asked.

Buca's voice drifted out of the darkness. "Our people are native to this planet. We traditionally hunted the mountains in nomadic bands, but colonists from Elia and other systems drove us aside. When the colonists came, some Maczhi copied them by building encampments. The Maczhi became dependent on supply shipments from Elia, but some of us kept the old ways."

"Do the colonists know about you?" Nunn asked. "Do they know you've been following them around and listening in on their conversations?"

Buca glanced in her direction and then went back to gazing outward into the dark. "They don't know about me. I make sure of it."

Chapter 7

Kellogg examined the thin scar on Peterman's side and checked the medical scanner. "You're all clear, Lieutenant. You can thank the captain for this."

Peterman put his shirt down. "Thank you, Captain."

LeMaine clapped him on the shoulder. "Don't let it happen again or you'll be busted down to private." LeMaine nodded toward the hollow entrance and lowered his voice to a murmur. "See if you can find out anything else about our new friend."

Peterman climbed up to the hollow entrance where Buca sat squinting across the landscape. He hadn't moved since he first showed up.

Kellogg went over to Polasek, who sat on the floor where he had fallen. Kellogg scanned his hip. "How are you feeling, Lieutenant?"

"I feel like shit. Thanks for asking, pal."

Kellogg laughed. "You must be feeling better if you can mouth off to me. Stand up and see if you can put weight on your leg."

He helped Polasek up. Polasek tried to shift his weight onto his injured hip and winced. "It still hurts."

Kellogg supported him while Polasek limped over to the shelf Peterman had just vacated. Kellogg lowered him onto it. "Stay put for now. You can guard O'Hara while we make another play for the outpost."

Kellogg handed Polasek his carbine and placed Polasek's pack next to him. Polasek kept flinching while he scooted back on the shelf and made himself as comfortable as possible, but he stayed sitting up while he checked and reloaded his weapon.

Kellogg crossed to LeMaine's side and they both looked down at O'Hara. The young sniper lay on his back on the shelf where Kellogg had operated on him.

O'Hara's fatigues lay open on either side of his chest to reveal a solid landscape of cuts, tears, incisions, cauterized seals, bruising, and swollen flesh. They covered his torso from his neck down to his navel, but at least his eyes were open.

He looked up at LeMaine with a mixture of desperation and fury. "You can't leave me here, Sir! Let me come with you!"

"Forget it, pal," Kellogg cut in. "You aren't going anywhere but back to the field hospital on Viahiri Prime. If I hear from Polasek that you're trying to get up, I'll have to sedate you."

LeMaine rested his hand on O'Hara's shoulder. "Rest easy, son. We aren't going into any action if I can help it. We're taking a walk in the park. You won't be missing anything."

O'Hara picked up his head like he might try to sit up, but he lacked the strength even to do that. "Don't leave me behind, Sir! How can I face the others like this?"

"They're leaving me behind, too, Sergeant," Polasek chimed in. "We can both be humiliated together."

O'Hara gasped in exasperation and collapsed back on the shelf. "At least give me a weapon, Sir. Don't leave me unarmed."

LeMaine glanced over at Kellogg and Kellogg nodded. LeMaine crossed to where Kellogg had discarded O'Hara's pack, fished in it, and brought back a single sidearm. "Here you go, son. Just don't try to get up. None of us wants to operate on you again. Understand?"

O'Hara turned away clutching his weapon. "Yes, Sir."

LeMaine gave O'Hara's shoulder one last squeeze. Kellogg passed his scanner over O'Hara's chest and then both he and LeMaine put on their packs and picked up their carbines.

LeMaine paused at the entrance to look back. O'Hara refused to look at him, but Polasek smiled and nodded while his hands went through the practiced routine of checking and adjusting his weapon.

LeMaine stepped out of the hollow to find Lemon, Monk, Heckler, and Nunn waiting for him. They stood guard in the sunshine and scanned the terrain around their gully.

Peterman and Buca approached from farther up the draw. They broke off their conversation when they reached the rest of the group. "Any sign out there?" LeMaine asked.

"The colonists have withdrawn," Buca announced. "They are no longer guarding you."

"Why not?"

"I didn't see. They pulled back in the night. Your path to the outpost is clear now."

"As clear as anything gets on this rock," Heckler muttered.

LeMaine checked his remote. "There they are. The colonists are moving away toward the north."

"They aren't even trying to conceal themselves," Nunn remarked. "I wonder why not."

"Probably to trick us," Lemon suggested.

"Never mind," LeMaine replied. "Let's get to the outpost before they come back. Move out, people."

He started up the draw. Peterman and Buca flanked him. The other four fell in behind with plenty of checking the ridges on either side.

LeMaine headed straight up the hill. He wanted to get out of this gully quickly so he could see as much of the countryside as possible. He was sick and tired of these assholes ambushing him.

Buca drew level with him and pulled ahead. LeMaine sped up. Just a few feet from the top, he heard a loud buzz and his fingers instinctively clamped on his weapon.

He swept it up, but at that instant, a deafening clack froze him in his tracks as ten cannons popped over the ridge. They all pointed down at the squad in a deadly ring.

Cezians snarled at the Hellhounds from behind each weapon. LeMaine braced himself to go down shooting, but the gunners didn't open fire.

The next second, forty more Cezians armed with fusion rifles swarmed over the hillsides to surround the squad. The Cezians yelled something in another language, rushed the squad in a horde, and circled the Hellhounds in weapons.

LeMaine's eye raced across the ridge. Shooting at these people would get him and his whole squad vaporized by anti-matter cannons.

The instant he hesitated, the Cezians snatched his weapon out of his hands. He grasped it automatically, but when they tore it out of his grip, he gave it up.

The Cezians disarmed the rest of the Hellhounds, but a second later, gunfire erupted inside the hollow. Someone screamed.

LeMaine spun around fast. "Polasek....!"

A thunderous blow clubbed LeMaine across the back of the head and he went down face first in the dirt.

He came to his senses lying on his back in a dim, musty enclosure. His eyelids fluttered and he looked up at Kellogg bending over him. The young medic had a giant black eye and a fat lip.

"Lie still, Sir. I need to check you out."

"What the hell is going......?" LeMaine tried to sit up.

Kellogg pushed him down. "Not so fast, Sir. You aren't clear for active duty until I say so."

LeMaine snorted. "You call this active duty?"

Kellogg smiled, but the sadness in his expression made LeMaine shudder. "Open your eyes."

"My eyes *are* open, Sergeant."

"Don't even bother arguing with him, Sir," Heckler grunted behind LeMaine. "The son of a bitch has been through the same damn thing with all of us. Now it's your turn."

"I say we put in to Command for a new medic," Nunn chimed in. "Someone easy-going.... someone mild-mannered...."

"Someone obedient," Lemon added. "Someone who doesn't understand their own medical authority."

LeMaine started to turn his head, but Kellogg gripped his chin and forced LeMaine to face him. "Look at me."

LeMaine stared up at his medic and blinked. Kellogg covered one of LeMaine's eyes with his palm and removed it before doing the same thing to the other eye. "What are you doing?"

"They took all my gear. I have to check you out the old-fashioned way. Just keep still or you'll make it take even longer."

Kellogg started patting LeMaine down. He squeezed and manhandled LeMaine's neck and skull, his shoulders, arms, ribs, and finally his legs.

"You can get up now, Sir."

"Are you sure?" LeMaine sneered. "I wouldn't want to put myself in danger or anything."

Monk laughed. "No sane person would want that."

LeMaine hauled himself up and winced. His head hurt and he rubbed his temple. Then he looked around.

The squad sat in a tiny room carved out of what looked like bare rock. There was barely enough space in the middle for LeMaine to lie down while the others kept their knees drawn in to make room for everyone.

LeMaine pulled himself over to the wall and sat down next to Monk. Even in the dim light, he saw all his people sporting the evidence of beatings. "Any word on O'Hara and Polasek?"

"Nothing," Heckler replied. "We've been in here ever since they captured us."

"Where are we?" LeMaine asked. "Did you see where they took us?"

"We're somewhere in the mountains," Nunn replied. "We went south after we left the hollow. We're in some kind of compound hidden in the middle of nowhere."

"There were a couple thousand Cezians all over the place," Lemon added. "I'd say whatever they're doing at the Grara Outpost is being carried out by a skeleton crew. This is their real headquarters."

LeMaine groaned. "Wonderful."

"Look on the bright side, Sir," Monk chimed in. "At least we're closer to using their communications system here."

LeMaine snorted. "That's you, Monk. Always looking on the bright side."

"Monk is right," Kellogg told him. "At least we don't have to walk into a potential shit storm to convince the Cezians to let us use it."

LeMaine laughed. "Oh, now you're joining in the joy parade? You're gonna put me out of business, Sergeant."

Kellogg sat down next to him. "Just doing my job, Sir."

"Now we just have to convince them we aren't here to help out those scumbag colonists," Nunn remarked.

"Easier said than done," LeMaine began. "If they think......"

At that moment, the door crashed open and hit Kellogg in the face. He shrank back against LeMaine to get out of the way as a bunch of armed Cezians stormed in.

They stepped on the Hellhounds' legs and kicked a few people aside before the Cezians hurled O'Hara and Polasek on the floor.

"Hey!" Lemon bellowed and started to stand up. "You bastards!"

LeMaine caught her arm and pulled her down when the Cezians glared at her. Heckler grabbed O'Hara and towed him out of the way. Polasek had to practically crawl onto Monk's lap to give the Cezians enough space to get out of the room.

The Cezians slammed the door and silence fell over the squad. Kellogg rotated onto his knees and bent over O'Hara, who still sprawled in Heckler's big arms. "You okay, man?"

O'Hara nodded up at the closed door with huge eyes. He opened his mouth to say something and coughed. A bloop of bloody saliva bubbled out of his mouth and ran down his chest that still showed between his open shirt.

"Holy shit!" Kellogg hissed. "Lie him down. Hurry up."

"Sir...." O'Hara's glazed eyes skimmed sideways to LeMaine.

LeMaine leaned forward and took O'Hara's hand. LeMaine struggled to keep his voice steady. "Easy, Sergeant. Just lie quiet and let Kellogg do his thing."

Kellogg shot LeMaine another black look. If the Cezians injured O'Hara, Kellogg wouldn't be able to do jack shit without his medical gear.

Monk arranged Polasek on the floor next to him, but they had to smash into LeMaine and each other to fit. "You okay, Sir?" Monk asked Polasek.

Polasek nodded, but he didn't say anything. Another terrible silence fell over the squad while Kellogg got to work on O'Hara. LeMaine pressed O'Hara's hand between his own, but he could already see it was hopeless.

Kellogg started palpitating O'Hara's chest. "Damn it!" he whispered. "I don't even have a damn scalpel to open him up and see where he's bleeding."

"Sir....?" O'Hara's eyes glided over to LeMaine's face again, but O'Hara didn't see anything anymore. His pupils dilated and he stared at something behind LeMaine's head.

"I'm here, son," LeMaine whispered. "We're all here."

Kellogg pressed one of the incisions he'd sealed last night. Blood oozed from the skin where the seal split.

LeMaine's throat constricted. Twenty years in the military and this never got any easier. If anything, it got harder every time he lost someone.

He placed his left hand against O'Hara's cheek. "You did real good, son. I'm proud of you. You did your family and your squad proud."

Monk turned away and looked at the wall, but at that moment, the door exploded off its hinges for the second time. A body hurtled into the room and stepped on O'Hara on its headlong plunge.

It crashed into the back wall and Buca tumbled down on top of Nunn. She grabbed him and dragged him into the Hellhounds' group as the Cezians charged in and pointed their weapons at the squad.

Chapter 8

LeMaine's instincts got the better of him and he flung himself forward. He jumped onto his knees, turned backward, and blocked Kellogg and O'Hara with his own body. "Don't shoot!" Five Cezians aimed their rifles at LeMaine's face. He raised his hands. "Don't shoot! We're unarmed!"

"Get down on the floor!" one of the Cezians bellowed in clear, unmistakable English. "Get away from that man."

"No!" LeMaine choked. "If you want to kill someone, kill me. This man is injured and he needs medical attention right away. If you don't return my medic's tool kit, this man will die. Is that what you want Elian Command to find out when word gets back to them? Do you want them to find out you let one of their soldiers die rather than give him medical treatment?"

LeMaine stammered to a halt and gasped to catch his breath. He no longer held out any hope that the Cezians would see sense in time to save O'Hara's life, but LeMaine had to try.

"Who are you?" the voice boomed from behind the aliens holding LeMaine at gunpoint.

"I told you at the outpost! I'm Captain LeMaine of the Elian Special Forces. We came to respond to a distress call. We had no idea what was going on with the colonists on this planet. We didn't know they were stealing your...."

"Quiet!" the voice thundered.

LeMaine flinched, but he didn't move. A long moment of tense silence ticked past. Every second brought him closer to the Cezians blowing his head off.

A scuffle broke out behind the Cezians, but he couldn't see anything beyond the guns pointed in his face. Out of the shadows, someone threw something hard and it crashed into LeMaine's chest.

He took a second to realize that it was a backpack—a backpack with a giant red cross patch on the front flap. It was Kellogg's backpack.

LeMaine pushed it behind him and instantly raised his hands again. "Thank you."

He heard Kellogg working fast behind him and LeMaine's heart skipped a beat. Did he dare to hope?

"Who are you really?" the voice snarled out of the dark. "You came here to help the colonists. You're military. You came to clear the aliens off this planet!"

"No!" LeMaine croaked. "We only defended ourselves against the Cezians. We didn't know about the colonists robbing you. We came here to find an Elian diplomat lost somewhere on this planet. Elian Command received a distress call and they assumed it came from the diplomat. We came to find her and get her to safety. That's all. I'm telling you the truth." He thought fast. "You have communications with Elian Command. You can confirm this for yourself."

No one answered him. He'd played his last card. If the Cezians were the ones who sent that distress call, they could contact Elian Command themselves. Command would find out the Hellhounds had been captured on this planet.

Then what? The Hellhounds had a reputation for handling anything. Command sent them to this planet to deal with the situation, not to get themselves into a life-threatening mess where they needed a rescue mission mounted for them, too.

That was the Hellhounds' job—*not* to need a rescue. It was LeMaine's job to make sure they didn't need a rescue.

LeMaine heard Kellogg whispering to his squad mates in the silence that followed. Was O'Hara dying right now?

LeMaine should be there. He should be holding O'Hara's hand right now, not trying to talk his way out of his whole squad getting annihilated.

He couldn't turn around, not when he finally explained his position to these people. If they didn't listen to him, he had a much bigger problem than O'Hara dying.

Someone shoved between the Cezians holding LeMaine at gunpoint. Another Cezian pushed to the forefront and glared down at him.

Something in the features looked more delicate than the others, and when the creature spoke, the deep rumbling voice did nothing to make her seem less feminine.

Her horned face and wicked fangs made her look hideous and deadly, but her eyes really sealed the deal. "You are Elian scum," she snarled. "Elians don't care for anything but conquering one planet after another. You're one of them. The Elian Command came here to finish the war the colonists started."

"No!" LeMaine couldn't speak above a whisper. "Do you think Command would send nine people with carbines to finish a war? We don't even have an aircraft."

Her eyes sliced from one side to the other measuring the squad. She must have seen that none of them posed any threat to her. "You will stay here while we confirm your story. If you're lying, you will all die."

She turned on her heel and the other Cezians backed out of the room. The door slammed again and the Hellhounds slumped. "Jesus Christ!" Heckler whispered.

LeMaine collapsed on the floor next to Kellogg. "How bad is it, Sergeant?"

"It's okay," Kellogg choked. "It's only a small tear in his trachea. I can fix it. He'll be all right."

LeMaine ran his fingers through his hair and realized his hands were shaking. Polasek clapped him on the shoulder and pulled LeMaine back against the wall. "You did good," Polasek whispered. "They'll confirm the order. They'll find out we came from Command."

LeMaine didn't answer. He leaned his head back against the wall, shut his eyes, and concentrated on getting his heart to slow down. He had to think. He had to think of something to do—anything to get his people out of this.

The *Renown*. He needed to access the *Renown's* navigation system, but he couldn't do that without the Cezians' help.

He glanced over at Buca. The Maczhi crouched between Heckler and Nunn. Blood dripped from Buca's nose and most of his face swelled up with bruising. He stared at the floor. He didn't look so hot to join the Elian Special Forces now.

A second later the door swung open. It creaked on its hinges instead of crashing aside and hitting anybody.

LeMaine shot upright in a flash. He got as far as kneeling in front of O'Hara, but the Cezians didn't charge in sticking their guns everywhere.

LeMaine braced himself and prepared for the worst, but the Cezians stayed outside in the hall. They aimed their guns at him, but they didn't enter the cell.

The female Cezian stood behind them baring her fangs at him. "You will come with me, Captain."

"No!" he blurted out. "I won't leave my people."

"You will leave them and come with me or they will all die," she hissed. "You will come, and if you don't answer my questions, you'll be the first to die."

LeMaine swallowed hard. "Give me your word you won't harm any of them while I'm gone."

A cruel smirk twisted her fanged mouth. "You talk of giving my word. The Elian Command gave us assurances that they would support our colony and negotiate citizenship for Cezians in the Elian system. The Elian Command and the Elian Assembly has broken every promise they ever made to us and you speak of giving my word!"

LeMaine lowered his eyes. He couldn't look at her. "I don't know about that. I'm just a soldier. I don't have anything to do with Command or the Assembly. I only care about protecting my people."

She measured him with a hard look and finally clamped her mouth shut. "Very well. You have my word that no one will enter this room until you come back." Her eyes dipped to O'Hara. "What happens to them before that doesn't concern me."

"Okay." He dropped forward to put his hands on the floor and push himself up. "I'm coming."

Polasek darted forward and gripped LeMaine's wrist. He gave LeMaine a sharp shake of his head as a warning, but LeMaine was already rocking backward onto his heels. "Stay here," he whispered. "Take over."

Polasek unwrapped his fingers from LeMaine's wrist and Polasek leaned back. His face fell into shadow where LeMaine couldn't see him. Monk kept his face turned away and didn't make eye contact, either.

LeMaine straightened up to face the Cezians and all their guns. He stepped across the threshold and turned back for one last look at his squad, but the Cezians slammed the door in his face.

LeMaine sighed and turned around again to face his captor. "Well? Here I am. What do you want to talk to me about? I already told you everything."

"Follow me, Captain." She turned on her heel and strode off down the corridor. LeMaine didn't move until one of the guards prodded him with his rifle.

LeMaine started forward. His head pounded from the blow that knocked him out, but he would still vastly prefer to be back in that room with his squad than out here with these aliens.

The female Cezian turned at an intersection and climbed some stairs to a long catwalk where it crossed a high stone wall. LeMaine looked down at dozens of Cezians going about their business.

Many stood guard on the walls while others worked on their cannons down on the ground.

Tall buildings dotted with windows lined the compound. Cezians of all ages crossed beneath him, leaned from the windows, and talked to each other. Lemon was right. There must be thousands of them living here.

"Did you know, Captain?" the female asked. "This is the only Cezian colony in the Elian system where Cezians can live under their own independent governance. Every other Cezian colony in the system is subject to exceptional regulation. The rules are designed to keep the Cezians down and prevent them from advancing or gaining too much of a market share over Elian citizens—and it works."

"Like I said, I don't know much about politics," he replied. "I'm just a soldier. I do my job and then I get assigned to another one."

"You say you came here to find and rescue a diplomat."

"That's right," LeMaine replied.

"Did your Command tell you anything about this diplomat?"

"Only that she's female and that she came here to negotiate with one of the alien groups here."

"Which group?" she asked.

"I don't know. That's classified and it wasn't necessary for me to know to carry out my mission. Command didn't know the Cezians were on this planet, so I assume she came here to negotiate with the Maczhi."

She spun around fast and hissed at him through her fangs. "The Maczhi!"

"Why not? They're Elian citizens. The colonists were interfering with the Maczhi's supply shipments, too, so the Maczhi would be entitled to diplomatic intervention."

She snarled at him. "I see you know more about politics than you want me to believe."

He shrugged. "I'm just trying to find her."

"How do you know she wants to be found?"

Now it was his turn to spin around. "You!"

She looked away. "Why are you so surprised?"

"You're......Cezian."

"You're very perceptive. Of course I'm Cezian. I came here to communicate between the Elian Assembly and the Cezians who took refuge on this planet from the cruel regulations oppressing them elsewhere."

"But you.... you joined them!" LeMaine couldn't stop staring at her. "You.... you went off the reservation. You joined the other side."

"I did much more than that. I organized this revolt to defend our people against the colonists. The Cezians were losing ground when I arrived. The colonists would have wiped them all out, but I took over their command and turned the tide."

LeMaine gulped. "Holy crap!"

"Well?" she demanded. "Now you've found me. Will you drag me back to Elia against my will? Will you report my betrayal to your Command and bring in the military to finish us off once and for all? All Elians view Cezians as bloodthirsty murderers. Don't deny it."

LeMaine scanned the ground beneath him while he scrambled for some way to react to this. She was right about one thing. Wider Elian society hated the Cezians. Public opinion leaned heavily in favor of either annihilating them all or driving them out and sending them back to their own system.

The Elian Assembly implemented plenty of controls to stop Cezians from competing with other races in business, academics, trade, and every other area. There were even limits on how much money a Cezian could keep in the banking system.

She interrupted his thoughts. "You asked what I wanted to talk to you about, Captain. I have a proposal for you."

"What is it? I already told you I'm not here to fight anybody's civil war for them. We don't have enough people to make a difference anyway."

"I don't want you to fight a civil war for us. I don't want to fight a civil war at all."

"What do you want?" LeMaine took a deep breath. "I'll do whatever it takes to ensure my people's safety."

She gazed across the compound at the Cezians living their lives on all sides. "What I ask will put them in more danger, but it's the only way you can get them off this planet."

"What is it?" he asked again.

"I want you to help us send another message to Elian Command."

"Why can't you do that now? Why can't you use the Grara array? Your people are already in possession of the building."

"The array at the Grara Outpost is broken beyond repair. It stopped working not long after we drove out the colonists. We sent the distress call, but the array stopped working before we could communicate any details with the message."

"Why have you been defending the outpost, then?"

"We did it to draw the colonists away from *this* compound. We wanted the colonists to think we were defending the array. We wanted them to think the array was critical to us and that we wanted to keep control of the only remaining communication system. As long as we held the Grara Outpost, they concentrated their attacks there and left our people alone."

LeMaine sighed. "Let me guess. There's another array."

"In the mountains to the south. We don't know if it works, but you have a communications specialist with you, am I right?"

LeMaine heaved another almighty sigh. "Yeah. I do."

"We need your help to get to the array, drive away any colonists who might be defending it, and reactivate it. Once we do that, I can contact Command and call in reinforcements. They'll come for me."

LeMaine snorted. "Yeah. They'll come for *you*."

"Well? Do we have a bargain?"

"Under one condition."

"What condition is that?"

"That you give my people enough time to recover from their injuries....and that you give my sniper the medical care he needs. I won't leave him in danger while we go trekking across the country."

She leveled him with a critical eye and then nodded. "I understand now and we will wait."

"Thank you. As soon as my people are all recovered, we'll be much more useful to you than we are now."

She waved to one side and they started walking down the wall in the direction they had come. LeMaine looked behind him. He didn't want to talk anymore. He wanted to get back to the squad, but she didn't notice.

She climbed down a different ladder to a different corridor. LeMaine got more and more agitated the farther she led him away from the squad. Was this a trap? Was she leading him to his execution after all?

She turned into a brightly lit passage lined with doors. "You haven't once asked me my name, Captain."

"Huh?" He looked behind him again. "Oh. Yeah. You're right."

She frowned when he turned around again. "It's Lulara."

He didn't hear her. He wanted to go back and check on O'Hara. LeMaine also wanted to check the rest of the squad for injuries. If they all got beaten up on their way in, they could have injuries of their own that needed treatment.

"I asked you a question, Captain. Are you listening to me?"

He struggled to drag his attention back to the present. "Huh? Oh, sorry."

"I asked you how long you've been in the service. You seem too old to command a squad like this."

"I guess I am."

She stopped in front of one of the doors. "You really care about your soldiers, don't you?"

"Of course I do. That's my job."

"No, it isn't that. You care about them more than a job."

He glanced around and finally settled on meeting her gaze, but he couldn't get away from her fast enough. "I guess that's part of the job, too. They're good kids. They deserve a commander who cares about them."

"I'll be around to check on you. Your medic can tell me when your people are ready to move."

She waved at the door behind him. He didn't know what she meant until the door opened from the inside. Two Cezians came out and LeMaine's stomach dropped when he saw the Hellhounds inside.

O'Hara lay stretched out on a medical exam table with a bunch of medical equipment hooked up to every part of his body. Tubes went into his nose and mouth and his eyes were taped shut.

Kellogg and a bunch of Cezians worked over him with Kellogg calling orders to everyone. Buca and the Hellhounds sat on other exam tables while more Cezians attended to their injuries.

A few Cezians were in the act of easing Polasek onto his back and helping him take off his fatigues so they could check his hip.

LeMaine took a step forward and the conversation with Lulara evaporated out of his head. He didn't give a damn what happened tomorrow. He was where he needed to be and now he could stop worrying about his people.

Chapter 9

LeMaine stopped next to O'Hara's bed and surveyed the young sniper's bare chest. "You don't look so hot, Sergeant.'

O'Hara burst out laughing. "Don't tell my girlfriend that, Sir. She thinks I'm stunning."

"What girlfriend?" Nunn called from her bed on the other side of the hospital ward. "You aren't talking about your scope again, are you, Romeo?"

O'Hara blushed and lowered his eyes, but he wouldn't stop laughing. "You got me, Nunn. I thought I was keeping our romance under wraps, but I guess I blew it."

"Don't worry, champ. Your secret is safe with me."

"It isn't safe with me, Prince Charming," Heckler chimed in. "As soon as we get home to Elia, every news outlet in the system is gonna hear about this."

The squad erupted in talk and laughter, but LeMaine didn't move. He kept scowling at O'Hara's chest until O'Hara pulled his shirt over his head and buttoned it up.

Kellogg came along and took something out from under O'Hara's bed. "Are you sure O'Hara is fit for service?" LeMaine asked Kellogg. "I don't want him busting himself at the worst possible time."

"You know I wouldn't clear him if he wasn't fit, Sir," Kellogg returned. "He'll be fine."

"His chest is still black and blue and most of the seals haven't completely healed."

"They look bad, but the discoloration is normal and the seals are solid." Kellogg cocked his head and eyed LeMaine. "What's on your mind, Sir? Is this really about O'Hara?"

LeMaine turned away and passed his hand across his eyes. "I guess not."

Kellogg went back to packing his kit. He took supplies from the Cezian hospital stores, replaced the blood transfusions, and recharged his equipment.

LeMaine strolled to the next bed where Polasek sat propped against a large bean bag. He was reading something on a handheld computer terminal the Cezians had given him. "How are you feeling, Lieutenant?" LeMaine asked.

Polasek didn't look up. "Fighting fit. You can stop asking. My condition hasn't deteriorated since you asked me half an hour ago."

LeMaine slumped down on his own bed. He was sick and tired of sitting around doing nothing, but the coming campaign to reach the second communications array gave him grave misgivings. Why?

He leaned back on his own pillows and checked his remote for at least the hundredth time this hour. He read the layout of the Nanov Outpost to the south. It had been sitting derelict for years. The charts no longer depicted enough detail for him to locate the transmission dish.

He didn't like this at all, but when he raised his eyes to survey the hospital wing, he got his answer. He didn't want to split up the Hellhounds.

This wouldn't be their first operation working on different fronts. His people could all handle themselves independently and some of them even thrived on it.

Their recent experience made him worry about them more than usual, though. Either way, he had gone too far in planning this assault to back out now. They had already waited too long.

Just then, Lulara waltzed in. She had been becoming progressively more civil since LeMaine agreed to help throw the colonists out of Nanov and use the communications array to call in the Elian Military.

She looked around once, and instead of coming over to talk to LeMaine, she approached Kellogg. They exchanged a few snatches of conversation and LeMaine's scalp prickled. This was it. Kellogg would tell her that the whole squad was cleared for active duty.

LeMaine got to his feet and pulled his pack out from under the table. He had packed it days ago so it would be ready when Kellogg gave the word.

Polasek and Heckler stood up, too. The rest of the squad started moving even before Kellogg finished giving his verdict. No one had to tell them it was go time.

Lulara turned around and saw the squad coming toward her with their gear ready. Monk checked his weapon right in front of her. She almost left, but she stopped in her tracks when she spotted Buca at the bed on the end of the ward.

He got up with the others and started collecting his gear. He had gathered it together since coming to the Cezians' Nulia Compound. He slung a backpack over his shoulder and fell in with the others gathering around Kellogg.

"Hold it." Lulara pointed at Buca. "You stay here."

"No way," Heckler countered. "He's coming with us."

"No," Lulara snapped. "He's a prisoner."

"Like hell he is!" Monk boomed. "He's one of us and he's coming with us. We need him."

"No." Lulara set her features into a scowl, squared her shoulders, and glared at the squad. She didn't see them gathering around her in more threatening postures. "He stays here. He isn't part of this operation."

LeMaine sauntered over extra slow. "I'll be the one to decide who is part of my squad and who isn't."

"And I'll be the one to decide who goes on this operation and who doesn't." She leveled Buca with a cruel glare. "If he goes, the deal is off and you can take your chances with the colonists yourselves. I was doing fine here without you before you showed up."

LeMaine swiveled in front of her to block her from the rest of the squad. "You want this mission to succeed as much as we do. If it fails, the Cezians will keep being second-class citizens in this system. We stand the best chance of accomplishing this job if Buca helps u s."

"No Maczhi is going on this mission. He stays. That's my last word." She whirled away and left the room without another word.

"Foul bitch!" Lemon hissed. "Let me at her, Sir. I'll slap some sense into that ugly head of hers."

"Who the hell does she think she is, telling us what to do?" Heckler growled. "She's supposed to be an Elian and she pulls this shit on military personnel."

LeMaine turned around to find Buca watching him. "It's all right, Captain," Buca murmured. "I'll stay behind."

"No way!" Nunn spat. "You're with us."

Buca shook his head and put his backpack down. "This mission is too important. You need to finish it and you need to Cezians to do that. I'll stay here."

"You don't have to do this," Peterman told him. "You're part of our squad now. This whole damn plan hinges on you."

Buca smiled down at him. "No, it doesn't. You know it doesn't. You don't have to spare my feelings. I can take it. I've been alone all my life." He glanced up at LeMaine and LeMaine's stomach twisted. "You know this is the only way, Captain. Go do it. Then I can be free."

LeMaine clasped Buca's shoulder hard. "I won't forget this. You deserve better than this."

"You're the only one who thinks so." Buca turned away and sat back down. "When I see you again, you'll tell me you were successful. Then, when the Elian Military shows up, I'll go with you. Then I'll be part of your squad for good."

"You're already part of our squad, pal," Monk told him. "You earned it."

Buca smiled at each Hellhound in turn, but LeMaine already recognized the truth in Buca's eyes. The squad had to leave and they couldn't afford to alienate Lulara or the Cezians.

"Let's go, Hellhounds," LeMaine told them and they followed him out of the hospital. They climbed down the stairs to the ground and emerged on a broad plateau adjoining the Nulia Compound.

They set off to cross it and slipped into a narrow defile on the other side. They wound down, down, down into the gully bottoms where they had to walk single file.

The gully twisted back and forth for a long time. An ooze of water seeped underfoot and eventually grew to a rivulet. It finally swelled to a little stream running down the mountain.

The stream passed through forests and finally merged with a larger river heading south. LeMaine ducked under a rocky overhand and took off his pack.

The rest of the Hellhounds got to work. Heckler took a waterproof bag out of his pack and put his two carbines and sidearms into it. He sealed it and stowed it in his pack along with his jacket. He took out a set of goggles and put them over his head.

"Make way for the Frog Man," Nunn teased.

"Mind your manners or I'll slap you with my flipper." Heckler put his pack back on and headed over to the river. "See you losers around the block."

"Take care of yourself, Heckler," LeMaine called after him.

"Me?" Heckler shot him a grin over his shoulder. "You know I'm the most important person in my life, Sir. If anyone is coming back from this mission, it's me."

He dove headfirst into the river and vanished. He didn't come up. In a second, the waves settled and the river kept moving on as though he was never there.

Nunn unzipped her pack and took out five blocks of Plaostine. She started cutting them in half and fitting the halves with primers. "What—only five?" Kellogg teased. "You're getting cautious in your old age, lady."

"Just wait 'til you see the other guy."

"You know where you have to go, Nunn?" LeMaine asked.

"You bet I do. Just watch out for the giant mushroom cloud."

"Don't blow yourself up while you're at it," Lemon interjected.

"I'll have Kellogg with me if I do."

"Don't joke about that," LeMaine cut in.

Lemon pulled a different black suit out of her pack and started unbuttoning her jacket. She peeled it off followed by her shirt.

"Boom-chicka-wow-wow! Take it all off, baby!" O'Hara hooted.

"Take a good look, shithead," Lemon snarled. "You aren't likely to see a girl anywhere else."

O'Hara shut his mouth real quick, but he kept smirking like a fool while she stripped off and pulled the suit over her underwear and backpack. She tugged the hood over her head and eventually arranged the hood to cover her face.

She adjusted a remote on her wrist and the suit changed. It shimmered and then changed to make her look like a Maczhi. It projected an image much larger than her real form.

This Maczhi slouched and dragged its knuckles like the starving aliens the Hellhounds first met. Her eyes sagged and goo crusted the lids.

"That's perfect, Lemon," LeMaine told her.

The creature rasped under its breath and spoke in a husky, broken tone. "Food.... neeed...."

Kellogg laughed at her. "Perfect."

Lemon high-fived him and then turned away, loped off up the riverbank, and disappeared into the woods.

Nunn put her Plaostine back in her pack and nodded to Kellogg. They bumped fists with Monk and Polasek before Nunn and Kellogg headed off in a different direction.

Polasek kept fiddling with his portable communications array before leaving with Peterman. "Any luck getting through the atmosphere?" LeMaine asked.

Polasek shook his head. "Nothing has changed. We're still using the same frequencies. We'll have to report this when we get home. Command should know about this."

Peterman bumped his shoulder. "Let's rock, Lieutenant. I don't like standing around."

Polasek nodded and packed up his stuff. They headed back north toward the Nulia Compound and left LeMaine, Monk, and O'Hara.

Monk stared at the ground when LeMaine approached him. LeMaine had to raise his arm all the way to grip his pilot's shoulder. "You know what you have to do, right, Monk?"

Monk nodded down at his boots and then squinted toward the river. "I just don't like splitting up the squad, Sir. Something about this job doesn't sit right with me. Maybe...."

"I know," LeMaine told him. "I feel the same way."

"Buca should be here. I shouldn't be doing this alone."

"I know, son. It sucks."

Monk pursed his lips and shrugged. "What the hell, right? This is nothing compared to that mess we got into on Zukion, right?" He snapped his carbine and hefted it to his shoulder. "See you around, Sir."

"See you around, Corporal."

LeMaine suffered another pang watching Monk walk off. Monk crossed the river a few hundred yards up the bank and disappeared into the trees opposite.

"You ready, Sir?" O'Hara asked.

LeMaine nodded. "Just don't bore me with your jokes on the way, Sergeant."

O'Hara laughed. "I wouldn't dream of it. You'd bust my ass without the others here to run interference."

LeMaine picked up his stuff, shouldered his pack, and headed south. O'Hara fell in behind him and hiked silently, but after an hour of steady travel, LeMaine started to wish he hadn't told O'Hara to keep quiet.

LeMaine missed his squad's endless chatter. Their attitude told him everything was all right. Not having them around made him jumpy. O'Hara usually only kept quiet when the shit was about to hit the fan or really was hitting it.

They walked all day until the sun started to go down. LeMaine followed his remote into the trees and called a halt where the forest ended at another tall hill. "We can stop here until morning."

O'Hara squatted down, took off his pack, pulled out one of his ration bars. He bit it off and his remote reflected off his pale eyes. "What do you suppose the others are up to?"

LeMaine grinned to himself in the dark. "Well, Nunn and Kellogg are probably holding the Wise Ass Galactic Championships now that you aren't around to defend your title."

O'Hara choked on his ration bar. "You're killing me, Sir."

LeMaine chuckled. "Heckler is probably communing with the crawdads at the bottom of a lake somewhere and...."

"Polasek and Peterman are solving the galaxy's most pressing diplomatic problems," O'Hara finished.

"And you're stuck with me. Sorry, Sergeant."

O'Hara only smiled. "I'm glad."

"You don't have to say that, Sergeant. You don't have to blow sunshine up my ass because you're worried about getting told off."

O'Hara glanced up and immediately looked away. "I actually like you telling me off. It tells me you care. Maybe that's why I shoot my mouth off so much."

LeMaine burst out laughing. "Now I know you're blowing smoke."

"Would you believe I was considered a good boy when I was younger?"

"No. I would definitely not believe that."

They both laughed and LeMaine took out a ration bar of his own. "You should get some sleep, Sergeant."

"Thanks, Sir, but I don't think I could sleep right now if I tried. I'm too keyed up."

Silence fell between them. They sat together in the dark eating their ration bars and watching the stars twirl through the heavens.

LeMaine kept checking his remote. The rest of the Hellhounds showed up on it for a while, but in a few hours, they passed out of range. They were too far away and they kept moving right up until LeMaine lost sight of them.

He rested his head and pack against a tree trunk. After several hours, O'Hara wrapped himself in his drop suit, curled up on the ground, and fell asleep. LeMaine watched him for a while before LeMaine's eyes drifted closed and he let himself go.

Chapter 10

LeMaine checked his remote and nodded to O'Hara. O'Hara nodded back and fitted his scope to his carbine before they climbed to the top of the last hill separating them from the Nanov Outpost.

LeMaine flattened himself behind the summit and peered over. A broad valley spread below him with the outpost sitting on the other side.

Twenty thermal cannons dotted the roof. Armed guards lined the parapet and more surrounded the compound. Tall guns mounted on towers swiveled in all directions, but LeMaine didn't see any gunners up there. They must be automated.

A silver river snaked right next to the walls. Forests surrounded the compound's back side in a protective fringe. Relief flooded LeMaine's heart when he saw that outpost's the layout matched Lulara's intelligence exactly. This just might actually work.

O'Hara sighted down his scope while LeMaine checked his remote. "Anything going on down there?" LeMaine asked.

"Plenty," O'Hara muttered against his stock. "We were right. The colonists are in the house and ready to rule the planet."

"Good luck with that. Any sign of our boy Macon?"

"He won't be out here with the grunts. He'll be inside shining his tiara and pearls."

LeMaine sighted down his carbine and took aim at the thermal cannons on the roof. He couldn't hit anything else at this distance, so he would leave the rest to O'Hara.

"Any sign of the others?" O'Hara asked.

"Heads up," LeMaine whispered. "We got company."

Something rustled in the bushes near the eastern wall. O'Hara and LeMaine both swept their carbines that way as a tall Maczhi sloped into view. Its shoulders hunched and it made little agonized grunting noises.

It tripped and stumbled on its way to the outpost. The guards on that side rushed the creature and shout echoed from the roof. Some of the cannons swiveled to aim down at the alien. A few more guards left their posts to help restrain the Maczhi from getting too close.

The Maczhi struggled and fought trying to get near the wall. It went into a hysterical tirade of yells, croaks, and calls. It didn't sound like any language LeMaine had ever heard.

"Holy shit, Sir!" O'Hara breathed. "I wish to hell I could get this on video. She's going all out!"

LeMaine also started to question whether this alien was a real Maczhi or Lemon in disguise. What if some innocent, starving Maczhi really had stumbled into a deadly battle?

The commotion escalated to a fevered pitch. More guards left their posts to wrestle the Maczhi away, but the creature proved too strong. It took at least seven guards helping out to stop it from reaching the wall. Others stood around watching and the gunners called down to their comrades on the ground.

The alien's yells echoed over the field to LeMaine's position, and at that moment, something slipped out of the woods on the opposite side of the outpost. It skimmed down the wall crouching against the stone before moving on. It was Nunn.

"Go on with your bad self, girlfriend!" O'Hara whispered. "That's right. Give 'em the full enchilada."

"She's planting more than ten," LeMaine remarked.

O'Hara smirked behind his scope. "She always was a sneaking little bitch. That's what I love about her. When it comes to blowing things up, she doesn't skimp on the Plaostine."

"Here comes Heckler."

The big Marine slithered out of the river right next to the wall. He emerged only up to his goggles, and when he saw the spot deserted, he climbed the bank, scaled the wall, and dropped down inside the compound.

"Any second now...." O'Hara muttered.

At his word, a deafening bellow echoed across the field and Monk stormed into view. He blasted out of the undergrowth at the base of the hill where LeMaine and O'Hara were hiding.

Monk thundered to the skies and all the guards and gunners jumped. They whirled around to face Monk and forgot all about their Maczhi captive.

Monk barged toward the compound getting closer all the time. The guards raised their rifles and called threats and warnings, but Monk only answered them with more roars and bellowed curses.

He swung up both his carbines and aimed at the guards blocking his path, but his size and the noise stopped them from making the first move. They inched closer to each other and backed away.

The gunners on the roof shouted down to their comrades and LeMaine thought he heard one of them yell, "Fire!"

A gunshot rang out from somewhere. LeMaine didn't see where it came from, but at that single echoing crack, the mounted cannons on the towers pivoted downward to aim at Monk.

"Now!" LeMaine roared and O'Hara opened up. He blasted off four shots, one at each cannon tower. All four guns detonated in clouds of smoke and sparks and the whole compound erupted in pandemonium.

Lemon ripped off her suit, pulled her carbine, and unloaded on the guards. They were all so intent on stopping Monk that they never saw her coming.

She mowed them down and Monk sprayed shots in all directions. He swiveled and cut down another dozen guards while Lemon raced over to his side. They turned shoulder to shoulder so they could face their enemies without hitting each other.

At that instant, a colossal boom shook the landscape and the wall around the compound vaporized. A series of explosions ran the circumference of the compound and blasted the rock apart.

"Go, baby, go!" O'Hara cheered, but he was shooting so fast he couldn't move. He popped off one shot after another and the gunners on the roof toppled onto their guns.

LeMaine fired as fast as he could squeeze. He leveled every guard and gunner he could see, but O'Hara got most of them.

LeMaine swatted O'Hara's shoulder. "Let's move!"

Both men sprang to their feet and took off running down the hill. Nunn's charges popped around the wall nearing the front and Monk and Lemon backed away from flying debris and.

LeMaine and O'Hara reached them and pulled Monk and Lemon the rest of the way out of danger when an almighty ka-boom blasted the wall apart from the inside. The four friends ducked under their arms until the rain of destruction cleared enough for them to advance.

The moment the wall evaporated, hundreds of armed Cezians charged out of the nearby forest. They roared in fury and converged on the compound in hordes.

"Go! Go! Go!" LeMaine ordered.

The four friends broke into a run and swarmed the compound. They converged on a large building sitting fifty feet back from where the wall used to be.

LeMaine and his people met Nunn, Kellogg, Heckler, Polasek, and Peterman coming the other way. "Did you have any luck?" LeMaine yelled to Polasek.

"I tried to patch in front from the forest, but it didn't work. The colonists must either be masking the array or it's really kaput. I don't want to find out which."

"Come with me." LeMaine grabbed Monk, Heckler, and Nunn. "Let's go. Follow us, Polasek."

The Hellhounds closed in a tight knot, but LeMaine couldn't see much with all the Cezians overrunning the compound. Their furious shrieks and the colonists' screams distracted him.

He pushed through the smoke getting closer to the compound building, but when he took another look, he halted.

"These are all civilians," Peterman yelled over the noise. "All the fighters must be inside."

LeMaine approached the front door, but that was a losing proposition. He motioned for his people to flank him on either side of the entrance. LeMaine crouched behind the threshold, held his breath, and flung the door open.

Fusion rifle fire erupted from inside. A few overly enthusiastic Cezians rushed the entrance and met their deaths as the gunshots spat from inside.

Lulara led the mob. She signaled her people to rush the compound when she saw the Hellhounds there, but LeMaine motioned her away. "Keep back! The colonists are defending the...."

Another explosion interrupted him and a hail of debris peppered his head. He blinked dust out of his eyes. "Nunn!"

"On it, Sir!" she called back.

She squatted down and Heckler and Monk both moved in to stand over her. They guarded her while she pulled more Plaostine from her pack, primed it, and then peeked through the windows.

She caught LeMaine's eye, pointed behind her, and he nodded. She tapped Monk and Heckler and the three friends inched away along the wall.

"We need another diversion," LeMaine yelled to Lemon.

"All mine, Sir!" O'Hara cut in. "I'll give you a diversion you won't forget."

He shouldered his carbine and sighted through the scope at something LeMaine didn't see. For all he could tell, O'Hara was aiming at an ordinary house.

O'Hara fired and the structure detonated in a catastrophic explosion. A pillar of fire billowed to the clouds, but O'Hara wasn't finished. He jerked aside and fired twice more. Each of his shots set off a devastating boom that made the Cezians and colonists duck.

"That will work, Sergeant," LeMaine yelled.

"I'm your man," O'Hara called back. "Just give me the word anytime you want to blow something up."

LeMaine looked around for Nunn, but she and the other two had passed out of sight behind the building.

LeMaine was just deciding what to do next when Nunn's head popped over a windowsill across the compound. She pulled her sleeve around her hand, punched her knuckles through the glass, pitched a block of Plaostine inside, and ducked out of sight again.

"Get down!" LeMaine hollered.

The Hellhounds crouched for cover and the compound shuddered with a muffled boom. "Go!" LeMaine bellowed. "Go now!"

He plowed into the compound as Nunn, Monk, and Heckler came climbing through the window. They met the rest of the squad in a carpet of bodies, but no communications array.

"Where is it?" LeMaine asked over his shoulder.

"This way." Polasek shoved past LeMaine and plunged deeper into the compound.

Everyone on the squad checked their remotes following Polasek to another door. He pushed it open and entered a dark stairwell descending into the ground. "Looks like the colonists are taking a page from the Cezians," Lemon remarked.

"Or the Cezians are taking a page from the colonists," Heckler countered.

Polasek stopped at the bottom and Kellogg bumped into him. "Shht! They're in here."

"How can you tell?" LeMaine frowned at his remote. "I'm not picking up anybody."

"They're masking it, remember? They can conceal themselves from remote detection. They wouldn't hide themselves and leave all their people exposed if they weren't guarding something important."

Polasek slipped off his backpack and left it on the stairs. Then he took a fresh grip on his carbine. "Give the word, Sir."

"You're in charge here, Lieutenant," LeMaine whispered. "Do what you gotta do."

"Yes. Sir."

He depressed the latch, but before he could turn it, Lemon grabbed his arm. "Hold it, Lieutenant. I have a better idea."

Before anyone could argue, she shoved her carbine into Kellogg's hands and she pulled her suit over her head.

"Good God!" Heckler groaned. "What is it this time?"

"Are you gonna attack them as the Leprechaun from Hell?" O'Hara asked.

"Real funny, jackass." She tugged the hood over her face and adjusted her remote. "I'll scare the ever-loving shit out of these assholes."

She touched her remote and, before her squad mates' eyes, she melted into a black puddle on the floor. The ooze swirled and undulated around Polasek's ankles.

Lemon's voice floated out of thin air. "Wait until you hear the screaming before you attack."

O'Hara snickered. "I can't wait to hear the screaming."

The puddle rippled over the floor to the crack beneath the door, flowed seamlessly under it, and vanished.

"How long do we have to wait?" Monk whispered.

Nunn opened her mouth to answer, but at that moment, a blood-curdling shriek sounded behind the door.

"Not very long, I'd say!" Polasek grabbed the door handle and charged through into a room. The other Hellhounds raced after him, but they stopped once they got inside.

A giant transmission dish occupied the huge chamber and pointed its face to the ceiling. A thick layer of dust covered everything. That dish hadn't been used in ages.

Thirty guards stood around it—or they used to. A blurry smear of something black twisted and contorted in front of them. It swirled one way and caught a guard by the arm.

The ooze swallowed his weapon and he screamed as the horror started to tow him into its grim depths. The puddle crawled up his arm getting closer to his shoulder and neck. He screeched and struggled trying to rake it off.

His comrades fired into the blackness, but the thing only coiled and undulated out of their way. It sucked the first guard into its dark heart and, with another terrified shriek, his neck snapped and he fell hard on the floor.

Guards on the other side wheeled and fired at the thing, but it only melted into a puddle at their feet. Both groups of guards wound up shooting at each other instead.

The puddle streaked across the floor toward the Hellhounds and the guards rotated to gun it down. They whirled to face the squad and LeMaine snapped out of his trance. The rest of the Hellhounds raised their carbines and unloaded on the guards.

The Hellhounds cut down the colonists and then took care of another ten who rushed into the room to follow up the attack.

The moment the Hellhounds cleared the room, LeMaine spun backward to face the door. "Fall in line! Stand ready to defend Polasek. Get busy, Lieutenant. Get that array running and make it snappy."

"On it, Sir."

Polasek grabbed his backpack from the stairs and shouldered through the squad to get to the array. LeMaine strode down the line of Hellhounds checking each one for injuries, but they were all unharmed. That wouldn't last long if the colonists had anything to say about it.

LeMaine halted at the far end of the line. "Any sign of Macon?"

Peterman shook his head. "Nothing in the compound or outside. If Polasek is right, Macon will use his technology to hide himself more than anyone. He'll go to any lengths to stop Command from bringing him to justice."

LeMaine frowned. He knew Peterman was right and LeMaine didn't like it at all. He wanted to get out of here and hunt Macon down.

LeMaine would like to be the guy who handed that bastard over to Command, but LeMaine had more important business right now.

Explosions and pounding footsteps echoed through the compound from upstairs. LeMaine took his place with the other Hellhounds and raised his rifle to defend the stairs.

Screams and deafening bellows drifted down from above, but when dozens of people pounded into view, a posse of Cezians stormed in led by Lulara.

She glared at LeMaine and then at Polasek working on the array. "What's the situation?"

"No idea." LeMaine didn't lower his gun. "Ask Polasek."

Lulara passed LeMaine and started talking to Polasek behind LeMaine's back. He didn't budge. He kept the stairs in sight in case any more colonists showed up.

Lulara reappeared at his side. "You can stand down. The compound is secure."

"You'll forgive me if I don't take your word for that. We'll stay here until we get the message away."

Lulara nodded. "You stay here. I'll clear the area upstairs."

She motioned her people away and the Cezians vacated the room. Polasek muttered to himself in the tense silence that followed.

No one moved for a long time. Things went quiet upstairs and LeMaine started to lower his guard when Lulara came back. "Okay, now the compound really is secure."

"Did you find Macon?" LeMaine asked.

"No. He isn't here."

LeMaine frowned. "That's weird."

"Not really, Sir," Peterman replied. "He wouldn't stand around waiting to get his head shot off. He's in hiding somewhere."

"Captain!" Polasek called.

LeMaine lowered his carbine, but no one else did. He strode over to Polasek, who stretched out on his back with his upper half buried under the array. "What's the status, Lieutenant?"

"We need a power source, Sir." Polasek stuck his head out and spotted Lulara. "Can you bring your generators up from Nulia?"

"That could take days."

"I can repair the array, but we can't send any transmission without power."

"What have the colonists been using for power?" Lulara asked.

Polasek bit back a grin. "They had three generators, but O'Hara blew them up on the way in."

Lulara grumbled under her breath, but a second later, she shrugged it off. "It doesn't matter. We have the array. That's more important. I'll send up to Nulia for a generator. You keep working on this, Lieutenant. I want to send the transmission as soon as the array is operational."

She strode out of the room and Polasek caught LeMaine's eye. Polasek opened and closed his fingers in a talking motion and made ridiculous faces mimicking Lulara behind her back.

LeMaine bit back a grin and returned to the rest of the Hellhounds. "Upstairs, all of you."

"Where are we going, Sir?" Kellogg asked.

"Don't you want us to stay here and guard Polasek?" Monk asked.

"We don't need to guard Polasek with all these Cezians around. They're as anxious as we are to get the array running. Right now, we have a date with our good buddy Macon."

Chapter 11

LeMaine and the Hellhounds strode out of the basement into the sunshine bathing the Nanov Outpost. The outpost lay in devastated wreckage on all sides.

The buildings that survived the Hellhounds' invasion only held up a few crumbling walls and piles of debris blocked the avenues between them.

Kellogg turned to O'Hara. "You just had to blow up those generators, didn't you?"

O'Hara shrugged. "Well...yeah."

A scuffle drew LeMaine's attention to the Cezians wrestling a bunch of colonists into line near where one of the generator buildings used to be. Lulara supervised her people shoving the colonists around.

A group of men lunged out of position and charged the Cezians. Curses and yells broke out on both sides and both groups fell on each other in furious attacks.

LeMaine strolled over to Lulara. "What's going on?"

"These people won't tell us where Macon is."

Another outbreak of fighting interrupted her. Four big men attacked the Cezians only to get driven back with blows and snarls.

"Alien vermin!" one of the colonists spat. "Get your filthy hands off me, you pieces of shit!"

"Let me handle this," LeMaine murmured to Lulara.

She let out a piercing whistle and the Cezians pulled back instantly. The colonists kept glaring and posturing while the Cezians withdrew to Lulara's side. Anyone could see both sides itching to start another fight.

LeMaine and Peterman approached the colonists and LeMaine lowered his voice to a murmur. "You people are all on your way up to the Kegao Prison, so do yourselves a big fat favor and tell us where Nelson Macon is."

The biggest colonist shot a withering sneer past LeMaine's shoulder toward the Cezians. "We won't do anything to benefit those sewer rats. They're a plague on this planet."

"You don't have anything to say about what happens to them. We're talking about you." LeMaine dodged his head in front of the guy's eyes so the colonist had no choice but to meet his gaze. "The only way you can hope to avoid a life sentence is to convince a judge you didn't know what Macon was doing. If you did know what he was doing, today will be the last day you ever see sunshine again. Do I make myself understood?"

At that moment, a deep boom trembled through the ground. The outpost's main building shuddered, and when everyone turned to look, the roof folded back and the giant transmission dish purred out on a hydraulic lift.

It rose into view with Polasek perched on the housing next to the dish. He grinned and waved down at LeMaine. "Got the dish working, Sir! Transmitting a message to Command now."

"What happened to needing a generator from Nulia?"

"Didn't need it after all!" Polasek chirped. "Turns out the outpost has an emergency generator underground. She's all up and running and the message is away....and the *Renown* is on her way in now."

LeMaine turned back to the colonist in front of him. "Well? Would you rather explain yourself to me or to the Elian Military Command?"

"Screw you—race traitor!" The man shut his mouth and then spat on the insignia on LeMaine's uniform.

LeMaine sighed and turned back to the Cezians. "They're all yours."

"No!" A different colonist lunged forward and grabbed LeMaine's arm. "Macon is hiding in the canyons farther south."

"Shut the hell up, Santana!" the first guy snapped. "Don't tell him anything."

The second guy shot his friend a terrified glance and then turned back to LeMaine. "They threatened us. They made us all come to this outpost to act as human shields for the array. They told us Command would kill us all if we didn't stop the Cezians from calling in the Military."

"Where's Macon?" LeMaine asked.

"He has a retreat location in the southern mountains...."

"You're a dead man, Santana!" the first colonist roared. He tried to lunge at the traitor, but Monk appeared out of nowhere, grabbed the guy, and yanked him out of line.

Monk wrestled him away from the rest of the colonists, shook him, and almost threw him toward the Cezians. "Keep your mouth shut if you don't want me turning you over to *them*."

Santana gulped hard and finally looked up at LeMaine. "His retreat is in a canyon where four plateaus meet from all four directions. You can't miss it."

LeMaine called up to the transmission dish. "Polasek—get down here!"

"You bet, Sir." Polasek hopped down to the ground and strolled over dusting off his hands. "What's up?"

LeMaine jerked his thumb at Polasek. "Explain to my lieutenant here how to disable your masking technology."

Santana opened his mouth and shut it more than once. "But…. I don't know how."

"I do," a third man piped up. "It's simple."

"Do it," LeMaine told him.

The guy strode away, and when the Cezians stepped in to stop him, Kellogg and Heckler blocked their path.

The guy came back a second later with what looked like a remote on a wrist strap. He held it out to Polasek. "It projects a magnetic field around the person wearing it. It blocks the frequency of any remote navigation emission trying to detect you."

Polasek frowned at the device. He went into the compound and came back with his backpack. He tinkered while the Hellhounds stood around and waiting.

"Do you really think this will work?" Lulara asked LeMaine.

He shrugged. "If we can't get it working now, Command will have the same problem when they show up to apprehend Macon. If Polasek can crack this frequency…."

"Got it!" Polasek called out. "It's pure genius!"

"Can you not get all ecstatic about electronics?" Nunn cut in.

"I have my scope and Polasek has his electronics," O'Hara added. "Don't knock it 'til you try it."

Polasek studied his array a little more. "This is weird. Each controller has its own frequency."

"Can you hack Macon's frequency?" LeMaine asked.

"I can't……but *she* can." Polasek stood up and nodded toward the horizon.

LeMaine's heart twisted as the *Renown* floated over the far hills and zoomed across the landscape on her way to the Nanov Outpost.

"My God!" Heckler breathed. "Did you ever see such a beautiful sight?"

Monk clapped him hard on the shoulder and the Hellhounds burst out laughing in pure relief. LeMaine felt his throat starting to choke up.

Polasek picked up his pack. "Let's rock and roll, Hellhounds! We got us a bogey to catch."

The Hellhounds took off running toward the *Renown* coming in to land on the field outside the compound. LeMaine started forward, jutted his chin toward Lulara, and then at the colonists. "Keep an eye on them for me....and try not to kill anyone, okay? We'll be back in a minute."

He picked up speed heading for the open hatch. He couldn't get off this planet fast enough.

He stepped inside to find the Hellhounds buckling their safety harnesses, reloading their carbines, and stowing the weapons and gear under their seats.

Their seats lined the rear compartment with Nunn, Heckler, Kellogg, and O'Hara on the port side. Lemon, Polasek, and Peterman faced them with one seat left empty at the end for LeMaine.

They all grinned at each other in delight that they were finally on their way home. They just had to wrap up one last detail.

LeMaine stuck his head into the cockpit to find Monk slaving over the controls. Polasek's communications array rested on the console at Monk's knee. Polasek's relay connected the *Renown's* navigation system.

"Can you use this to find Macon?" LeMaine called over the noise of the engines winding up.

"Let's find out," Monk yelled back.

LeMaine took the seat next to Monk, buckled himself in, and checked the navigation chart. "Take us out."

The *Renown* shuddered as she lifted off. The ship whizzed higher and mountains slipped by the cockpit. Wherever that cocksucker Macon was hiding, LeMaine hoped he was enjoying his last minutes of freedom.

The ship vibrated as Monk throttled faster. "Coming up to the retreat!" he yelled.

"Any sign yet?"

Monk nodded down at the chart. "Seventeen life signs—all human."

LeMaine read the signs on the chart and spotted a small identity signature near one of them. *Nelson Macon. Wanted For Murder, Conspiracy, and Inciting Insurrection. Evilia Settlement.*

"What do you know?" LeMaine muttered.

"Sir?" Monk yelled.

"Now I know why Peterman recognized that asshole's name."

Monk wheeled the *Renown* into a long canyon and the ship picked up speed zooming between sheer walls. The seventeen life signs clustered in one spot beyond where the four plateaus met. Santana was right. No one could miss it.

Monk vaulted over the last plateau and dropped down the other side. A large compound lay tucked in the opposite canyon with a dozen good-sized racer craft parked in the courtyard.

"Well, well, well!" LeMaine called to Monk. "It looks like weapons, food, and medical supplies aren't the only things our boy Macon has been stealing."

"Heads up, Sir!" Monk bellowed. "They're lifting off!"

Monk whizzed over the compound as a whole bunch of people scurried from the buildings. They ran to their racers and loaded up before launching into the air above the plateaus.

"Keep a bead on Macon!" LeMaine ordered. "Don't let that son of a bitch get away!"

"Holy shit!" Monk yanked his stick hard to port and ripped the *Renown* out of a racer's path as it veered toward her. Monk barely dodged a collision only to run into the rest of the racers converging on the *Renown*.

"Macon's making a break for it!" LeMaine yelled. "They're covering his escape."

"Son of a bitch!" Monk thundered as three racers opened fire and peppered the *Renown* with shots.

"Lock and load, Hellhounds!" LeMaine bellowed over his shoulder. "We got a road-runner on our hands."

The Hellhounds unbuckled and clambered out of their seats. Each of them opened a slot behind their seats and climbed into their cannon placements on the ship's sides.

The placements blinked on one after another on the dashboard in front of LeMaine, but he didn't see them. He switched on his own placement at Monk's side and the cannon controls slid out of the dashboard.

He grasped them and wheeled his cannon around to return the colonists' fire. They peeled off into the clouds and Monk rocketed through them to hunt Macon down.

A second later, the racers veered and accelerated to overtake the *Renown*. They crept up on either side and the Hellhounds opened fire without mercy. The cannons rattled the ship on both sides.

"Eat some of that, suckers!" Heckler roared.

"Come on, baby!" Kellogg slammed his cannon back to the rear as another four racers streaked past his placement. "You know you want some of this."

"Watch out, Lieutenant!" Peterman yelled. "Coming in fast to starboard."

"All over it, son," Polasek called back. "Keep an eye on that bitch above you."

Peterman rotated his cannon back the other way and hammered an incoming racer with everything he had. The enemy plunged in a headlong dive to collide with the *Renown*, but Peterman attacked with so many shots that the racer exploded right against his placement.

"Peterman got one!" Polasek called across the compartment. "Peterman: one. Hellhounds: zero!"

"Oh, hell no!" O'Hara hollered back. "I am NOT getting beat by Peterman."

"This one's all yours, sweetheart!" Nunn told him. "You and me, baby. Come on!"

"I'm with you!" O'Hara and Nunn both brought their cannons around to target another racer hurtling alongside.

They both laid into their enemy, but the racer gave back as good as it got. Monk dodged to port and smashed the racer sideways.

The little craft ricocheted off the cliff walls, and before anyone could do anything, Kellogg spun his cannon backward and pounded the racer into a cloud of debris.

"Ha ha!" Kellogg crowed. "Yeah, baby! Kellogg: one!"

"You little shit!" Nunn snarled. "I'm gonna kick your ass for that."

"You gotta catch me first, honey!" A devastating smash distracted Kellogg and all four Hellhounds on the port side whirled to see what caused it.

"Polasek: one!" Peterman hollered from starboard. "You slackers better get busy if you want to catch up."

Monk dipped over another plateau and tilted down into a different canyon. He left the racers behind, but only for a second before they all dove in to follow the *Renown*.

A single racer streaked far and away trying to outrun the *Renown* while the others ran interference.

LeMaine trained his cannon on Macon's craft, but Macon was still too far away. The vessel swerved back and forth winding through the narrow defiles. "Can you catch up with him?" LeMaine asked.

Another crash answered him as a pursuit racer pelted head over heel and exploded into the cliff face. "Peterman: two!" Peterman yelled out.

"You're banned, Peterman!" Lemon called back. "Stop shooting! Leave some for the rest of us."

Peterman's laughter drifted to LeMaine's ears, but he barely heard it. He frowned at the navigation chart. It still showed Macon's racer with the *Renown* hot on its heels. Macon's identity signature traveled next to the racer, but LeMaine wasn't looking at that.

He pointed to a different dot blinking on the plateau starboard to the *Renown*. "What the hell is that?"

Monk frowned at it and almost crashed the ship into a wall. "No damn way! It can't be."

LeMaine forgot to target Macon's racer. He even forgot to keep track of the Hellhounds' kill count mounting behind him.

The dot streaked along the plateau moving impossibly fast. The chart displayed only one recognizable identifier: *Maczhi.*

In front of LeMaine's eyes, the dot rocketed forward going faster than either Macon or the *Renown*. In a second, a different racer overtook Macon and pulled farther ahead. It plunged over a rise and dropped into one of the canyons.

"Wheel him, Monk!" LeMaine took a fresh grip on his cannon controls. "Steer him into that canyon."

Monk locked his teeth and wrestled the ship hard to starboard. He put on a burst of speed and the *Renown* crawled right up on Macon's ass.

LeMaine opened fire and plastered Macon's racer with gunfire. LeMaine concentrated his attack on the port wing, and when Macon dodged, LeMaine's shots smashed into the cliff next to the Macon's craft.

Macon fell right into LeMaine's trap, veered hard to starboard, streaked into the canyon, and picked up speed closing on that dot.

"Faster!" LeMaine hollered. "Faster!"

"I can't fly any faster!" Monk roared. "We'll crash...."

At that moment, Macon whizzed around another corner and nearly collided with the stranger racer. It sat parked on the ground with its engines idling. Macon reacted in a heartbeat and ripped backward to vault over the stranger.

Macon's vessel screamed over it, missed it by a whisker, and the unknown racer opened fire into Macon's underside. One shot ripped the starboard wing off and next hit smashed into the racer's tail.

Macon's craft cartwheeled in the air, somersaulted, and twirled away with a cloud of smoke billowing from its rear end. It smashed into one of the cliffs and dropped with an almighty crash right next to the ship that shot it down.

Chapter 12

L eMaine unbuckled his harness and climbed into the rear compartment to find all the Hellhounds leaving their cannon placements. "Arm up to deploy," he ordered.

They took out their carbines and the whole squad stalked outside. They paused next to the strange racer while the hatch buzzed down to the ground. Buca stepped out carrying a fusion rifle. It looked curiously like the ones the Cezians had been using.

He glanced over at Macon's racer and then at the squad. Heckler strode up to him, grabbed Buca hard by the back of the neck, and shook him. "Ha ha! What did I tell you? You're an official Hellhound now, boy. That was spectacular!"

"Buca: one. Macon: zero," Polasek added and the whole squad burst out laughing.

Buca caught LeMaine's eyes and shrugged. "I guess I lied when I agreed to stay behind at the Nulia Compound."

LeMaine couldn't help but grin back at him. "I suppose I'll have to overlook it this one time." He nodded toward Buca's racer. "Do I really want to know where you got that?"

"No, you don't.... unless you really want to ...." Buca hesitated and then grinned. "Sir."

"Listen to this guy!" Heckler shook Buca again. "I told you he's one of us. You're gonna fit right in back on Elia, pal."

"Do the Cezians even know you're gone?" Kellogg asked.

Buca laughed for the first time. "I didn't tell them I was leaving."

A crash drew everyone's attention to the wreck a few feet away. The whole squad watched a steel panel crack off Macon's racer and crash to the ground.

A plume of dust rose from the spot. The racer shuddered as a human arm burst through a section of crumpled metal and waved in space for a second.

The next moment, a dusty head poked out after the arm and a grimy face blinked through the smoke. Macon waved the dust away and coughed before he recognized the Hellhounds standing around observing him.

"Which one of his limbs should we pull off first?" Kellogg asked.

"Let's start with his eyelids," Lemon snarled.

"Or his fingernails," Heckler added.

"Let's turn him over to the Cezians," Peterman suggested.

Macon smirked up at them with his chest and shoulders sticking through the gap in his racer. "Hey, folks! Good to see you again."

"I say we let Buca arrest him," LeMaine announced.

Buca whipped around to gape at him. "Really?"

"Sure. I can't think of a worse fate for him than to get manhandled by a piece of alien scum like you." The other Hellhounds laughed in Macon's face. "Go on, son. Apprehend your fugitive."

Buca didn't move. He stared down at Macon while he hauled himself the rest of the way out of the wreckage. He did his best to present himself before the Hellhounds, but with all that dust and grime covering him, he didn't make a very good impression.

Macon tried to ignore Buca and beamed at the Hellhounds like they were his closest friends. "That was a nice piece of flying back there. I didn't think you'd catch up with me."

"We did," Monk boomed. "Nice try, though."

"You maybe want to get yourself some trained gunners to cover your ass next time." Polasek clapped Peterman on the back. "Even little old Peterman beat them."

"And Kellogg," Kellogg added and everyone laughed again.

LeMaine found himself joining in their laughter, especially when Macon's expression changed the moment he realized they were laughing at him instead of with him.

Macon frowned. "How did you guys find me, anyway?"

"Funny thing about that," O'Hara mused. "Our boy Polasek here got the Nanov array up and running. The Elian Military Command is on its way here as we speak."

"And your loyal followers gave you up first thing," Nunn added. "They couldn't sell you out fast enough to save their sorry lives."

"And Polasek also figured out how to hack your masking technology," Lemon went on.

"I'm sure Command will be very interested to get their hands on it," LeMaine finished. "They'll be able to use this technology to make sure idiots like you don't mess with Elian citizens again." He nodded to Buca. "If you would be so kind as to do the honors, son...."

Buca strode forward and took hold of Macon's elbow. Macon started to struggle, but Buca overpowered him. "Hey! You can't do this to me! Get this alien pest off me!"

"Get used to getting arrested by Elian citizens, asshole!" O'Hara called out.

Buca marched Macon back to the *Renown* with Macon protesting all the way. Buca halted in the compartment and looked around. "What do I do with him?"

"Put him here." Heckler pulled down an extra seat on the port side.

Macon gave one last futile effort to break Buca's iron grip. "You can't do this to me! I have rights, you know. I'm a patriot! I'm responsible for preserving the human race from this filth!"

"I would love to hear you explain that to a judge." LeMaine nodded to Buca who shoved Macon into the seat.

The other Hellhounds wrestled the safety harness around Macon's shoulders and LeMaine put a security lock on it to hold the shithead in place.

Polasek pulled down another extra seat on the starboard side right next to Lemon. "You sit over here, pal."

"What about my racer?" Buca asked.

"Do you want to take that back to Elia with you?" Kellogg asked.

Buca's eyes darted around the compartment. "I guess not."

"You won't need it," Nunn told him. "You'll be riding in the *Renown* all the time."

"Except when you're getting shot at," O'Hara added.

"Buckle up, Hellhounds," LeMaine ordered. "We're outta here."

The others took their positions and LeMaine rode in the cockpit on the way back to Nanov. He heard the squad talking, laughing, and teasing all the way there. He loved that sound.

Monk soared out of the canyons and the *Renown* floated over the plateaus, but when Monk cleared the mountains, his face drained of color. "Holy hell!"

"Steady, Corporal," LeMaine told him. "We're among friends here."

Monk slowed, but the squad only had one direction left to go. The *Renown* flew into a giant flock of Elian warships descending through the atmosphere. The *Renown* seemed so small compared to them.

Monk landed between three giant warships parked right outside the ruins of the Nanov Outpost. Now came the reckoning.

LeMaine went into the compartment and the conversation died when the rest of his squad saw his expression. "You're with me, Polasek. Peterman, you're in charge."

"Yes, Sir."

"The rest of you stay put. Don't let me see your faces out there until I give you the word."

Polasek followed LeMaine outside and LeMaine saw at a glance where he had to go. His commanding officer, Colonel Elias Nicholson, and Colonel Nicholson's auxiliary, Commander Russell Lodge, stood near the mountain of rubble the Hellhounds made of the outpost.

The two officers and two other people were talking to Lulara. LeMaine didn't recognize the other two, but based on, he assumed from their clothes that they were members of the Elian Assembly.

"It's been nice serving under you, Sir," Polasek murmured in his ear.

"Not so fast, Lieutenant."

LeMaine pulled up in front of Colonel Nicholson and saluted. "Sir!"

"At ease, Captain. Mission accomplished. Well done."

"Thank you, Sir. I'm sorry about the condition of this outpost."

Colonel Nicholson waved that away. "Shit happens, right? You saved the dish. That's what's important."

"And the diplomat," Commander Lodge added. "You'll probably get another decoration for this."

"I don't want another decoration, Sir."

"Lulara tells me some of your people received medical treatment in the Nulia Compound," Colonel Nicholson went on. "Have all your subordinates recovered from their injuries?"

"Yes, Sir, thanks to the Cezians."

"Did you apprehend Nelson Macon?" Commander Lodge asked.

"As a matter of fact, it was a Maczhi operative who apprehended Macon....and this Maczhi is requesting a post on my squad as compensation."

Colonel Nicholson raised his eyebrows. "That's unusual."

"I'd like to offer my personal recommendation that his request be granted. He's an exceptional individual. He'd be an asset to my squad and we'd all be delighted to have him."

Colonel Nicholson and Commander Lodge exchanged glances. "We would have to take that under advisement, Captain."

"If you want to put me in for another decoration, Sir, I'd be happy to forego any recognition for this mission in exchange for having this man posted to my squad until you make a decision about accepting him."

Colonel Nicholson frowned at him, but LeMaine held the colonel's gaze. LeMaine didn't come this far to let Buca down again.

"Well, I've learned not to question you when it comes to managing this squad, Captain," Colonel Nicholson finally agreed. "Request granted. Consider this Maczhi posted to your squad at the rank of corporal."

"Thank you, Sir. The other Hellhounds will be thrilled."

"Where is Macon?" Lulara cut in

"He's on the *Renown*."

"I want to see him," she growled. "I want to see him taken into Command custody."

LeMaine nodded to Polasek. Polasek hurried back to the *Renown*, and a second later, Buca came out jerking Macon along by the arm.

Macon's insults drifted across the field, but Buca didn't look sideways at him. He marched Macon up to the colonel and jostled Macon into position where Lulara could see him.

"I demand to be taken into custody by a human crew!" Macon snapped. "This is a gross violation of my rights as an Elian citizen."

"As a matter of fact, Sir," Colonel Nicholson returned in his frostiest tone, "this Maczhi is now a member of the Elian Military Command as of five minutes ago. He is empowered to arrest lawbreakers anywhere in the Elian system, and since you've been wanted for years, any Elian citizen would be entitled to detain you either way."

"Take a good look, Macon," Lulara hissed. "I want my face to be the last thing you see before you disappear forever."

Macon curled his lip at her. "You won't get away with this. We'll come back. We'll be victorious in the end."

"You tried to rid this planet of aliens so you could claim it for humans," she countered. "In the end, the opposite happened. Thanks to you, all the humans on this planet are being dragged off as traitors to Elia. The only Elian citizens left on this planet will be aliens. You might want to think about that while you're rotting in prison. Just remember what your campaign of blood purity actually accomplished."

A bunch of security guards approached from Colonel Nicholson's warship, the *Silmion*. They took Macon from Buca and marched Macon into the *Silmion* where LeMaine lost sight of him.

"I can't quite believe it's over," Lulara murmured in a much softer tone than LeMaine had ever heard from her before. "I never thought I'd really see him get arrested."

"It isn't over," Colonel Nicholson replied. "It's only just starting. The Cezians have a lot of work to do to prepare for citizenship and the Maczhi have work to do to rebuild after this disaster." He turned to Buca. "Are you sure you want this, son? You don't have to leave. Your people could use a man like you on this planet. You could be a leader to t hem."

"No, I won't stay," Buca replied. "My place is elsewhere."

"You might want to think about that," Commander Lodge added. "Life in the Elian Special Forces isn't all it's cracked up to be. Just ask Captain LeMaine."

Buca nodded, but he didn't look away from the two officers. "Thank you, Sir, but I can see what it's like."

Chapter 13

"I said no," LeMaine snapped. "How many more times do I have to say it?"

"Keep your voice down!" Commander Lodge hissed low. "He'll hear you."

"I hope he does. I hope he hears me sticking up for him because you sure as hell won't."

Commander Lodge's features hardened and he glared at LeMaine. "Watch your tone, Captain. You're way out of line."

"Oh, really? From where I'm standing, it looks to me like you're the one out of line."

"You have to admit it's highly out of order," Commander Lodge went on. "I mean, what sane person won't even talk to their own family?"

"Buca, apparently," LeMaine replied.

"It's downright bizarre. He's an Elian citizen. He should start acting like one."

LeMaine rolled his eyes to Heaven. "Oh, please, Russell. We've been over this a thousand times. When are you gonna give me a break? Give *him* a break."

"I'm serious. Don't you even wonder what's going on in his head?"

Commander Lodge cast a furtive glance behind LeMaine. LeMaine didn't have to wonder what the commander saw back there because LeMaine already knew.

LeMaine planted himself in front of the enlisted quarters in the Nulia Compound. Elian Military Command had spent the last three weeks moving the transmission dish from Nanov to Nulia so the Cezians could use it to communicate with Elia.

Now Command was using the compound as their remote headquarters on Ziea while they finalized negotiations between the Cezians and the Maczhi about the planet's future.

The Hellhounds were housed in the enlisted quarters. LeMaine spent so much time here that he basically lived here, too. He slept in the officer's wing, but that was it.

Anyone looking through the open door would see Buca lounging on his bunk with the other Hellhounds. He still hadn't gotten the hang of their incessant jokes and teasing, but he enjoyed their company. He became progressively more relaxed as the weeks went on—unlike Colonel Nicholson and Commander Lodge who became more agitated and aggressive every day.

Peterman stood at LeMaine's side through this whole painful interview and didn't interrupt once. LeMaine also didn't have to turn around to see Monk standing guard at the enlisted quarters entrance.

Monk didn't say anything. He stared straight in front of him and acted like he couldn't hear their conversation at all, but his presence bore mute witness that the Hellhounds were there in spirit.

Monk's hulking frame took the place of the whole squad in barring these officers from entering the quarters. None of them would let these officers near Buca again.

"These negotiations could be the most sensitive and the most important in recent history," Commander Lodge went on. "We need Buca with us."

"That's shit, Russell," LeMaine countered. "You don't need him at all and you know it. He hasn't been part of Maczhi society for years. He's a loner."

"He's Maczhi," Colonel Nicholson interjected. "We need another Maczhi just like we need Lulara to negotiate with the Cezians."

"Lulara is a trained diplomat attached to the Elian Assembly," LeMaine countered. "Buca didn't sign on to the diplomatic corps. He signed on to my squad. Why don't you take Monk to negotiate with the Maczhi? You'll have better luck."

"Show a little respect," Colonel Nicholson added. "We came all this way to salvage a situation that was on the brink of civil war

"As I recall, the war was already over by the time you showed up," LeMaine returned. "It was over because of Buca."

"This is nonsense." Commander Lodge sidestepped LeMaine. "I'm going in there to talk to him."

LeMaine sidestepped just as fast and straight-armed the commander backward. "Stop right there. You're not going in there. I said no."

Commander Lodge hissed through gritted teeth. "Take your hand down now, Owen. I won't tell you again."

"And I won't tell *you* again. You aren't going in there. You've already talked to Buca at least fifty times. You've pestered him non-stop for three weeks to help you negotiate with the Maczhi and he's already said no at least fifty times. I won't let you go in there and get in his face again. He did his part to bring peace to this planet. Now just leave him alone."

"Get out of the way, Captain," Colonel Nicholson whispered. "This is highly out of order."

"No, it isn't. You posted this man to my command. Now it's my job to protect his safety and wellbeing from anything that might threaten it, including Command itself. How many times does a man have to say no before you'll listen? You won't listen to him, so now you'll listen to me."

"He won't even talk to his own family," Commander Lodge insisted. "It's freakish."

"So what if he won't talk to his family? What he does with his family is his business. The last time I checked, Command doesn't make anyone sign on the dotted line saying Command will have decision-making power over service people's relationships with their families."

"This is too important to let it go, Owen," Colonel Nicholson insisted. "He's in the service now. We'll order him to do it if we have to. Then he'll have to do it."

LeMaine pursed his lips, but he kept his temper. He was prepared to stand here for hours—days, even—if it meant the two officers would finally leave Buca alone.

He drew in a deep breath to steady his nerves. "He won't do it if you order him to. You'll only drive him out of the service and then we'll have lost one of the best people the Hellhounds have ever had. Are you really willing to sacrifice that because you won't take no for an answer? I thought you were smarter than that."

"Don't get insulting, Captain," Colonel Nicholson snapped. "You're still in the service yourself. Show some respect."

"Respect is earned, Sir, and right now, you and Commander Lodge here are rapidly destroying the last shred of respect I ever had for you. If you don't show some respect for this man's decisions, I don't really see how you can expect anyone to respect you."

Commander Lodge whipped around and accosted Peterman. "Will you talk some sense into this man, Lieutenant? Make him see reason."

"I can't do that, Sir," Peterman replied in his even tone, "because I absolutely agree with everything Captain LeMaine is saying. You've badgered Buca day and night since you first showed up on this planet and he's steadfastly held his ground. Your treatment of him would never be tolerated anywhere else in the Elian Military and could even get you charged with criminal harassment in civil court. Frankly, I'm shocked that you could treat one of your own enlisted people like this."

"This is outrageous!" Commander Lodge exclaimed. "He won't even talk to other Maczhi! Who acts like that? It isn't normal."

"Maybe that's why he keeps saying no. Did you ever think of that?" Peterman asked. "And while we're at it, Sir, I would remind you that there are plenty of human Elians in the service who don't speak to their families, either. So unless you're prepared to make this a regular military policy, I would advise you to drop it."

Commander Lodge glared at Peterman with smoke billowing out of his ears. Then he glared at LeMaine. "This isn't over."

"Yes. It is," LeMaine returned. "Don't let me see you near Buca again—unless you plan to award him a decoration for valor and service to the Elian people."

Commander Lodge stormed off and left LeMaine facing Colonel Nicholson, but LeMaine still didn't move. He was prepared to take a dishonorable discharge over this. He didn't shoulder the responsibility for his people's very lives to see them treated this way.

"I sure hope you aren't making a terrible mistake, Owen," Colonel Nicholson whispered.

"I'm not, Sir."

Colonel Nicholson shot one more sidelong glance into the enlisted quarters. Laughter drifted from inside so at least someone in this shithole was still enjoying themselves.

Colonel Nicholson gave LeMaine another appraising glance and nodded. "I'll see you in a little while, Owen."

"Yes, Sir."

Colonel Nicholson strolled off much more calmly than Commander Lodge did. The colonel's footsteps faded around the corner and eventually disappeared. Silence descended except for snorting and guffawing coming from inside the quarters.

LeMaine stayed where he was for a long time. He kept waiting for one of them to come back and start all over again, but they didn't.

He finally turned around and found Peterson at his side. "You okay?" Peterman murmured.

"Yeah." LeMaine passed his hand across his eyes. "Thanks for saying that."

"You did real good. You kept your composure a hell of a lot better than I would have."

LeMaine's head shot up and he had to smile at his young lieutenant. LeMaine couldn't think of anything to say beyond thanking Peterman again, so LeMaine didn't say anything.

He glanced over to find Monk looking down at him. Monk's eyes told LeMaine that Monk heard every word, which meant the rest of the Hellhounds would know as soon as

LeMaine turned his back on them. At least LeMaine would be able to look them in the eye when this was all over.

He stepped into the quarters and scanned his squad. Kellogg was putting on a show for the others. He had shoved a small spherical ball up his nostril and was puffing out his cheeks and his other nostril while he pretended to try to blast the ball out.

Nunn, Lemon, Heckler, and O'Hara fell over themselves laughing. Buca reclined on his own bunk watching them with a mild smile on his face.

He turned as LeMaine entered and Buca's eyes found LeMaine's. Did he know? No one in Command knew anything about the Maczhi. Buca's hearing might be good enough to hear the whole exchange, too, for all LeMaine knew.

Buca regarded LeMaine with a questioning gaze, but LeMaine couldn't think of anything to say to him, either. If LeMaine sticking up for Buca didn't work, nothing would. LeMaine had done all he could. What happened next was anybody's guess.

Peterman bumped his elbow and snapped LeMaine out of his trance. He left the quarters and Monk stayed behind when LeMaine and Peterman walked off to follow Commander Lodge and Colonel Nicholson.

LeMaine's mind went blank on his way downstairs. He didn't want to think about the Cezians or the Maczhi or the negotiations or this mission or anything else. He didn't want to think at all anymore period, but Peterman brought him back to reality.

"You ready for this?"

"I don't really have a choice, do I?" LeMaine muttered. "Never accept a promotion, Lieutenant. Rising in rank is a curse."

Peterman chuckled. "Some other disaster will flare up in another part of the system and they'll pull the squad off this planet. They won't keep us here forever."

"Christ, I hope you're right! I don't know how much more of this I can take."

"They need us in combat," Peterman replied. "We're too important to waste our time with this."

"I wish I could believe that."

Peterman squeezed his shoulder and relief flooded LeMaine's being. "Maybe you should join the diplomatic corps so you can understand the fine print."

Peterman and LeMaine turned into the conference room where they'd spent most of the last three weeks.

A large contingent of Cezians packed one side of the room. They talked loud and fast in their harsh, guttural language. Lulara stood in the center of the mob talking and gesticulating as wildly as her fellow Cezians.

A group of Maczhi clustered in a far corner murmuring to each other under their breath. They kept casting furtive glances toward the Cezians and then whispering some more.

Colonel Nicholson, Commander Lodge, and some of the diplomatic people stood at the end of a long table that stretched down the center of the room.

None of the three groups went near the table. Besides the Maczhi glancing at the Cezians, everyone present did their best to ignore everyone else.

LeMaine and Peterman crossed the threshold and the whole room fell instantly silent as all three groups turned to stare at LeMaine.

The Cezians glared at him with their hard, flinty eyes, but that was nothing new. Even Lulara glared at him.

He was starting to get used to that, but he couldn't get used to Commander Lodge and Colonel Nicholson glaring at him. Or rather, Commander Lodge glared. Colonel Nicholson only looked sad, which was somehow so much worse.

Only the Maczhi looked even marginally friendly. They actually looked relieved when LeMaine finally showed up.

He summoned all his resolve and approached the table, pulled out a chair at the end, and sat down. Peterman stood at his elbow.

One by one, the rest of the delegates inched toward the table, pulled out their chairs, and sat down. The Cezians and the Maczhi lined up on both sides while the Command and diplomatic people occupied the far end of the table. No one said a word and a heavy weight of tension fell over the room.

Colonel Nicholson finally leaned forward, rested his elbows on the table, and cleared his throat. "Welcome back, everyone. Thank you for joining us, Captain. Now....to continue our discussion from yesterday.... Lulara, you wanted to discuss the Maczhi's hunting territory that overlaps the areas currently occupied by the Cezians."

Lulara leaned forward, too. "Thank you, Colonel. As I understand it...."

She started talking and LeMaine tuned out. He didn't have to say a word in these meetings. Only his presence mattered.

The Maczhi and the Cezians kept glancing at him throughout the meeting. This had disconcerted him at first, but later, he realized that both sides were looking to him for encouragement and support. His presence somehow gave them some assurance that the Elian Military Command couldn't.

In a few minutes, the Maczhi started stating their concerns and desires. The negotiations developed and revolved around both races' needs and compromises they were willing to make to get what they wanted.

The longer LeMaine spent in this room, the more resolved he became never to let Buca set foot in here. That man knew what he was doing when he refused to take part in these negotiations. LeMaine envied him that.

Chapter 14

The Hellhounds slouched against the *Renown* hull, chewed their ration bars, and shot the breeze. Monk tinkered with the ship while Polasek fiddled with his communications array. "I still can't crack these damn frequencies!" he complained. "Every time I get one dialed in, the atmosphere fluctuates and I lose the signal."

"Don't you ever take a break from that god damn array?" Lemon snapped. "You're at ease, Lieutenant. Take advantage of it."

"I can't relax until I figure this out." Polasek tried something else, and when he didn't get the effect he wanted, he bumped his fist down on the array. "Hold a signal, you stupid machine!"

"Breaking it isn't likely to make it work better, pal," Heckler growled.

"Stroke it and whisper sweet nothings to it," Kellogg suggested. "That's what O'Hara does with his scope."

O'Hara clutched at his heart, gagged, and pretended to collapse to his knees. "Aarrgh! I'm hit!"

The others laughed and LeMaine bit back a smirk. The Hellhounds had been cracking jokes non-stop since they brought in Nelson Macon.

They'd been effectively on shore leave while LeMaine and Peterman got roped into helping out with the final negotiations. Now the negotiations were over and the Elian Military Command would be vacating this planet for good.

Lulara had been up to her neck in negotiating the details of the Cezians finally being declared Elian citizens. The Maczhi were doing better. Now they were receiving their rightful share of supplies coming out to Ziea from the rest of the Elian system.

After LeMaine's disastrous confrontation with Colonel Nicholson and Commander Lodge, they finally got the message and left Buca alone. They had also become painfully formal with LeMaine himself, but at least they never mentioned Buca again.

LeMaine and Peterman got no such luck. The Cezians and the Maczhi both insisted that LeMaine be intimately involved in all the arrangements. After three straight weeks of back-and-forth communications between the parties, he was ready to get out of here and go back to being just a regular soldier.

O'Hara got to his feet and resumed his position between Polasek and Nunn. O'Hara started eating his ration bar when Polasek shook his fist at his array again. "Damn you!"

"Let me know when you've had enough, Lieutenant," O'Hara quipped. "I'll shoot it for you and put you out of your misery."

A snap of footsteps out in the forest made everyone look up. Buca came striding down the mountainside from miles out in the wilderness.

LeMaine pushed himself off the *Renown* and stepped forward to meet him. "Did you see your family?"

Buca nodded. "I saw them."

"Are you ready to go, then?" Nunn asked.

"I'm ready."

LeMaine studied him, but LeMaine didn't ask what transpired between Buca and the other Maczhi in the mountains. Buca had remained unusually tightlipped every time any of the Hellhounds tried to find out about his life, his family, or his background.

LeMaine let the subject alone. Maybe after Buca had been with the Hellhounds for a while, he would open up to his squad mates. Then again, maybe he wouldn't. LeMaine had never met any man more capable of keeping to himself.

LeMaine squeezed Buca's shoulder. "Let's go."

They loaded up in the *Renown* and Monk flew them back to Nulia. Most of the Elian fleet had moved to Nulia, too. Most of the warships were already gone when he *Renown* landed outside the compound.

LeMaine and Peterman disembarked to meet Colonel Nicholson and Commander Lodge. The two officers accompanied Lulara to meet them.

LeMaine extended his hand to Lulara. "I guess this is goodbye. Next time, maybe don't make your mission so classified. That will make it easier for rescue crews to find you."

She laughed and shook his hand. "Thank you, Captain. I appreciate you coming out to find me."

"Hey! You were doing just fine on your own before I showed up, right? The Cezians are lucky to have you."

"The Cezians will have to be lucky to have someone else for a while. I'm being recalled to Elia to report to the Assembly." She cast a nostalgic gaze toward the compound. "I'm going to miss this place. I wish I was staying."

"Lulara has an unusual request, Captain," Commander Lodge interjected.

LeMaine spun around, but when he confronted the commander, Lodge didn't glare the way he had been these last few days. Some of the stiffness left his expression. His eyes softened to something closer to what they had been before this whole disagreement sprang up.

Maybe he and Colonel Nicholson were finally ready to let it go, now that Buca was leaving the planet for good.

"What's the request?" LeMaine asked.

"Lulara wants to ride back to Elia on the *Renown*," Lodge replied

"God, why?" LeMaine exclaimed. "You don't want to get sandwiched in the back of a little craft like that with a bunch of grunts."

She beamed at him. "Actually, that's exactly what I want."

"Can you believe this?" Colonel Nicholson smiled at Lulara and then, to LeMaine's relief, he smiled at LeMaine, too. "She would rather ride with the Hellhounds than enjoy a diplomatic-class stateroom on the *Silmion*."

Lulara smirked at LeMaine. "Can you blame me?"

He had to laugh along with her. "I guess I can't. Getting a sore backside on the *Renown* is my favorite way to travel."

"Do you have room with your new squad member?" Commander Lodge asked.

"Yeah, we'll make it work. Well, come on. Just don't expect any room service on the way." LeMaine saluted Colonel Nicholson. "Thank you, Sir. I'll see you back on Elia."

"Report to me once you debrief your squad, Captain. We have another situation developing on Basirus and we need to deploy the Hellhounds right away."

"I can't wait, Sir."

LeMaine saluted Commander Lodge and escorted Lulara back to the *Renown*. "Your squad won't be offended that I'm riding with you, will they?" she asked.

"They won't be offended by you, but you might be offended by them. Just try not to take their jokes too seriously. They aren't what you call diplomatic."

She laughed. "I'll try to blend in with the natives."

He stepped into the hatch and interrupted a particularly rude joke going on between Kellogg and O'Hara. "And then the Clamestran says to the Zuaphan, 'Go wash your tentacles before you touch my......'"

Kellogg broke off and his jaw dropped when Lulara walked in. O'Hara turned around to see what Kellogg was staring at and O'Hara almost fell out of his seat. Only his safety harness stopped him from toppling to the floor.

"What the hell is she doing here?" Lemon blurted out.

"She's riding back to Elia with us, Sergeant," LeMaine replied, "so behave yourself because, if anyone is riding on the roof, it's you."

"You need your hair blow-dried anyway, honey," Heckler added.

Monk stuck his head out of the cockpit. "Could you check the fuel mixture again, Sir? I think it might be...." He gulped and his eyes popped when he saw Lulara.

"Lulara is riding back to Elia with us, Monk, so do us all a favor and don't pull any of your fancy tricks." LeMaine pulled down the spare seat, which just so happened to be right next to Buca. "You can strap in here."

She hesitated to sit down. Buca kept his eyes turned straight ahead and his expression perfectly blank. He showed no sign of even being aware of a Cezian sitting next to him.

His reaction snapped her out it. The rest of the squad watched her and LeMaine didn't say anything to ease the tension. She wanted to ride with the Hellhounds and Buca was a Hellhound now. She better get used to it.

The Cezians were citizens now, too, which meant they better warm up to the rest of the Elian population real quick. This might be the first time a Cezian and a Maczhi sat next to each other, but it sure as hell wouldn't be the last.

She sat down and started pulling on her harness. Le Maine went up to the cockpit and buckled in next to Monk. "Take us out, Corporal."

Monk fired the engines and LeMaine leaned back in his seat as Ziea passed beyond the cockpit window for the last time. He wouldn't be sorry never to see this planet again as long as he lived.

Pretty soon, the landscape shrank away and the curve of horizon dwindled. The stars prickled the sky and the *Renown* floated out into space. LeMaine heaved a long sigh, shut his eyes, and rested his head back against his seat.

Voices bounced back and forth in the rear compartment and Lulara's joined in with the rest of the Hellhounds. LeMaine even heard Buca talking. Maybe he and Lulara might actually say a few words to each other on the trip back to Elia.

"What about taking a look at that fuel mixture, Sir?" Monk asked.

LeMaine opened his eyes and looked down at the dashboard. He stuck out his hand to adjust the dial on the fuel mixture when a shuddering slam jostled the *Renown* hard to starboard.

"What the hell was that?" both he and Monk asked at the same time.

"What the hell!" Polasek yelled from the back.

LeMaine surged forward in his seat and searched the controls for any sign of malfunction when another brutal crash pulverized the ship from behind.

"What the hell is going on?" LeMaine bellowed at Monk.

"How the hell should I know?" Monk seized the stick in both meaty fists and fought the ship to regain control. "We're losing attitude."

"The port engine is out!" LeMaine attacked the controls, but no matter what he did, the ship wouldn't stabilize.

The engines screamed trying to compensate for both Monk's movements and the malfunction that LeMaine still couldn't identify.

LeMaine switched over to an internal reading on the engines when a punishing blast struck the *Renown* across the nose. The ship whipped in a complete circle and kept on spinning.

"Shots fired!" Monk roared.

"Where?" LeMaine yelled back. "Where are they coming from?"

"You tell me! I got my hands full over here!"

LeMaine scrambled to read the surrounding space, but he couldn't pick up anything. He was just switching over to the *Renown's* sensor logs of the last five seconds when the sensors flashed an alert.

"Incoming!" he yelled just in time for another crash to pound the port wing.

"We're hit!" Monk screamed. "We lost the port engine! She's out of control!"

LeMaine craned his head back. "Lock and load, all of you!"

The Hellhounds started to unbuckle their harnesses when another cruel blow struck the ship broadside. Nunn and Heckler pitched across the compartment and landed on top of Polasek and Lemon.

LeMaine caught a flash of green and blue winking across the window in front of him. All the black of space vanished as a planet rushed the *Renown* in a blur.

"Monk....!"

"I'm trying, Sir! She's dead in the water!"

LeMaine stretched farther around and raised his voice with all his might. "Strap in! Brace for impact! We're going down!"

Chapter 15

LeMaine barely had time to duck his head before a massive tree trunk hurtled toward the cockpit window. He tucked his chin and threw his arms in front of his face just in time.

The trunk smashed into the window and shattered glass peppered his cheeks and forehead. The *Renown* skidded to starboard and went spinning off into the forest.

LeMaine cracked one eyelid and spotted trees and debris flying at him from all directions. "Get down!" he yelled.

He doubled over and wrapped his arms around his knees, but Monk remained sitting bolt upright in the pilot's seat to LeMaine's left. Monk crushed the stick in both fists and struggled in vain to wrestle the *Renown* under control.

"Get down, Monk!" LeMaine bellowed, but Monk didn't respond. Snapping, cracking, smashing, and ripping noises echoed through the *Renown's* hull.

Screams, bellows, and more slams came from the rear compartment where the rest of the Hellhounds sat strapped into their places. LeMaine hated to think what was going on back there.

The next instant, another brutal smash struck the ship hard on the port side. The *Renown* whipped sideways and LeMaine's weight slammed against his safety harness. He grunted in pain and tried to right himself against vertigo as the ship spun four more revolutions.

He felt sick to his stomach and struggled to pull his head up when a catastrophic blow punched the ship downward from above. The *Renown* crashed into the ground and lay still.

LeMaine stayed curled in a ball fighting to breathe. His harness dug into his ribs. Broken glass sprinkled somewhere out of sight.

Groans from the rear compartment made him look up. The *Renown's* dashboard was completely dead. Thick leafy branches blocked the broken window. LeMaine couldn't see anything beyond it.

He glanced over at Monk and LeMaine immediately started clawing at his own harness to get it off. "Monk!" he yelled. He fumbled to unclip the buckle and sprang over to the pilot's seat.

Monk sat upright in his seat with a giant branch impaled through his upper chest. Monk's stunned eyes traced around the cockpit and crossed LeMaine's face several times without seeing him. "Sir.... I don't feel so good."

LeMaine touched Monk's shoulder and dropped his hand right away. "Hang on, Monk," LeMaine croaked. "We'll get you out of here."

"Sir...."

"Kellogg!" LeMaine bellowed into the rear compartment. "Kellogg—get up here now!"

No one answered him. LeMaine ducked into the rear compartment and his heart dropped into his shoes. Nunn and Heckler lay bent and broken on the floor. Nunn lay face down with Heckler's muscular frame sprawled across her back. Neither of them was moving.

Kellogg sat slumped and unconscious in his harness. His face was black and blue. Blood dripped from his nose and scalp to cover one eye and cheek.

"Son of a bitch!" LeMaine sprang over to Kellogg and scrambled under the seat looking for something. "Where the hell is Kellogg's medical kit?"

"Here, Sir." O'Hara stretched his arm above his head and pulled down a scuffed tan backpack from the equipment rack. He flung it over to LeMaine and LeMaine caught it.

"Let me help you, Sir." Polasek unclipped himself and knelt down next to LeMaine.

"Shit!" LeMaine hissed. "If anything happens to him...."

Polasek glanced forward to the cockpit, but he didn't say anything. LeMaine went to work with a vengeance and pulled out Kellogg's medical scanner. He ran it over Kellogg's head, but he couldn't find anything wrong.

"He has a concussion. That's all," he whispered. "See if you can get the smelling salts out of there."

"Where are they?" Polasek asked.

"No idea. Just find them. Monk...." He didn't finish.

LeMaine swiveled to one side and started scanning Heckler. LeMaine couldn't even curse when he read the screen. Heckler's spine had snapped and his body prevented LeMaine even from finding out what was wrong with Nunn.

LeMaine cast a desperate look around the compartment. O'Hara still sat in his harness. Peterman had released himself from his own safety rig and was bending over Lemon in the seat near him.

Two other passengers occupied the *Renown's* personnel positions. Buca still sat in his harness. He examined Lulara's unconscious form.

O'Hara shifted in his seat and caught LeMaine's attention. "Unbuckle yourself, Sergeant," LeMaine ordered. "I need you to help me move Heckler."

"I can't, Sir." O'Hara squirmed to yank against his harness. "The buckle is jammed. I need you to hand me that extrication tool so I can cut the straps."

"What the hell!" someone bellowed from behind LeMaine. "Don't touch me! Get off me! I'll kill you!"

LeMaine whipped around again to find Polasek kneeling in front of Kellogg. The young medic flailed trying to fight Polasek off.

"Easy, Sergeant," Polasek told him. "It's okay. You're on the *Renown*. You were unconscious."

Kellogg blinked at Polasek and then looked around. His expression changed in a flash and he grabbed his buckle. "Holy Christ!"

"Slow down, Sergeant," LeMaine told him. "You have a concussion."

Kellogg sprang out of his seat and grabbed the scanner out of LeMaine's hands. "Give me that!"

LeMaine didn't fight him. "If you really want to do something, go up front and help Monk."

Kellogg took one look at Heckler and Nunn and then grabbed his pack. He disappeared into the cockpit and LeMaine heard Kellogg cursing. LeMaine didn't want to think about how Kellogg was going to get Monk out of the pilot's seat or even save Monk's life.

LeMaine drew in one breath and thought fast. He tossed the extrication tool to O'Hara and then waved to Polasek and Peterman. "Help me move Heckler."

The three men surrounded Heckler and O'Hara joined them in getting hold of Heckler's limbs. They heaved him off of Nunn and laid him on the floor.

"Now what do we do?" Polasek asked.

"There's nothing we can do for Heckler," LeMaine replied. "We just have to wait for Kellogg."

LeMaine made another check of the other passengers. Lemon rubbed her head and groaned, but LeMaine didn't see anything else wrong with her. He went over to Buca. "How is she?"

"She's unconscious." Buca patted Lulara down. "I can't find anything else wrong with her."

"Leave her where she is. Don't move her."

Buca straightened up and looked around. "Will they live?"

"Who knows? Wait here. I have to talk to Kellogg." LeMaine stuck his head into the cockpit. "I need your scanner."

"To hell with that!" Kellogg yelled. "Get me a saw or something to cut this branch."

LeMaine glanced behind him. The *Renown* didn't have a saw.

"What are you standing there for?" Kellogg snapped. "Hurry up. We have to get him out of this seat. Find me something to cut this branch."

LeMaine hesitated. "I...uh...."

"Give me the laser scalpel from the kit. Hurry up, Sir."

LeMaine snapped out of his trance and pounced on Kellogg's kit. It lay open on LeMaine's old seat. He shoved the scalpel into Kellogg's hand.

"Get over here, Sir," Kellogg ordered. "I need you to catch his weight as soon as I release him."

LeMaine tried to wedge himself around Monk, but the pilot's enormous body left barely enough room for Kellogg, let alone another person.

LeMaine ended up propping one knee against the dashboard. He pressed Monk's shoulders back against the seat while Kellogg sliced off the front of the branch. It fell in Monk's lap.

Monk blinked down at it and his bleary eyes rotated up to LeMaine's face. "Sir.... the *Renown*...."

"You don't worry about the *Renown*, son. Just sit tight. We're gonna get you out of here."

"Lean him forward," Kellogg panted. "Just a little."

LeMaine tried to release his hold on Monk, but Monk didn't move. "Shit!" Kellogg hissed.

"The shots.... Sir...." Monk drawled. "They came from.... Iumia...."

"Okay, son," LeMaine murmured. "I'll take it from here. Just try to sit tight and we'll...."

Kellogg snarled something under his breath. The scalpel hissed and spluttered behind Monk's back.

"Sir.... I might be...." Monk's head dropped and his chin fell on his chest. LeMaine pressed his two fingers to Monk's neck. He couldn't feel a pulse, but he didn't tell Kellogg that.

Kellogg cursed a few more times and Monk slumped the rest of the way forward. His weight fell into LeMaine's and Kellogg's arms.

"Damn it, he's heavy!" Kellogg growled. "Anybody back there?" he yelled behind him. "A little help up here!"

Polasek stuck his head through. "What do you.... holy shit!"

"Help us!" LeMaine ordered. "O'Hara! Peterman! Get up here!"

The cockpit got a whole lot more crowded when O'Hara, Peterman, and Polasek wedged themselves inside. They all struggled to manhandle Monk's body out of the pilot's seat.

"Easy!" Kellogg gasped. "Swivel him sideways. Pick up his legs, Sir. That's it. Lie him down."

"We can't get him out on his back," Peterman pointed out. "He's too wide."

"We'll have to turn him on his side." Kellogg directed Polasek to rotate Monk sideways. That was the only way his massive shoulders could fit through the narrow gap to the rear compartment.

Buca glanced in. "Can I help with anything?"

"Get hold of Monk's shoulders. Polasek, get in the back, get out your communications array, and find out where we are. Monk said we're on Iumia. Find out how far we are from any help."

Polasek and Buca changed places and the four men ferried Monk into the back, but not without banging him into things, changing their grip several times, and almost dropping him on the floor.

The bloody hole in Monk's back and the matching one in his chest surrounded the sawn-off piece of branch six inches thick. LeMaine dreaded the moment when Kellogg actually started working on Monk.

Chapter 16

LeMaine and the others laid Monk down next to Heckler, but at least Nunn was sitting up. She sat in the seat by Lulara, who was also awake and pressing a rag to a cut on her scalp.

Kellogg pounced on Monk and Kellogg started ripping his backpack open. He grabbed his scanner, pointed it briefly at Heckler, and turned all his attention to Monk.

"Do you need me to stick around and help out?" LeMaine asked him.

Kellogg waved him away. "Go. I'll handle this."

"The rest of you arm up. We need to secure the area and see what's what outside." LeMaine went over to Nunn. "How are you doing, Corporal?"

"I'll live, Sir." She glanced toward the rear hatch. "Can I come with you?"

LeMaine waited until Kellogg put his scanner down. LeMaine pointed it at Nunn and scanned down her body. "You can come, Corporal."

She pumped her fist and started loading up her carbine. LeMaine did a quick check on Lemon and Lulara. "You better stay here, Madam Ambassador."

"You wish." Lulara glanced at the bloody rag and set it aside. "I'm coming with you."

"No, you're not. You aren't on this squad. Stay put and we'll find out how to get you to Elia like we planned."

"I'm not on your squad, so you can't tell me what to do. You snap orders to your Hellhounds, LeMaine. I'll make my own decisions."

"I guess I can still decide whether to issue you with a weapon," LeMaine countered. "Are you going out there unarmed?"

O'Hara snorted and LeMaine became aware of Polasek, Peterman, O'Hara, Buca, Nunn, and Lemon all watching the exchange. O'Hara and Lemon even had the audacity to grin at LeMaine facing off against a registered Elian diplomat.

"Fine." Lulara sat back down. "I'll get you for this."

LeMaine waved at the other Hellhounds. "What the hell are you looking at? I told you to arm up."

The others went to work loading their guns and collecting their packs from under their seats. LeMaine checked their gear while he readied his own weapon.

He made sure not to look at Kellogg cutting into the block of wood embedded in Monk's chest. LeMaine signaled O'Hara and Buca to stand guard while he opened the hatch.

The hatch hit the ground and the crew aimed their carbines outward at thick, impenetrable undergrowth. Branches and leaves blocked the exit.

"I'm gonna go out on a limb and say it isn't dangerous," O'Hara quipped.

"Be careful, Sergeant," Peterman returned. "One of them might slap some sense into that thick head of yours."

O'Hara started to laugh when a high-pitched whistle broke the stillness. It howled out of the sky and the Hellhounds ducked.

The next instant, a rocket smashed into the ground somewhere out of sight. The impact jostled the *Renown* and threw all the Hellhounds off their feet. Kellogg dove forward and covered Monk with his body.

Lulara lunged forward and landed on the floor next to LeMaine. "Can I have a weapon now?"

"Give the lady a weapon!" he yelled over his shoulder.

Buca shoved a carbine into her hands and she scrambled to check it. O'Hara swept his gun back and forth across the bushes outside. "Where are they? Where are the shots coming from?"

"How should I know?" LeMaine yelled back. "Polasek!"

Polasek crawled over to LeMaine pulling his backpack with him. Polasek opened it on the floor to reveal his remote communications array. At least that was still working.

"We're five miles west of Saevis," Polasek yelled as four more rockets pounded nearby. "It's the biggest city on Iumia."

"Where are the shots coming from?" LeMaine bellowed. "Who's shooting at us?"

Another cluster of explosions shook the *Renown*. The trees outside swayed and rustled, but LeMaine still couldn't see anything out there. The blasts struck so close to each other that he couldn't tell how many rockets had landed.

Polasek checked his array. "They're coming from the atmosphere. Someone is shelling the city....and missing."

LeMaine staggered to his feet and fell against the hull. "Move it out! We have to get to the city."

He glanced behind him and caught Kellogg's eye. Kellogg, Monk, and Heckler weren't going anywhere.

LeMaine didn't want to leave them, but he couldn't stay here. He didn't want to go out into a dangerous situation without Kellogg, but maybe LeMaine could find a safer place for them than the *Renown*.

He took a quick glance at the remote panel on his sleeve. No other life signs were showing up outside the *Renown*.

He ventured outside the hatch making sure to cover every angle. He ducked again as more rockets hammered the forest, but they didn't hit the *Renown*. They didn't sound so close, now that LeMaine listened with a clear head.

He pushed some branches out of the way and peered through. A huge city sprawled across the floor of a nearby valley. The *Renown* had landed high on a mountain overlooking Saevis.

The city looked so close and inviting, but that was an illusion. In front of his eyes, twenty more rockets whistled through the atmosphere and detonated inside the city. They landed far away from each other and more rockets fell all the time.

"Are we really going down there, Sir?" Nunn asked at LeMaine's shoulder.

"We sure as hell aren't staying here. Move out."

The Hellhounds forced their way through the bushes and broke into open ground. Tall trees gave a little bit of cover, and when LeMaine looked back, he couldn't see the *Renown* at all. The bushes concealed it completely, so that was some comfort.

He waited, but no more rockets landed out here. "Maybe they just missed," Nunn suggested.

"Who?" Lemon asked.

"Does it matter?" O'Hara asked. "They're shooting at us."

"They aren't shooting at us," Peterman pointed out. "They're shooting at the city."

"So why are we going there?" Nunn asked. "We'd be walking right into their fire."

"We can't get off the planet without the *Renown*," O'Hara replied, "or without contacting Elian Command to come and get us."

"We can't contact Command from here," Polasek told them. "My array isn't strong enough and the *Renown's* is dead. We have to go down to the city to contact anybody."

"Cut the chit-chat," LeMaine ordered. "Fan out. You'll be less likely to get hit that way....and keep an eye on your remotes for anyone coming."

The Hellhounds spread out and started down the mountain. LeMaine swept his weapon back and forth. O'Hara and Buca brought up the rear and kept casting backward glances toward the *Renown*, but no more rockets threatened the squad. Maybe those shots really were misses.

The bombardment of Saevis became more intense with every passing minute. Polasek hustled up next to LeMaine. "Monk said the shots that hit the *Renown* came from this planet."

"He might have been mistaken," LeMaine replied. "He was out of his mind when he said that and we couldn't see much while the attack was going on."

Polasek glanced behind him toward the rest of the squad and lowered his voice to a murmur. "We were inside the Elian system when we got hit. Whoever shot at us must have done it from an Elian planet."

"That doesn't concern us now, Lieutenant. Our only mission is to get off this planet alive."

"It concerns us if the shooter was on this planet," Polasek countered. "We could be walking right into their arms."

"That will make them easy to find, then."

Polasek dropped back and left LeMaine to his thoughts. He didn't want to think about someone inside the Elian system shooting at an Elian Military craft.

A second later, though, Peterman sped up to reach LeMaine's side. "What did you do to Polasek, Sir?"

LeMaine looked up. "Huh? Nothing."

"He wants me to talk some sense into you."

LeMaine chuckled. "Someone has to, I guess."

"He thinks you're nuts for going into a city that's under bombardment."

LeMaine examined Peterman on the side. "Do *you* think I'm nuts for going into a city that's under bombardment?"

Peterman shrugged. "You're the boss here, not me."

"I'm asking your opinion. You're the same rank as Polasek. You're practically my second second-in-command."

Peterman laughed. "They don't make bars for that rank, Sir."

"Either way, we need to send word for help and we can't do it up here. If I had to guess, I'd say...."

LeMaine dodged behind a tree and brought his carbine to his shoulder when his remote buzzed. He waved the rest of the squad to seek cover as a group of people climbed the mountain on an intercept course for the squad's position.

The Hellhounds aimed their carbines down the hill and LeMaine caught a glimpse of O'Hara fitting his scope to his weapon.

LeMaine strained his eyes to see who the strangers were. They came within range and he saw at a glance that they were all armed.

He thought fast. If the Hellhounds got into a firefight with these people, his best bet would be to draw the strangers away from the *Renown*. Kellogg wouldn't be able to defend Monk and Heckler on his own.

Then again, the strangers were hiking on a straight course for the crash site. They acted like they already knew about the ship. What was their plan—to eliminate the squad and scavenge the *Renown* for parts?

If they wanted the ship, LeMaine should evacuate Kellogg and the two injured Hellhounds. The *Renown* wasn't much good for anything anyway.

LeMaine couldn't evacuate Kellogg and the other two. LeMaine and his whole squad couldn't move two injured men, not under fire from these strangers.

The strangers filed into view and LeMaine emerged just far enough from behind his tree to make himself visible but without exposing himself. "Hold it right there! Don't take another step! Elian Special Forces! Identify yourselves."

An old Kressak with waist-length white hair halted and raised his arms on both sides. He didn't make any move to grab the carbine slung across his back. He left it hanging by its strap and his crooked, broken, yellow teeth showed when he grinned.

His skin sagged from watery eyes, but he stood up straight and looked LeMaine straight in the eye. "We were looking for you. We detected your ship falling through the atmosphere."

"Did you shoot our ship down?" LeMaine demanded. "The shot that grounded us came from this planet."

"No shots came from this planet," the Kressak rasped. "We're under bombardment as you can see."

The Kressak's sharp eyes darted from one tree trunk to another evaluating the Hellhounds one at a time. LeMaine checked the rest of the strangers and frowned.

The other members of the approaching group belonged to three different species. The group of seven included two other Kressaks, two Andaaths, and two Ampherai. Those three species shouldn't be working together.

The first Kressak saw him hesitate. "We came to get you. We need your help. We need the Elian Military and we can't contact them."

"You.... want *our* help?" LeMaine glanced over at Peterman, but the squad negotiator kept his cheek firmly sealed to his weapon. Peterman didn't offer to explain any of this to LeMaine. "We were on our way down to the city to ask for *your* help. We can't contact Command. Our ship is wrecked."

The Kressak grinned even more widely and lowered his hands. "You better come with us."

LeMaine didn't move. He didn't want to put his gun down, but before he could decide what to do, Peterman stepped out from behind his tree. He lowered his weapon and showed himself right out in the open where any of the strangers could shoot him if they wanted to.

"I'm Lieutenant Stuart Peterman. I'm the Command negotiator on this squad and this is Captain Owen LeMaine, our commanding officer."

The Kressak nodded. "I know. I read your signature when you entered the atmosphere."

"If you know all that, what are you doing out here?" LeMaine demanded.

"We're doing the same thing out here that you're doing. We're hiding from the bombardment. Come with us. We have communications equipment and we need help to fix it. We need to call in the Elian Military before the enemy destroys us all."

"Who?" O'Hara called out from behind his tree. "Who's the enemy?"

The Kressak grinned directly at the young sniper. "If we knew that, we wouldn't need help to fix our communications equipment."

LeMaine looked the other way and Polasek shrugged at him. Either this whole thing was a trick to lure the Hellhounds into a trap or these Iumians were serious.

Just then, another barrage of rockets plunged through the atmosphere. Distant booms echoed out of the city and the whole situation crystalized in LeMaine's mind.

An Elian Military transport getting shot down inside the Elian system was bad enough. All the nearby planets belonged to the Elian inner ring. They were all fiercely Elian. None of them harbored any hostile elements that would ever dream of raising a weapon against a Military ship like the *Renown*.

Now a major rocket bombardment of a central Elian city was going on right in front of LeMaine's eyes. Those rockets could only come from space within the Elian central ring. Who in God's name was bombing an Elian city from inside Elia? The whole galaxy must be going crazy.

LeMaine lowered his carbine and nodded to the other Hellhounds. O'Hara, Polasek, and Nunn stepped out, but Buca and Lulara stayed where they were. They didn't come out until all the other Hellhounds lowered their guns and exposed themselves to the strangers.

The old Kressak stalked up to LeMaine. "Welcome, Captain. I am Aalgik.

"What's going on here?" LeMaine asked. "Who would bomb your city like this?"

"As soon as we get our communications system operational, we'll both know. Follow me."

Chapter 17

LeMaine dodged out from behind a tree, swept his carbine across the landscape, and immediately pulled his head out of sight.

The forest ended in a ragged fringe with a stretch of field between the Hellhounds' position and a bunch of houses. Skyscrapers and other buildings rose beyond Saevis's outer neighborhoods. LeMaine couldn't see where the city ended on its other side.

Continuous rocket strikes screamed out of the atmosphere and boomed through the city. Several rockets hit a massive tower and detonated it outward in a catastrophic eruption of rubble, dust, and exploding gas.

The tower groaned and the ground trembled beneath LeMaine's feet as the structure started to collapse.

"The bunker is under that first big skyscraper," Aalgik murmured in LeMaine's ear. "We'll have to run for it."

"You're insane!" O'Hara hissed from farther behind LeMaine's back. "We'll never get in there alive."

"We've gotten in and out alive many times," Aalgik replied. "We can do it again."

"What do you mean by 'many times'?" LeMaine asked. "Just how long has this bombardment been going on?"

Aalgik bared his ugly teeth in a grin. "Long enough. If we're going, we should go now before it gets any worse."

LeMaine glanced behind him. The other Hellhounds clustered in a group and squinted through the last scraps of cover at the way ahead. None of them looked particularly enthusiastic about this project.

"Are you sure the bunker is protected?" LeMaine asked. "How do we know your equipment isn't getting destroyed in this attack?"

"It isn't. We're going. If you're coming with us, come now."

Aalgik darted out from behind the tree before LeMaine could reply. The rest of the Iumians burst out of their hiding place at the same time and charged onto the field.

"Go!" LeMaine ordered and he raced after them. Running into a rocket strike might not be the wisest thing he ever did in his career. Then again, it was better than sitting on Iumia with no communications and no way off the planet.

The other Hellhounds fell in behind him. As soon as they showed themselves, the rockets pelting the city swiveled over to target the squad.

LeMaine sprang from one side to the other trying to catch any glimpse of the rockets before they landed on top of him. He ran at full speed to catch up with the Iumians, but they turned out to be a lot faster than he expected.

Buca caught up with LeMaine and gained on the Iumians. Lulara came up behind Buca and the two of them ran side by side ahead of the other Hellhounds.

LeMaine veered to his right to avoid another rocket smashing into the ground right next to him. He stole a glance behind him to make sure the other Hellhounds were keeping up.

He turned forward to check how far they were from the city when an almighty crash detonated right in front of him.

Dirt, sod, and shrapnel whipped him in the face, but his legs didn't connect to his brain fast enough. He hurtled through the explosion and almost stepped on Buca crouching on the ground. Lulara lay face down in the dirt.

LeMaine stopped to check on them and the rest of the Hellhounds swarmed around him. "Keep moving! Follow the Iumians!"

"Go, Captain!" Buca yelled. "I'll take her."

LeMaine hesitated one more second as Buca heaved Lulara off the ground. He strapped her arm around his shoulder and took off at a fast run. He dragged her feet over the grass.

LeMaine spun backward and aimed his carbine behind him. He didn't see any other people on his remote, but he checked anyway just to be sure. He stayed in that position and followed Buca all the way into the city.

The Hellhounds outstripped the trio and LeMaine lost sight of them. Buca careened behind a building and propped Lulara against the wall while LeMaine stood guard. He checked and rechecked the surroundings to make sure no one threatened his people.

"She's hit, Captain," Buca panted. "I can't do anything for her."

LeMaine backed into the corner, made one more check of the area, and turned around. Blood and cuts crisscrossed Lulara's face. Her eyelids hung three-quarters closed, but she was still breathing.

LeMaine patted her down. Blood soaked her clothes, but he didn't have time to find out what was wrong with her.

"Let's hope the Iumians have a medic on the other end." LeMaine turned to Buca. "How are you doing? Can you still carry her?"

Buca dipped a single nod. "I can carry her."

"Let's go, then."

"Where do we go? We lost the Iumians."

LeMaine squinted at the sky. "Aalgik said the bunker was under that skyscraper. Let's head for that. I'll cover you."

"Take this." Buca handed over his carbine. "I can't use it."

LeMaine draped the weapon's strap across his chest while Buca repositioned Lulara on his shoulder. LeMaine scanned the street. "It's all clear. Follow me."

He stepped outside and started forward, but much more slowly this time. Buca stumbled from one corner to another while LeMaine cleared the way. He searched every alley and side avenue before he nodded for Buca to come forward.

The skyscraper in the distance got closer, but LeMaine still couldn't see the bottom of it. He also didn't know how to get into it once he found it.

He could only hope the Iumians would show themselves and that they would do it before Lulara died on him. That would be the cherry on top of the cake—if a registered Elian diplomat died on his watch.

He made it four more blocks before Buca didn't respond to LeMaine's nods. Buca backed Lulara into a shadowy alley and lowered her to the ground.

LeMaine backed in next to them. "What's up? Is she gone?"

"I'm not sure." Buca bent over her and pried back her eyelids. "She started making a strange sound in her throat. I don't know enough about Cezians. She may be dying."

LeMaine pressed his fingers to her throat. "She still has a pulse and she's still breathing."

"How close are we?" Buca asked.

"Not that far. I'll go ahead and check for the entrance. You stay here and guard her." LeMaine handed Buca back his carbine. "I'll come back and get you when I know where we're going."

"Are you sure?" Buca asked. "I can come with you. We can leave her here and...."

"No. We won't leave her here alone. Just keep an eye on her. I'll be right back."

LeMaine stood up and aimed his carbine out at the street. He almost went out into the open when he heard gunfire—the unmistakable gunfire of Elian carbines.

He swung his weapon in that direction, and before he could move, the other Hellhounds and the Iumians hurtled past him.

Laser fire zinged out of nowhere and one of the shots hit Lemon in the spine. She pitched onto her chest, struggled to crawl a few paces, and then flipped onto her back. She bellowed in rage and opened fire with her carbine.

The other Hellhounds and their Iumian friends scattered into corners and hiding places all over the street. Nunn, O'Hara, and Peterman skidded across the ground and took shelter behind a low wall by another building. Polasek and three Iumians hid behind the corners of an alley up ahead.

Only Lemon remained exposed and unprotected in the middle of the street as more lasers scattered across the area.

LeMaine didn't hesitate. He stormed into the street laying down a carpet of carbine fire. He sidestepped toward Lemon and dropped on his knee next to her. He jammed his carbine into his shoulder to target whoever was shooting at his people....and he froze.

A bunch of aliens advanced up the street returning fire on the Hellhounds' position. LeMaine almost forgot to shoot when he saw who the enemy was.

Lemon didn't forget to shoot. She howled in fury and unloaded on them. Three of the enemy turned their laser rifles in LeMaine's direction and he snapped out of his shock.

He squeezed his trigger, but at that moment, Buca stepped in front of him and unloaded on the advancing aliens. He hit five of them including two that had been about to blow LeMaine away.

LeMaine grabbed Lemon by the collar and hauled her sideways toward Lulara. Lemon remained sitting up and added her fire to Buca's. They sent the enemy into hiding, too, but the strange aliens didn't leave.

LeMaine leapt for the corner and he and Buca returned fire. The aliens kept to their hiding places, and with the Hellhounds and the Iumians under cover, the enemy couldn't hit anybody.

The aliens retreated and they didn't show themselves again. LeMaine jerked his chin at Buca and they both tiptoed into the street. Nunn, O'Hara, Peterman, and Polasek came out, but when they finally made it to the aliens' position, there was nobody there.

"Let's get the hell out of here," Nunn panted. "Aalgik said the bunker is only two blocks away.

O'Hara looked around. "Where's Lulara?"

"She's over there," Buca replied. "She's injured."

"Hey!" Lemon yelled from out of sight. "You might want to come and get this ugly bitch! She's going down fast!"

The five remaining Hellhounds returned to the alley where Buca and LeMaine left Lemon and Lulara. LeMaine heard them talking, but he didn't leave the spot.

He trained his weapon from one side street to the other. He didn't want to leave. Those aliens might come back at any time and he didn't want them to catch him off guard.

The Hellhounds reemerged. Buca supported Lulara's lifeless body while O'Hara and Peterman shared Lemon's weight between them.

Polasek paused there and cocked his head at LeMaine. "Are you coming, Sir?"

LeMaine shot one more appraising look at the surroundings and backed away. He rejoined the squad, but he didn't turn around. He defended their rear while Nunn went in front.

They crossed the last few blocks at a painful snail's pace, but no one came. The Hellhonds arrived at the skyscraper and found Aalgik and a few other Iumians waiting for them.

The natives waved the Hellhounds into a doorway that dropped into an underground passage. The door clanged shut and blocked out the sound of the bombardment.

Chapter 18

Aalgik hurried ahead of the Hellhounds and opened another fortified door deep under the skyscraper. The passage kept dropping, and without any windows, LeMaine couldn't tell how far underground the squad had traveled.

The inner door led to a small, cramped room crowded with people from several different races. Most were Kressaks, Andaaths, and Ampherai in the same proportions as the original group that intercepted the Hellhounds.

The rest were a strange collection of Icids, Zuvuks, Xuvax, and Shalgu. Three Shalgu rushed the squad and started working on Lemon and Lulara.

LeMaine moved back and went over to Aalgik. "Where's your communications system?"

"It's deeper underground. We have to make sure the bunker is secure before we take any strangers down there."

"We're hardly strangers," Nunn interjected. "You were the one who brought us here. You asked us to come and help you."

Aalgik grinned at her. "I wasn't referring to you, my dear. I was talking about the Axichis."

"Axichis!" Polasek exclaimed. "We don't have to worry about them. They're our allies."

"You need to take some intergalactic relations classes, Lieutenant," LeMaine told him. "Those were Axichis outside just now. They attacked us in plain view."

Polasek gaped at him. "That's impossible! The Axichis have a free trade agreement with Elia. They're the one neighboring system we don't have to worry about."

"I think you mean they're the one neighboring system we *didn't* have to worry about. They're here now." LeMaine faced Aaglik. "We need to access your communications system as soon as possible. We need to contact Command immediately."

"Wait a minute." Aaglik turned to some of his comrades. "Open it."

Three Andaaths approached one wall behind the other Iumians. They did something to the wall that LeMaine didn't see and several hidden panels opened to reveal a vast communications array embedded in the chamber.

Polasek hurried over and started examining all the readings with interest. "What do you need our help for? These are working fine."

"These show us readings within Saevis," Aaglik replied. "They aren't powerful enough to reach Elia or even to scan off the planet. We need our underground array for that."

"How can an underground array reach off the planet?" Peterman asked. "It would need to be above ground for that."

"It *was* above ground," Aaglik replied. "We moved it when the bombardment started."

LeMaine pricked up his ears. "You didn't tell me how long this bombardment has been going on. You said that before. How long have the Axichis been attacking Iumia?"

Aaglik grinned again, but that grin gave LeMaine the creeps. It expressed no warmth or mirth at all. "We've been sending reports of an Axichis military buildup for years, but the Elian Military Command always discounted our evidence. They said what you just said—that the Axichis are our allies and we can't do anything to interfere with the free trade agreement. They didn't want to sour diplomatic relations."

LeMaine glanced over at Lulara. He had a certified Elian diplomat with him right now, but she wasn't in any condition to help him.

Aaglik prodded one of his Andaaths. "Show him."

The Andaath brought up a different set of schematics. It showed the planetary rotation of all the celestial bodies in the Elian system.

"This is Iumia's normal orbit pattern around the sun." Aaglik traced it with his finger. "We first noticed the Axichis building up their military on their side of the border.... here."

He pointed to the place where Iumia's orbit passed the most closely to Elia's border with the Axichis system.

"Of all the Elian planets in our system, Iumia passes the closest to Axichis space," Aaglik went on. "At our closest pass, we picked up signatures of ships, ammunition depots, and troop movements on the Axichis side."

LeMaine glanced over at Polasek at the same time Polasek glanced at him.

"That was five years ago," Aaglik went on. "We orbited away from Axichis space so we couldn't send any further evidence. Command chose to ignore our warning."

"And now Iumia is back in the same position in its orbit," Peterman added.

"Precisely," Aaglik replied, "which is why they're attacking us now. If the Axichis gain a foothold on Iumia, they'll have a base inside Elia. The planet will orbit back inside the system and carry the Axichis deeper into Elian space. They'll be within striking range of several other planets and then...."

His finger followed Iumia around the sun until its orbit synchronized with Elia's. The two planets passed within a few million kilometers of each other. If the Axichis conquered Iumia or even established a base on the planet, they would be able to bombard Elia at close range.

LeMaine spun away and went over to Lulara and Lemon. Lemon was sitting up and one of the Ampherai was spraying something on her back.

"Aargh!" Lemon roared. "What the hell are you doing to me? Just electrolyze the damn things and be done with it."

"We don't use electrolyzation," Aaglik told her. "This will fuse the broken bones without causing unconsciousness."

Peterman cocked his head. "Does Command know about this?"

"They do," Aaglik replied. "We sent them prototypes when the system was first invented. Command shelved the prototypes and never developed the technique for widespread use."

Peterman leaned in close and watched a fizzy substance simmering on Lemon's skin. "Kellogg will definitely want to know about this."

"He can want to know about it all he likes," Nunn pointed out. "He won't be able to use it if Command doesn't approve it for use."

The Ampherai medic who was working on Lemon sprayed a second substance on top of the first and her eyes popped when she turned around. "The pain is gone."

The medic stood up. "The bone is fused now. You're free to move around."

"Just like that? I don't have to...do anything?"

"The system works instantly," Aaglik replied.

Lemon got to her feet and twisted her waist from right to left. "How is it, Sergeant?" LeMaine asked.

"Great. Excellent. Fantastic."

O'Hara clapped the medic hard on the shoulder and the man jumped. "You're gonna put Kellogg out of business. He won't be happy."

"He's never happy unless someone's on the verge of death," Lemon grumbled.

"And you're always giving him something to do, aren't you?" Nunn chimed in.

"Cut the shit," LeMaine ordered. "What's the story with Lulara?"

At his word, a Kressak medic did something to Lulara and she opened her eyes. Her face was still purple with bruising, but her eyes rotated around the room. "Captain...."

"I'm here." LeMaine crossed to her side and squeezed her hand. "How you doing, Ambassador?"

She tried to laugh and winced. "I feel like shit."

"Lie still. These people are fixing you up."

"What happened?" she groaned. "I don't remember anything."

"You got hit by a rocket. Buca carried you the rest of the way."

She tried to turn her head to look at Buca, but she ended up wincing again. "Try to keep still," the medic told her. "Your spine is broken, but I can repair it."

"Buca...." she rasped.

Buca didn't move. He hung back against the wall and didn't join in the general conversation. He shrank even farther back when Lulara drew both the Hellhounds' and the Iumians' attention to him.

Lulara's eyes swiveled back to LeMaine. "Bring him here, Captain.... please. I need to.... tell him something."

LeMaine nodded at Buca, but Buca still hesitated. The other Hellhounds moved out of the way to give him a clear path to Lulara's side, but Buca still took a few more minutes to decide to do it.

He inched forward cautiously still holding his carbine. He pointed at the ceiling, but his posture left no room to doubt how he felt about being summoned to Luara's side.

He looked down at her smashed face. Her eyelids didn't quite work right, but her eyes fixed on him with their old ferocity and Buca stiffened for the worst.

"Buca...." she choked. "I'm.... sorry. I'm sorry I treated you that way....at Nulia. It was.... uncalled for. You.... you should have been the diplomat. You should have.... represented the Maczhi...."

"No," he interrupted. "I shouldn't. I didn't. I don't."

"You do," she husked. "You're.... the best of the Maczhi. I'm sorry. I should have.... treated you with more respect. I...beg your pardon.... on behalf of the Cezians. When I get to Elia...."

She gulped and broke off. Buca stared down at her. LeMaine couldn't read Buca's reaction. LeMaine couldn't tell if Buca had any reaction at all. Did he feel anything about Lulara's apology?

The medic stepped in and pointed a medical scanner at Lulara's head. "No more talking. I need to repair her spine now and I need her to keep still." The medic waved to Aaglik. "Take them downstairs. There's no danger."

Aaglik nodded and motioned to LeMaine. "Follow me, Captain. I'll take you to our communications system."

LeMaine tore himself away with difficulty. Aaglik went to the end of the wall of panels, grabbed the last panel, and the whole bank pulled out to reveal a hidden door.

The rest of the Hellhounds followed Aaglik into a dark stairway, but Buca didn't move from Lulara's side. He stared down at her ruined face while the medic started to spray whatever that stuff was on the side of her neck.

LeMaine paused on the threshold. "Are you coming, Corporal?"

Buca looked over his shoulder at LeMaine. That was the first time LeMaine called Buca by his rank title, but Buca remained totally impassive.

If Buca decided to stay with Lulara, LeMaine wouldn't argue. If this moment turned the tide on Cezian-Maczhi relations, LeMaine wouldn't interfere.

Buca cast one more long, penetrating look down at Lulara. "I'm coming."

He turned away and passed LeMaine on the way downstairs. LeMaine shut the door behind him and cut off the sound of Lulara howling in pain when the medic repaired her spine.

Chapter 19

L eMaine and the Hellhounds followed the stairs to a vast underground room packed to the walls with electronic equipment. "Holy smokes!" Polasek breathed. "This is incredible!"

"We've lost him, Sir," O'Hara teased. "Polasek has died and gone to tech nerd paradise."

Polasek didn't hear him. He tiptoed forward trying to see everything at once. "Is that a data itemizer? I thought only Command used those."

"They do." Aaglik crossed to a large bank of processor stacks set up on shelves across one wall. The shelves rose to the ceiling and stood at least four feet out from the wall. "This is our system. It got damaged when we evacuated from the surface."

"When was that?" LeMaine asked.

"We started evacuating four years ago. Command told us our evidence was meaningless and the Military refused to fortify Iumia for our next orbital pass close to the Axichis system. Some of us saw the need to take proactive steps to defend ourselves and prepare for a potential Axichis invasion."

"Smart," Nunn observed.

"We left the array on the surface through the rest of our orbit so we could continue to communicate with the rest of the system and with Command. We only moved it down here two weeks ago."

"Polasek!" LeMaine called over his shoulder. "Leave that alone and come over here."

Polasek tore himself away from all the other equipment and turned his rapt gaze on the shelves. "Can you fix it?" LeMaine asked.

Polasek didn't answer. He ripped open his backpack and hooked his remote array to the Iumian system. "Oh, it's so simple! The codex is damaged."

"That's what I said," Aaglik growled. "Can you repair it?"

"No, but I can replace it."

"How?" LeMaine asked.

"With my codex." Polasek attacked his remote array, flipped it over, and with a few clever flicks of his wrist, he broke it open and laid the circuitry bare.

"Is this a good idea?" Peterman asked. "If you cannibalize your array, you won't be able to contact Command anywhere else."

"I won't need to contact Command anywhere else because I'll be able to contact them here."

Polasek unscrewed something from his array, wedged his wiry body between two shelves, and grunted and groaned fitting his codex to the Iumian array.

"How about you hook yourself up to it and be done?" Peterman asked. "Then you can communicate with Command anytime you want to."

O'Hara and Nunn snorted and Buca actually smiled. "Shit!" Polasek muttered. "There! It should be working now."

Aaglik did something to the array and one of the Kressak technicians across the room called out, "We're through! Elian Military Command is hailing us."

LeMaine and Aaglik hurried over. LeMaine's heart soared when he looked down at the weathered face of his own superior officer, Colonel Elias Nicholson. He gasped when he saw LeMaine. "Jesus, Owen! We thought you were all dead."

"We came pretty close, Sir. Some of my people are still hanging by a thread. Can you send us an evac on the double?"

"Are you insane? The whole system is at war. Don't tell me you don't know!"

LeMaine and Aaglik exchanged glances. "We didn't know. The Iumian communications system was nonoperational until a few minutes ago. The Axichis are bombarding Iumia and they've landed ground troops in the city. They're trying to take the planet."

"I hate to be the one to break it to you, Captain, but they're overrunning the whole system. You have to extend our apologies to the Iumians. You can tell them we're paying the price now for not believing them. The Axichis did a hell of a lot more than invade Iumia. Their whole invasion force is over the border. It's open warfare! The whole damn Military is out there fighting them. They've got us on the ropes! I'm sorry, Owen, but you and the Iumians are on your own for now."

LeMaine puffed out his cheeks. "That is truly unfortunate, Sir."

"I wish I could tell you something else, but if it comes down to your safety and the safety of your squad, just go grey and disappear until hostilities are over. Don't engage the Axichis if you don't have to. Just hold out until we can secure the rest of the system."

"How long is that likely to take?"

Colonel Nicholson shrugged. "Who the hell knows? None of us expects you to retake Iumia with nine people."

LeMaine winced and cast a pained glance at what was left of his squad. Peterman. Polasek. Nunn. O'Hara. Lemon. Buca. He had six people. That was it. He wouldn't be taking anything with so few, but he didn't tell Colonel Nicholson that.

"We'll do our best, Sir."

Colonel Nicholson started to say, "I know it's asking a lot, but I was wondering if you wouldn't mind...." when an explosion rocked the image feed. The colonel jolted to his right, steadied himself, and looked up at the ceiling.

"I gotta go, Owen. We're under constant bombardment here. I don't know if...." He had to pause while more blasts jostled his communications system on the other end. "Listen to me!" he shouted into the feed. "If you can get to the...."

The feed snapped and flickered off. "What happened?" LeMaine asked the technician at his side. "Did the codex go out or something?"

"There's nothing wrong with the array," Polasek told him. "The problem is on their end."

"If Command is under bombardment, that means the Axichis are attacking Elia itself. Nowhere is safe, and quite frankly, I didn't swear an oath to defend the system from enemies foreign and domestic to hide under a rock while the whole place is at war." LeMaine turned to Aaglik. "We have to get out of here. Do you have any serviceable spacecraft at all—anything we can use to rejoin the military?"

"We have a few, but most of them are either derelict or in disrepair."

"Too bad we don't have Monk with us," Lemon remarked. "Then we might be able to repair the *Renown*."

"We don't need Monk. I can repair the *Renown*."

All eyes turned to Buca. He spoke so seldom that, when he did, he commanded attention from everyone.

"You didn't say you could repair the *Renown* when we first crashed," O'Hara countered. "Why didn't you say something then?"

"I was following the orders of my commanding officer." Buca glanced over at LeMaine. "Isn't that what I signed on to do?"

"Forget the *Renown*," LeMaine countered. "It's too far away and we would have to go through the bombardment to reach it. Where are these ships?"

Aaglik started to turn away when one of the technicians yelled out. "Incoming Axichis bombing run! They're targeting the main colony."

Everyone rushed over to the man's station. Multiple scanner and video feeds from all over the city showed squadrons of Axichis fighter craft swooping over the city. They plummeted out of the atmosphere, raced between the buildings that were still standing, and pounded the surface with hundreds of rockets.

"What are they targeting?" LeMaine asked.

"The main colony," the technician replied. "It's where the rest of the Iumians congregated when we evacuated the surface. They denied the danger and stayed where they were. They're the only Iumians left to target."

Aaglik took one look and spun away. "Marshal every pilot to the airfield! Get every ship we have in the air—now!"

"We're coming with you," LeMaine told him. "We might not be able to do much with so few people, but this is our war, too. We'll help you fight it."

"Very well. Come, then."

Aaglik hurried up the stairs with the Hellhounds right behind him. LeMaine dropped back to Buca's side. "What would you need to repair the *Renown*? What equipment and supplies?"

"I don't need anything. The problem is electrical, not mechanical." Buca cocked his head to examine LeMaine. "You said forget the *Renown*. Did you change your mind?"

"Not now. I'm thinking later—after things settle down."

"If the Iumians have working craft, we won't need the *Renown*. We can take one of theirs to leave the planet."

"That shows how much you know about the Elian Military, pal. Iumia is a civilian planet. They don't have fighter craft except what already belongs to the Military and all of those will already be deployed against the Axichis. The Iumians won't have any fighter craft as well-armed as the *Renown*."

"Why did you say to forget it, then? Why not repair it now?"

"We don't have time."

Aaglik entered the upstairs room, but it was deserted. LeMaine didn't give himself time to think about where Lulara was right now.

Aaglik pulled out a different section of the paneled wall, passed down a horizontal corridor, and came out in a long gallery packed with people. Most of them were also Kressads, Andaaths, and Ampherai and they were all armed to the teeth.

"Pay attention!" Aaglik called over the crowd and everyone fell silent to listen.

"We're going out to the airfield to get as many of our ships in the air as we can. If you can get off the ground, go to the main colony. Do what you can to draw the Axichis away from the civilians, but don't do anything stupid. If your ship is completely unarmed, don't get close enough to get shot. Once the Axichis see our craft launching, we're hoping they'll break off their attack and come after us instead. Lead them away, land somewhere, and get out. Don't throw your lives away! Understand?"

Most of his listeners nodded.

"The rest of you do your best to defend and clear a path for our pilots to reach the airfield. Don't waste time trying to repair anything." Aaglik turned to three young Kressads standing against the wall. "You boys will head for the cannons. Fourteenth Division will defend you as best they can. Understand?"

Four people stepped out of the crowd—two Andaaths and two Ampherai. They approached the three young gunners and joined them.

"If there are no questions...."

LeMaine shot out a hand. "Hold it. You're sending four people to defend these guys? If you have cannons to cover the fighter crafts' launch, they'll need a hell of a lot more than four people."

"This is all we can spare. We have too few pilots and too few to guard them. We just have to make do with what we have. If there are no more questions, let's go."

"Hold it," LeMaine interrupted.

"What is it, Captain? We don't have much time."

"We can defend the gunners. The Hellhounds will go with them. We'll be more good to you there than trying to fly your ships."

"I'll go with the pilots, Captain," Buca cut in. "I will be more good to you there."

"Good," LeMaine replied. "Let's roll."

At his word, the Iumians turned their backs on him. They all mobbed to the other end of the gallery. LeMaine didn't see where they were going until he got there.

Another door opened into another corridor. It wound through what looked like a vast underground complex of interconnected rooms, chambers, control stations, and God only knew what else.

The Iumians picked up the pace and everyone checked their weapons. Talk broke out up and down the defenders and someone bumped LeMaine's elbow. "I'm Erias." One of the young Kressak gunners stuck out his hand to LeMaine. "These are my brothers, Thaki and Kaex."

"Captain Owen LeMaine...and these are my Hellhounds. Good to meet you." He shook the young man's hand. "How much experience do you have with the cannon?"

"Enough. All three of us were Elian Military.... though not as elite as your squad. We were posted to Soclitese during the last skirmish against the Fuslai. We've all seen plenty of action."

LeMaine examined the young man more closely. "You don't say?"

Erias nodded. "You won't be disappointed in us."

"We were at Soclitese, too." LeMaine jerked his thumb over his shoulder. "Polasek, Peterman, and our medic Kellogg were all in the firing line with me when we overran the Fuslai base. We would have been dead without the cannon cover."

Erias cracked a toothy grin. He didn't look as ghastly as Aaglik. "And we would have been dead without the firing line defending us. It's an honor to meet anyone who was at Soclitese."

"We'll see how much of an honor it is when we get out of this mess." LeMaine squinted through another door at the city outside. "This one could get messy."

"I'm sure of it." Erias pushed forward and paused on the threshold.

Unlike the other entrances to the Iumians' underground bunker, two giant concrete-slab doors flanked this one. They led into a huge, broad avenue lined on both sides with monstrous skyscrapers.

The shattered stubs of broken-off trees gave mute testimony that this was once the center of a thriving, luxurious city. Now it was a wasteland.

Chapter 20

Continuous rocket fire streaked out of the sky and pounded Saevis to ruin. Buildings on all sides crumbled in the bombardment. Clouds of dust and scrap twirled through the air in tornados of shrapnel and debris.

The Iumians in front of the Hellhounds raced into the open and bolted as far as they could into the city until they disappeared. Some just ran for it and didn't even try to defend themselves. They dodged rockets and some got caught in erupting plumes of spinning wreckage blasting out of buildings and the ground.

At the same time, Axichis fighter craft screamed through the mayhem plastering everything in sight. They wheeled between buildings, vaulted obstacles, and hammered the running Iumians with countless rockets.

Some Iumians paused to aim their weapons at the fighters, but LeMaine didn't see the defenders hitting anything. The Axichis were just too fast and too well-armed.

He paused on the threshold to scan the area and Buca dodged around him. The Maczhi charged into the chaos and vanished before LeMaine could say anything.

"There he goes," O'Hara murmured. "He came, he saw, he conquered. I hope he's all right out there."

"He'll be fine." Lemon snapped her Crossfire cartridge into her carbine. "It's our asses we have to worry about now."

LeMaine turned around to check his people. "Where are these cannons we have to get to?"

"Two miles northwest," Thaki replied. "They're hidden on a parapet behind the battlements."

"I don't know where that is so you'll have to lead us. Go!"

LeMaine plunged into the mayhem with the three gunners and the Hellhounds racing after him. LeMaine swept his carbine up to the skies, but he didn't try to shoot. He had to save his ammunition and he couldn't target the Axichis fighters anyway.

The group crossed four blocks before the gunners veered off to the left. "This way!"

The Hellhounds surrounded the gunners. The party moved away from the pilots trying to reach the airfield. The Hellhounds left the Axichis bombardment behind. Not as much debris whirled in the air here and the Axichis didn't seem to notice anyone trying to reach any cannon.

LeMaine didn't trust that situation to last long. The three gunners slotted between buildings and twisted and turned through a maze of streets. LeMaine swiveled backward to keep the Axichis in sight when the gunners came to a low hill and started climbing it.

LeMaine couldn't see any cannon at the top. A low building stretched across the hilltop. Trees and flowerbeds decorated the exterior and the grounds. It reminded him of a library or a museum, not a cannon placement.

The gunners picked up speed clambering toward it. This had to be the place. Nunn, O'Hara, and Peterman flanked them on both sides. Lemon and Polasek guarded the gunners' rear. LeMaine took a position farther down the slope to make himself the first line of defense in case anyone came out of the city to stop them.

No one came. The battle rotated and boomed out of the city. LeMaine could see much more of it from here. Axichis fighters spiraled around a dense knot of buildings far in the distance. A towering column of smoke, ash, and fragments cycled above the spot. That must be the airfield. The Iumian pilots were taking one hell of a pounding.

A shout went up from the gunners. LeMaine glanced over his shoulder just in time to see a cluster of rockets shriek out of the atmosphere. They smashed into the cannon placement with such a deafening ka-boom that the shockwave blasted the three gunners off their feet.

Thaki and Erias hurtled past Nunn and Peterman. A whoof of pelting debris swallowed Kaex and then smacked Nunn, Peterman, and O'Hara in their faces.

LeMaine charged them, but he already knew it was too late. A waft of breeze blew the smoke aside. He could see where he was going, but he already knew the cannon placement was gone.

He scrambled to Peterman's side. "Lieutenant!"

"I'm.... okay," Peterman rolled onto his side and started to get up.

LeMaine sprang from one person to the other and then waded into the dust cloud. He found Kaex flat on his back, but LeMaine couldn't help him now. He grabbed the young Kressad by the collar and dragged him back down the hill.

Lemon was helping Erias to his feet. Thaki doubled over with his hands on his knees while Polasek squatted next to him. Peterman was helping Nunn and O'Hara retreat to a safe distance.

LeMaine dragged Kaex over to Thaki, dropped on his knees, and cast one painful glance toward where the cannon placement used to be. Then he turned his attention to the young man. "So much for that brilliant plan."

"What now, Captain?" Erias asked.

LeMaine examined Kaex. He was out cold, but when LeMaine checked him over, he couldn't find any other injuries.

"There's nothing we can do for him here." He glanced up at Thaki and then at Erias. "One or both of you should take him back to the bunker. We'll go on to the airfield and see if we can get any of the fighters away."

"I'll take him. Take this." Thaki passed his weapon to Erias, grabbed Kaex by the wrist, and hauled his brother onto his shoulder. "Thank you, Captain."

"Thanks for nothing, you mean. Get your brother to safety. If you make it and you have time, rendezvous with us at the airfield."

"Yes, Sir. How will I find you?"

"Just follow the explosions." LeMaine clapped the young man on the shoulder. "Go! Hellhounds—move it out!"

LeMaine took off running back the way he came with the Hellhounds right on his heels. He didn't have to check where he was going. He just had to head for the thickest Axichis attack.

The enemy fighter craft howled in a tornado of engine noise and exploding rockets. The funnel of dust, smoke, and wreckage got tighter and denser. They must really be laying into the airfield with a vengeance.

LeMaine couldn't hope the Iumians were getting closer to their objective. For all the effort and resource the Axichis were putting into this assault, LeMaine didn't see a single Iumian ship in the air.

LeMaine didn't bother to aim his weapon at the enemy now. He bent his head and ran for all he was worth. He had to cross as much of the city as possible while he still held out some hope of helping the Iumians. With the Axichis laying down such a devastating assault, he dreaded to think what condition the Iumian ships would be in once he got there.

He raced ahead checking behind him every few blocks to make sure the Hellhounds stayed with him. Erias kept to the center of the pack moving fast and easily.

LeMaine veered around one last corner and pulled to a dead stop. The airfield—or whatever the Axichis were bombarding—was still several blocks away.

Right in front of him, a bunch of Axichis ships descended to street level, but they didn't land. They hovered twenty feet off the ground while hundreds of Axichis ground troops sprang down to the pavement.

LeMaine took a split second to realize what was happening, jerked up his carbine, and opened fire. All the Hellhounds swiveled into line on either side and they opened fire on the Axichis.

The Hellhounds cut down several dozen before the Axichis figured out that someone was shooting at them. The ground troops spun around and brought their weapons up. The transport ships also wheeled and lasers erupted from their undersides.

LeMaine scooted backward so fast he stumbled over Polasek. Polasek and Erias caught him and the whole squad dodged behind a nearby building.

"Keep it up!" LeMaine roared above the noise. "Draw them away from the airfield."

The squad took cover until the Axichis cut their fire. LeMaine peeked out and, as he expected, the Axichis started to turn away. He unloaded again and all the Hellhounds joined in to help out.

The Axichis responded even more furiously. They advanced up the street to hunt down the Hellhounds, but that only played into LeMaine's plans. He held his ground until the enemy got within a block of his position.

He signaled his people and they retreated to a safe distance, but they didn't leave. They kept harassing the Axichis to distract them from the airfield.

The battle raged another block with the Hellhounds retreating and the Axichis advancing to stop them when, without warning, all the Axichis broke off. They cut their fire, glanced around, and then turned away. In a few seconds, they all filed in the opposite direction—in the direction they'd been going when they first landed.

"What the hell are they doing?" Lemon panted in LeMaine's ear. "They wouldn't just give up."

"They're going to the airfield, obviously," Peterman replied. "They got orders to focus on their mission instead of fighting some pissant Hellhounds causing a nuisance."

"You're the only pissant here, Lieutenant," O'Hara teased. "You've been causing me a nuisance since I first posted to this squad."

"I'll cause you a lot more than a nuisance if you don't watch your mouth, Sergeant," Peterman returned. "I'm still your superior officer and I can always bite your ankles if you make me mad."

Nunn and O'Hara laughed. Erias raised his eyebrows at them and then glanced at LeMaine, but LeMaine wasn't listening. "We have to keep at them. Let's go. We can pick off a few more and maybe even slow them down."

He started forward, and after a few blocks, he overtook the Axichis again. They marched in a loose company and searched the surrounding streets for any other resistance, but they didn't find anyone.

LeMaine waved to Nunn and Polasek. They skimmed sideways to the other side of the street while Lemon, O'Hara, and Peterman took the opposite flank. LeMaine beckoned Erias to come with him and they snuck up right behind the Axichis troops.

LeMaine raised his carbine and Erias did the same thing. LeMaine waited a second and savored the delicious sensation of holding the Axichis in his power. He could kill them whenever he wanted.

He caught Erias glancing at him and LeMaine dipped his chin. Both men opened fire at the same time. They mowed down as many Axichis as they could before the rest of the troops spun around.

The enemy rounded on him and raised their guns, but LeMaine and Erias were already bolting away. The Axichis charged after them and opened fire just as the two attackers skidded behind a different corner.

The Axichis gave chase and ran straight into the Hellhounds' trap. Twenty Axichis followed LeMaine and Erias between the two positions. LeMaine staggered under cover and the Hellhounds dropped their enemies in the dust.

As soon as their comrades realized the trick, the surviving Axichis broke off and returned to their steady march for the airfield. The Hellhounds regrouped and LeMaine waved everyone forward to do it all again.

The distant bombardment got louder. LeMaine tiptoed up behind the Axichis for another ambush only to discover them engaged in a pitched battle against the Iumians.

LeMaine recognized a few defenders from the bunker. They hunkered behind overturned vehicles and shattered walls. The Axichis returned fire, but they couldn't advance with so many Iumians blocking their way.

LeMaine swiped his forefinger at the Hellhounds and they all took up protected spots behind the Axichis. The Hellhounds added their fire to the mix and pinned the Axichis between themselves and the Iumians.

LeMaine jerked his carbine from one enemy target to the next. Erias and Lemon flanked him on either side and the Axichis line started to break.

Peterman yelled something from farther to LeMaine's left. LeMaine glanced that way to see Peterman pointing at the sky.

Axichis fighter craft cartwheeled and revolved over the airfield, but LeMaine spotted a few Iumian ships up there, too. They didn't match the Axichis' firepower or speed, but at least they were trying.

LeMaine pulled his head down and dove over to Erias. "Can you fly?"

Erias shrugged. "I'm no slouch."

"You, Peterman, and Nunn come with me."

"Where are we going?"

LeMaine jutted his chin toward the impenetrable cloud blocking any view of the airfield. "We're gonna take a little ride."

Chapter 21

LeMaine shouted his orders to Peterman who translated them down the Hellhounds' line. Lemon, O'Hara, and Polasek readied themselves for a full-scale assault of the Axichis position.

The Iumians laid into the Axichis with every gun blazing. LeMaine noticed the Iumians concentrating on one small section of the Axichis flank.

A dozen Axichis went down and left a gap there. "Now!" LeMaine yelled and sprang out of hiding. He charged the spot rotating his carbine to his right. Peterman and Polasek joined him on that side while Lemon, Nunn, and O'Hara covered the left.

Erias dashed through the middle, broke the Axichis line, and kept on sprinting for the Iumian side. A shout raced through the Iumians and they split apart to let him through. They rotated their guns in either direction to give him a clear path.

The Hellhounds carved a channel through the enemy and LeMaine whipped around backward to defend his squad. The Hellhounds rotated outward to face the Axichis guns while they inched in retreat to join the Iumians.

"Break for it!" LeMaine roared as soon as he drew level with the Iumians. "Get to the ships! Fall back!"

The whole line wavered and the Iumians started to retreat. The Axichis advanced to pressure them and then sealed the breach. There was no getting out. The Hellhounds had to get to the airfield or die trying.

LeMaine bumped into somebody and almost stepped on a Kressad shooting past LeMaine's shoulder. LeMaine readjusted his position, but when he turned back to the fight, he braced himself for the worst.

The Axichis took advantage of the lull to push farther forward. More Axichis appeared from behind where the Hellhounds just had been. They joined their comrades and forced the Iumians to retreat even further.

LeMaine sprayed shots at the enemy, but when he tried to put some distance between himself and them, he ran into a brick wall behind him. He scanned up and down it, but he didn't see any opening.

He tried to shout to the Iumians near him to find out how to get onto the airfield, but he didn't have a chance. The Axichis surged forward, and this time, nothing stopped them from pushing right up against the Iumian flank.

LeMaine hunkered down shooting everything in sight. The Axichis overran the placements the Iumians just used to cover themselves. The Axichis pinned the Iumians and the Hellhounds against the wall with no way out.

Some Andaath LeMaine didn't know grabbed his arm and hauled LeMaine to the right. He didn't know what the guy wanted, but LeMaine could only hope the Iumian wanted to lead him to some escape route.

He followed in that direction and overtook Lemon, Polasek, and a bunch of Iumians heading the same way. They had to stop every few steps to defend themselves against the Axichis fire.

The Andaath leading LeMaine hustled him faster. They covered another ten painstaking when the Axichis unleashed a massive laser that smashed into the wall right in front of Nunn.

The brick exploded in her face and she toppled into the Iumians nearest her. They pulled her out of the way just in time, but now a giant pile of rubble blocked the Hellhounds' only avenue to safety—if there was any.

LeMaine dropped to one knee to take cover. A few other Iumians joined him and he lost sight of the rest of his squad.

He aimed outward at the Axichis, but he could already see it was hopeless. Too many Axichis blockaded the street and now the Axichis fighter craft pivoted their assault toward the ground battle.

LeMaine squinted through smoke and dust trying to acquire a target. Acrid fumes stung his eyes and nose. He could barely see anything, much less the Axichis hiding behind the barricade.

An Axichis fighter craft whistled out of the atmosphere, cartwheeled over the battle, and scattered lasers across the street. One of them smashed a few feet to LeMaine's right. Screams echoed in his ears, but he didn't have time to see who got hit. Was Nunn dead now.... or O'Hara?

Another three craft shrieked overhead hammering the area with dozens of lasers. One would hit LeMaine any second now and then it would be over. At least he would die fighting Elia's enemies.

He never thought he'd live to see the day when he called the Axichis his enemies, but that was someone else's problem now. The same four fighters flipped in midair and came tilting in for another pass.

He refused to look up. His carbine wouldn't do any good against the fighter craft, so he glued his weapon to his cheek and concentrated everything on shooting as many Axichis ground troops as possible.

He couldn't stop himself from hearing the fighter craft coming, though. Their engines shrieked in his ears getting closer by the second. Here it came.

The telltale sizzle of a laser zinged closer, but nothing interrupted his relentless shooting. How much Crossfire gel did he have left in his cartridge? He wouldn't get a second to reload once his ammunition ran out.

He relaxed waiting for the laser to end his life when, without warning, a devastating smash pounded the air around his head. He ducked automatically, but when he realized he wasn't dead yet, he looked up to see an Axichis fighter slam into the pavement between him and the ground troops.

He wasn't hallucinated. An Axichis fighter was definitely smoking on the ground. The wreckage and plumes of burning fuel blocked the Axichis from the Iumian position.

The Iumians sprang to their feet, pumped their fists at the skies, and shouted and whistled. LeMaine looked up. A different ship whirled and slalomed through the atmosphere. It dodged Axichis shots, spun around, and came racing back to assault the Axichis fighters.

The ship wobbled over LeMaine's head and he blinked up at Erias sitting in the cockpit.

All the Axichis broke off to turn their lasers on Erias. He ripped his ship sideways and sprinted for the atmosphere leading them away.

Before the Iumians finished celebrating Erias's victory, the Axichis ground troops broke cover. They swarmed across the street, left the wrecked fighter behind, and invaded the Iumians' position.

LeMaine raised his carbine, but another Iumian grabbed him to pull him away. LeMaine didn't fight it, but he didn't stop shooting, either. He and Lemon wound up in the back defending the Iumians' retreat.

They ran up against the fallen pile of brick again, and with the Axichis fighter blocking the street, they were really trapped now. The Axichis closed in to finish the defenders off when carbine fire erupted through the smoke.

The haze cleared just enough for LeMaine to see a shadowy figure standing on top of the fallen Axichis fighter craft. A square-shouldered man fired down into the Axichis troops. No, that was wrong. There were several of them up there and they all attacked the Axichis from behind.

The Axichis whirled away to defend themselves as Iumians emerged from all over. The fighters on top of the Axichis craft climbed down it and cut their way through the Axichis line. Nothing stood against them.

LeMaine's heart soared and he opened fire. The newcomers drove the Axichis back within the Hellhounds' range and Axichis troops tumbled in all directions.

Another cloud passed across the battlefield as the newcomers advanced to join the Hellhounds. LeMaine's throat choked up watching Kellogg and Heckler lead the Iumians.

Kellogg shot LeMaine one wild grin and then went back to dropping the enemy right and left. Heckler pivoted sideways to finish off the last Axichis ground troops.

Kellogg and Heckler pulled up in front of LeMaine and Heckler clapped LeMaine on the shoulder. "Damn, it's good to see you, Sir."

LeMaine swallowed with difficulty. "Not as good as it is to see you, Corporal. How's your back?"

"Kellogg cleared me for active duty, so here I am. You got any complaints? You talk to him."

"I would never complain about having you around, son. How's Monk?"

"He's back at the bunker with the Iumians, but he's fine," Kellogg replied. "He just needs to rest some before he gets back on his feet."

LeMaine gripped the young medic by the back of the neck and shook him. "You're the best, Kellogg. Have I ever told you that?"

Kellogg blushed and looked away. "You're embarrassing me, Sir."

"Let's get the hell out of here." LeMaine glanced behind him. The Iumians were making their way around the pile of brick.

LeMaine didn't see the other Hellhounds. They must be inside the airfield and he could still hear gunfire in there. The Axichis weren't gone and fighter craft still zoomed back and forth overhead.

Kellogg and Heckler joined LeMaine heading for the airfield. The brick wall ended thirty yards along. The group turned into the field and ran into another raging battle covering nearly the whole airfield.

Lemon, Nunn, Polasek, and Peterman hunkered behind an overturned tanker vehicle. It blocked the way to at least fifty Iumian ships dotting the airfield as far as the eye could see. Some bore the obvious signs of rust and decay, but quite a few looked serviceable.

LeMaine couldn't tell from here which might be operational, but another company of Axichis occupied all his attention right now. Several dozen Iumians returned Axichis fire from positions all over the field.

The Axichis flanked the field on the north side. Their line snaked out of sight between Iumian craft. The Axichis inched forward to drive the Iumian forces off the field. The Axichis filed between the Iumian craft staking out more and more territory. The Iumians couldn't reach any craft over there.

LeMaine, Kellogg, and Heckler fired on the enemy from behind the brick wall. The three men drove the Axichis farther east. The Hellhounds cleared a few more craft from Axichis control, but the Iumian pilots still couldn't advance.

Erias came somersaulting back and drew fire from the Axichis air assault, but one craft couldn't do much on its own. The defenders had to get more ships in the air one way or the other.

LeMaine yelled to Kellogg and Heckler. They pushed deeper into the airfield, but too soon, the Axichis split and half of them turned their guns on the Hellhounds.

LeMaine and his men dodged behind a derelict Iumian ship. This one couldn't possibly get off the ground. It had no landing gear and rust had rotted away most of the hull. Axichis shots peppered the hull and rusty splinters pelted LeMaine's shoulder.

LeMaine skidded out of sight and Kellogg plowed into him from the side. "The bastards!" Kellogg bellowed. "Who the hell do they think they are?"

LeMaine didn't answer. He leapt to his feet and Kellogg did the same. They traded shots with the Axichis, but the Hellhounds couldn't make any progress like this. The whole battle ground to a standstill with neither side gaining any advantage.

LeMaine assessed the situation for some way to turn the tide. The minute he stuck his head up, two more figures stormed out of the smoke beyond the Axichis position. They came from the east and appeared so fast they took the Axichis completely by surprise.

LeMaine only saw two of them and his heart] stopped when Thaki and Lulara opened fire on the Axichis from behind. The two newcomers spread out to cover as much of the east side as possible and stopped the Axichis from retreating.

The instant Thaki and Lulara appeared, a lone fighter craft rocketed out of the Iumian line. LeMaine took a second to recognize Buca sprinting at impossible speed straight into the Axichis guns.

Seven Iumians broke cover at the same time. They raced after Buca and sprayed shots all over the Axichis position to make the enemy duck for cover.

Buca never hesitated for an instant. He blasted through the Axichis troops, skidded behind them before they could react, and he vanished inside an Iumian ship standing right behind the Axichis.

The Axichis tried to round on him, but he was already gone. Thaki and Lulara moved in along with Iumians. "Go!" LeMaine bellowed. "Move it!"

Chapter 22

LeMaine sprang out of his hiding place with Kellogg and Heckler at his side. The other Hellhounds and the Iumians advanced from behind their sheltered positions. The combined group closed a dragnet around the remaining Axichis.

The Axichis started to retreat off the field and a shout went up from the Iumians. "Get in the air! All you pilots get to your craft—now!"

LeMaine checked over his shoulder and spotted Aaglik among the Iumians. LeMaine hustled over to him. "Do you have any extra craft? Put us in the air, too. We can help you."

Aaglik nodded, but he was too busy to talk to LeMaine right now. LeMaine went from one Hellhound to the next checking that everyone was okay.

O'Hara had a gash across his cheek and blood soaked Lemon's arm, but neither of them seemed to realize they were injured.

Thaki took off with the other pilots. In half a second, craft vaulted off the ground all over the field. Fifty Iumians held the surviving Axichis at gunpoint while the pilots got as many ships away as possible.

Aaglik turned to LeMaine. "How many do you have?"

"Besides Buca? There are eight of us. I don't know about Lulara."

"Good. Come with me."

LeMaine flagged the Hellhounds and they all followed Aaglik across the field. Aaglik pointed to five craft parked against a different brick wall. "You'll need one pilot and one gunner for every ship. Can all of you fly?"

"We can handle it," LeMaine replied.

"Do it, then. Get those cocksuckers off our planet."

"Kellogg, you go with Heckler," LeMaine ordered. "Peterman, you can keep O'Hara in line and Polasek can take Lemon. You're with me, Nunn."

Nunn rubbed her hands with glee. "Goody! I get to shake up the captain."

"No one's shaking anybody up. Just do the job."

"Except the Axichis, right?" O'Hara asked.

LeMaine pretended not to notice the maniacal gleam in his Hellhounds' eyes. Just the thought of shooting someone made them all way too happy.

He turned his back on them and headed for the nearest ship. He and Nunn had to pry the hatch open, but when they got inside, the craft looked well-maintained. Aaglik wouldn't give them a ship that didn't work.

Nunn hopped into the pilot's seat. "Strap in and hold onto your ass, Sir! We're going to town!"

LeMaine groaned. "Tell me again why I signed up for this."

She cackled with glee and started switching on the controls. "Be grateful you get to man the guns. We can switch places if you really want to."

"Not a chance."

She laughed again and her hands flew over the controls. She rotated her chair right and left adjusting and fiddling with everything. The engines cycled up to launch power.

LeMaine headed for the rear compartment. The ship's fuselage opened into two identical capsules at each end. One was the pilot's cockpit.

A full glass shield enclosed the Crossfire cannon placement. It gave a completely spherical view of the outside world except for the part attached to the ship.

LeMaine strapped himself in, slipped on his headset, and the controls blinked on in front of him. The giant cannon hung off the ship's back end with the firing mechanism inside the bubble.

LeMaine grabbed the weapon and a surge of power flowed into the gun. The rotational coupling attaching it to the ship loosened and became smooth and almost lightweight in his hands.

He swung his seat from side to side. He could move the gun in any direction except directly backward into the ship itself.

He swung the other way as a whole posse of Axichis ships rolled in from the west. Lasers carpeted the airfield, but just as fast, two more Iumian vessels shrieked out of the mayhem.

Five explosions rocked the airfield. "Get us the hell up there, Nunn!" LeMaine ordered.

"Getting us up there!" She ripped the ship off the ground so fast that LeMaine's stomach dropped. "Be careful what you wish for, Sir!"

Kellogg's voice barked through the headset. "Don't leave me hanging, girl! I'm keeping 'em warm for ya."

"Pull it around to the west," Peterman called in LeMaine's other ear. "Drive them into Buca's guns. He's the fastest."

LeMaine looked everywhere for the battle, but so much shit and crap blocked his view that he couldn't see the Axichis much less his own people.

"Coming in for dinner!" Nunn announced.

A pounding stutter of gunfire peppered the hull right next to LeMaine's bubble. "What the hell are you doing, you crazy bitch!" he yelled over his shoulder.

"On your starboard flank, Sir!" Heckler rumbled in LeMaine's ear. "Buca and Erias are holding the northern side. Move in to cut them in half, Nunn."

"You got it, pal!" She slammed the ship hard to port. LeMaine looked everywhere and finally saw what Heckler was talking about.

Nunn flew straight into the enemy's teeth. A dozen Axichis fighters spiraled out of the dust cloud and she aimed the ship's nose directly between them.

LeMaine barely had time to bring his gun up and open fire before the Axichis hurtled on either side of him, but Nunn kept right on going.

"Perfect!" Kellogg crowed. "You missed your calling with your Plaostine explosions."

"Don't tempt me!"

"Are we fighting a battle here or what?" LeMaine interrupted.

"You bet." Nunn wheeled in another devastating arc. She started racing back the way she came. This time, she flew into a part of the battle where LeMaine could see exactly what was going on.

Two fighters occupied a position on the airfield's western side. They looked different from the ships Aaglik gave the Hellhounds. Each had one position instead of two.

Buca and Erias manned them, and right then, three Hellhounds wheeled out of the chaos driving a bunch of Axichis before them. Cannon fire erupted from all three. The Axichis scattered and parted to save themselves. They tried to flee and ran straight into Buca and Erias.

"Like shooting fish in a barrel," Heckler growled.

"Seven more coming in from the north," Peterman announced.

"Hey!" O'Hara called. "Buca is taking all the kill count."

"We'll have to throw him out if this keeps up," Nunn added.

"Bring it around to the east," Polasek ordered. "Get behind them, Kellogg. Nunn, you take the south side."

"On it." She blasted away from the battle and flew far away from any enemy, but LeMaine understood this game now.

She peeled so far sideways that LeMaine looked straight down at the ground battle. The Iumians faced off against the Axichis and surged to drive the enemy off the airfield.

The next minute, Nunn righted their craft and LeMaine pulled his cannon up ready to fire. He didn't see anything for a minute.

Then she blasted out of the dust cloud and almost collided with twenty Axichis locked in a deadly struggle with the other Hellhounds.

"Get back, you cocksuckers!" Heckler roared.

"Reel 'em in, Sir!" O'Hara yelled.

"Come to Papa," LeMaine snarled and opened fire.

His shots pounded the Axichis from one side. Erias and Buca launched forward from the other side, but LeMaine was already doing too much damage.

"LeMaine, one!" Polasek screamed.

"LeMaine, two—four—eight!" Kellogg cackled. "Holy shit, he's rubbing our noses in it!"

LeMaine had to laugh. "Watch and learn, son. Watch and learn."

Buca laughed. "How many do I have?"

"You aren't part of this," Nunn told him. "You mind your own business."

Buca laughed again and Polasek veered away. "I'm running around the block to check the turkeys."

"We're coming with you," LeMaine told him. "Take us around to the west, Nunn."

"You got it, Sir."

She gunned the engines, plunged through the dust cloud, and made a circuit of the airfield. She ran into Polasek's fighter in no time. "Are they gone?"

"No such luck," LeMaine replied. "Beat it back to the battle and let's see if we can drive the ground troops back."

Nunn turned a somersault in midair and LeMaine's weight slammed against his harness. His stomach turned over at the same time, but he stopped himself from telling her to quit screwing around. The Hellhounds deserved a little fun after today.

The squad assembled over the ground battle, but by the time they got into position, the Iumians had already driven the Axichis away into the city streets.

Nunn circled the enemy, but the Axichis buried themselves in the city. "Those vermin won't leave the bunker alone," LeMaine remarked. "They'll come back to shit on our parade again. Mark my words."

"What do you want to do, Sir?" Polasek asked. "Should we stay up here and make sure more Axichis don't land?"

"Sir!" Nunn called over her shoulder. "The bunker is hailing you. Aaglik is asking for communications."

"Patch it through."

One of the bubble's displays flickered to life in front of LeMaine and Aaglik's ancient face appeared. "Well done, Captain."

"What do you want us to do? You're in charge here. Do you want us to stay up here and guard the airfield? The bastards will come back as soon as we leave."

"I'm sending out my own pilots to take your place. You should see them approaching the airfield from the west."

Nunn did something on her controls and a chart of the city showed up next to Aaglik's face. Thirty dots migrated closer to the airfield.

"I see them," LeMaine replied.

"Land on the airfield and hand over our vessels to the Iumian pilots."

LeMaine frowned. "Should I be taking offense at that?"

Aaglik grinned his ghastliest grin. "No, Captain. I have a much more important job for you and your squad—one my people can't do."

"What is it?"

"These ships are all very nice, but there's another battle craft on the planet that can do a much better job of defending Iumia from the Axichis. We need you to get it, but you can be sure you'll have to fight your way to it."

LeMaine puffed out his cheeks and let go of his cannon. "You're talking about the *Renown*."

"She's much stronger than anything else we have on this planet. We have to get her in the air. When the Axichis see you trying to reach the ship, they'll try to stop you. We'll give you whatever air support we can, but it will be dangerous. You'll have to repair the ship under fire."

LeMaine nodded. "All right, but we'll need Monk for an operation like that."

Chapter 23

Nunn landed the Iumian fighter craft on the tarmac. She and LeMaine climbed down just as a whole mob of Iumians streamed onto the airfield. They surrounded the Hellhounds as Peterman, Polasek, Kellogg, Buca, and Erias all landed.

Half the new arrivals rotated backward to defend the ships while their crews loaded up. The Iumians exchange a few flinty nods with LeMaine, but the natives didn't waste time talking.

"Move it out, Hellhounds. Beat it back to the bunker." LeMaine squinted at the wrecked city all around him. "I don't suppose the enemy will give us any trouble now."

"They're licking their wounds," Kellogg remarked.

"They aren't licking anything, chump," Heckler snarled. "They're arming for another assault."

"Let's go." LeMaine hesitated. "Erias...."

"I'm with you, Sir."

"Right." LeMaine started forward. He kept his carbine ready, but he was right. The Axichis didn't show themselves, but he felt their presence lying low in this city. They were biding their time before their next attack.

The Hellhounds made their way back to the bunker and the mood lightened considerably, now that they were leaving the enemy behind.

O'Hara hustled up to Buca's side. "So.... how many did you get?"

"I didn't count them," Buca replied.

"You are gonna HAVE to change that," Nunn told him. "Kill count is everything."

"Why is it everything?" Buca asked.

"Listen to this guy!" Heckler punched Buca's shoulder. "He's too humble to be a Hellhound."

"You need to grow yourself a head about five times the size," O'Hara told Buca.

"Like O'Hara's," Kellogg added and the others laughed.

"Hey!" O'Hara protested. "I can't help it if I'm awesome."

"An awesome pain in the ass," Polasek corrected.

"What do you mean?" Buca glanced from one Hellhound to the next. "Why would I want to grow my head to five times the size?"

The others laughed at him, but Buca kept looking between them in confusion. "It means you need to get all stuck on how awesome you are so no one can stand your company," Peterman explained.

"Like O'Hara," Kellogg added and everyone exploded.

"Go on, son," LeMaine chimed in. "Tell us how many you hit. Don't hold back. We can take it."

"You beat the captain," Heckler added. "That's something to be proud of."

"Don't worry," Polasek added. "He doesn't hold grudges."

"He'll just beat your ass next time," Peterman finished and the squad laughed some more.

LeMaine bit back a chuckle. He didn't get much chance to beat the Hellhounds in a shooting spree. When he did, he could take the friendly ribbing with the best of them.

"You're not going to tell us, are you?" Nunn prompted. "We'll just have to wait until you're on the *Renown* where you can't hide your numbers from us."

"You really want to know?" Buca asked.

"Of course!" O'Hara replied. "Don't keep us in suspense. At least let us know what we're up against."

Buca looked away. "Thirty-seven."

A hushed gasp went through the group. No one spoke for a second until Heckler hissed through gritted teeth. "Shit on a stick!"

"That's it!" Lemon muttered. "I'll kill him."

Buca looked around at his squad mates. "Did I say something wrong?"

"They're all hurt and shit 'cuz you showed 'em up," LeMaine told him. "Don't take it personally."

"The captain never does," Peterman added and the tension evaporated.

LeMaine squeezed Buca's shoulder. "You did real good, son. You should be proud of yourself."

"Maybe I should cut it back next time," Buca began.

"No!" all the Hellhounds yelled at once.

"For the love of Christ, don't start taking it easy on us," Heckler growled. "We can't stand that."

"Not even O'Hara can stand it," Lemon added.

"Are you sure?" Buca asked. "I don't even have a place on the *Renown*. Maybe I should...."

"NO!" they all roared.

"Don't even think about it," Kellogg countered.

"We'll really kick your ass if you do," Nunn told Buca.

"If you can catch him first, you mean," Peterman corrected.

Erias turned to LeMaine. "Is it always like this?"

LeMaine laughed. "Pretty much. You just can't shut these Hellhounds up, not even when someone is shooting at them."

"Why would we want to shut up?" Nunn asked. "We do our best shooting when we're mouthing off."

"*You* sure as hell do," Lemon fired back.

"You see?" LeMaine told Erias. "You have to do special jaw exercises just to get posted to this squad. That's the only way you can talk fast enough to keep up with these delinquents. You can tell Buca is new. He doesn't talk as much."

"Even Peterman can sling the shit with the best of 'em," Kellogg added.

"No one beats O'Hara's mouth, though," Polasek pointed out. "He can get the captain to reprimand him by every ten minutes if he really tries."

"Shit, he even pissed off Peterman earlier," Nunn reminded everyone, "and that's saying something."

Erias kept glancing back and forth between the speakers. Then he shook his head. "It was never like this on my squad."

"Sounds like you were on the wrong squad," LeMaine replied.

"Our lieutenant would never let anyone step out of line like this. He couldn't stand horsing around."

"Sounds like an asshole," Heckler growled. "Captain LeMaine is straight up."

"Thanks, Corporal," LeMaine countered. "You're not too shabby yourself."

"I do my best, Sir."

"Just don't start mouthing off to him," O'Hara advised. "You're nowhere near good-looking enough to get away with it."

"Who exactly are you talking to?" Peterman asked.

O'Hara shrugged. "The whole squad. Why do you think the captain puts up with me?" He shot LeMaine a winning smile. "You know you can't live without me, Sir."

"Yeah," LeMaine sneered. "When I retire, I'm gonna get me a ten-year supply of your wisecracks from the *Renown's* logs so I can listen to you mouthing off to me for the rest of my natural life."

The others laughed even louder. "You're yanking our chain, Sir," Kellogg replied. "You know you'll never retire."

"He'd get too lonely without us," O'Hara added.

Erias glanced over at LeMaine. "You actually put up with this?"

LeMaine grinned at him. "I'm a glutton for punishment."

"You must be."

LeMaine cast an affectionate glance around at his squad and didn't answer. He didn't mind the Hellhounds badgering him with their jokes and side remarks. It bonded them and gave them a powerful connection to each other.

The Hellhounds would do anything for each other and for LeMaine. He would do anything for them, too, including throwing himself in front of a gun to save any one of them.

He valued each of them like a member of his own family. In his heart of hearts, he knew his own management of this squad made them protect and help each other through the worst.

This easy-going back-and-forth of playful jabs and letting nearly all pretense of command drop away when they weren't in combat—it brought them all together in loyalty and mutual protection. The squad stood or fell on that and LeMaine wouldn't have it any other way.

He pitied other squads in the Elian Military like Erias's old company. They never had any fun. Their commanding officers took all the enjoyment and comradery out of the process. What was the point of joining the military without that?

LeMaine didn't understand it. He never wanted to be part of a squad like that and he made sure the Hellhounds never went that way. He appreciated Nunn, Kellogg, and O'Hara for keeping it that way.

Even the more reserved squad members like Polasek and Peterman had warmed up after being in the group long enough. Buca wasn't there yet, but he would be. He wouldn't be able to help himself. That was the way the Hellhounds worked. They got into your head and your heart until you couldn't imagine leaving them.

Kellogg was right. LeMaine would never retire. He would never leave this squad, which meant he would probably die in combat. He could live with that.

Erias guided the squad back to the bunker entrance. More Iumian fighters converged from all over the city, but just as many left the bunker on their way back out.

The squad returned to the underground command center where they met back up with Aaglik. "Thank you, Captain," he told LeMaine. "We couldn't have done it without you."

LeMaine looked around. "Where's Monk....and Lulara?"

"I'm right here, Captain." Lulara stepped out of a corner along with Thaki.

Thaki embraced Erias. "How's Kaex?"

"He's with the medics." Thaki caught LeMaine's eye. "Thank you for bringing my brother back, Captain."

"We're the ones who should be thanking him." LeMaine turned back to Aaglik. "I need to see Monk before we talk about anything else."

"I'll take you," Erias interjected. "I want to see Kaex."

"At ease, Hellhounds," LeMaine ordered. "Reload your weapons and prepare for another maneuver."

"Yes, Sir," Polasek replied.

Erias led LeMaine out of the room. They returned to the long corridor leading to the bunker's outer opening. Erias turned into a hospital room crowded with beds.

Deafening roars greeted LeMaine the instant he stepped inside. "Get your filthy hands off me! Let me go! I'll tear every last stinking one of you apart if you......!"

LeMaine strode over to Monk. Five or six Andaaths were trying without much success to restrain him and stop him from leaving the hospital. "What's the problem, Corporal?"

Monk shook the medics' hands off his giant arms. "I was trying to rejoin my squad, Sir, but these bastards wouldn't let me go. They were trying to keep me a prisoner here."

LeMaine glanced down at Monk's chest where Kellogg had cut Monk's shirt away. The shirt hung in tattered shreds over his bulging chiseled muscles.

A perfectly round scar of new skin covered the spot where the branch had penetrated Monk's chest. A few raw incisions crisscrossed his sternum. They had sealed well enough, but they were still fresh.

"Didn't Kellogg tell you to sit tight while you heal up?" LeMaine asked.

Monk glared at him and then looked away. "Yes, Sir."

"Did Kellogg tell you that you weren't cleared for active duty, Corporal?"

"Yes, Sir," Monk mumbled.

"What part of that didn't you understand? You know Kellogg's authority exceeds even mine when it comes to medical matters."

Monk scowled at the floor. "Yes, Sir."

"I should bust you downtown for trying to disobey orders like this. I should leave you here sitting on your ass while the rest of us go out to repair the *Renown*. How would you like that, Corporal?"

Monk's head shot up and his eyes fell out of his sockets. "You can't, Sir! Don't leave me here! She's my ship!"

"Actually, she's my ship, Corporal. It's lucky for you we need you on this mission or you'd be doing a hell of a lot more than sitting in a hospital ward while the Hellhounds get the job done."

Monk wilted and his huge shoulders slumped. "Yes, Sir. You're right."

"I know I'm right." LeMaine squeezed Monk's shoulder. "Now suit up and see if these Iumians have another uniform big enough to fit you. We need you. That's the only reason you're coming with us."

The medics retreated out of range when Monk got to his feet. LeMaine turned to the next bed where Kaex lay on his back. His face had turned purple since Thaki brought him back from the cannon placements.

Erias stood by his side and ran his fingers through Kaex's hair. "I'm here, boy. You're safe."

Kaex's eyes rotated from side to side without seeing anything. The whites had also turned brilliant red. "Erias.... the cannons...."

"You don't worry about the cannons anymore, boy. You stay here and rest up. I'll deal with the cannons."

"Erias...." Kaex husked.

LeMaine went over and patted Erias on the back. "Are you sure you want to come with us? Maybe you should stay here."

"No," Erias murmured. "I'm going. This is our fight. He wouldn't want me to sit it out just because he got hurt."

Chapter 24

Aaglik ran his finger over a large projected chart of the area around Saevis. "We want to distract the Axichis from what's going on. We'll send out the decoy squad here...."

He traced a route from the bunker back along the track the Hellhounds had taken to enter this city.

"Once the Axichis attack the decoys, I'll give the word for the Hellhounds to launch from the airfield."

"How do we know the Axichis won't leave a patrol over the airfield?" Nunn interrupted.

"We're counting on them leaving a patrol so we'll launch a decoy squad from there, too," Aaglik replied. "Erias and Thaki will lead the dummy fleet into the air first. They'll engage the Axichis and then the Hellhounds will launch."

"They'll notice us as soon as we make a break for the *Renown*," Kellogg pointed out. "They'll notice a different grouping moving away from the city."

"That's why the dummy group will lead the Axichis out of the city. They'll set up a distraction at the halfway point between Saevis and the *Renown*. When the Hellhounds launch and head in that direction, it will look like they're going to reinforce the first group."

"So how do we get to the *Renown*?" Peterman asked.

"As soon as you join the first group, the whole Iumian force will migrate over the forest. You'll make it look like you're fleeing or that the Axichis are driving you that way. You'll make it look like the Axichis shot you down and you'll land in the forest."

"So long as they don't shoot us down for real," Heckler growled.

"It doesn't matter as long as we reach the *Renown*," Buca added. "Once we get the ship in the air, we can fight the Axichis from there."

"Exactly," Aaglik agreed.

"So how do we repair the ship without supplies?" Monk asked.

"I've already discussed this with Buca," Aaglik replied. "He feels confident he can repair the ship with regular tools."

"Are you sure?" LeMaine asked. "We're taking one hell of a risk with this operation. We don't want to get all the way out there and wind up empty-handed."

"I can fix it," he replied.

"How?" Monk asked.

"What about the hull?" Lemon asked. "The ship was shot to pieces on atmospheric entry."

"We don't need to repair the hull," Buca replied. "We'll be inside the atmosphere."

"That doesn't help us get off this piece of shit planet." Lemon caught the Iumians glaring at her and she made a face. "No offense."

"Your objective will only be to bring the *Renown* back here for full repair," Aaglik replied. "Were the cannon placements intact?"

Buca nodded. "They were when we left the ship. As long as the Axichis didn't attack after we left, the hull breaches won't interfere with flight."

LeMaine listened to the quiet confidence in the newest Hellhounds' voice. LeMaine stopped himself from asking Buca again if he was sure he could get the *Renown* off the ground. LeMaine trusted Buca. Buca wouldn't say he could do it unless he knew for certain he could.

Monk wasn't so easily convinced. "How do you plan to get power to the ship's controls?"

"The *Renown* uses a Lensyx power system, doesn't it?" Buca replied. "Lensyx is highly combustible. If the Axichis hit the power supply on entry, the *Renown* would have exploded with all of us on board. She didn't, which means the power supply was undamaged. All we have to do is reconnect it to the engines."

"Assuming the engines weren't damaged," O'Hara replied.

"They weren't," Buca replied in his steady tone. "Lensyx combusts as soon as it makes contact with oxygen. If any part of the engine system had been damaged, the same combustion would have taken place."

"What about Crossfire gel?" Heckler asked. "How do we know the ship still has a full ammo complement."

"It has as much Crossfire gel on board as it had when we crashed," Kellogg replied. "No one has touched it since we landed."

"We still have the spare capacitors, too," Polasek added. "If any of the gel reserves got hit, we can restock them from the capacitors."

"Are there any more questions?" Aaglik asked.

The Hellhounds exchanged glances. LeMaine still saw plenty of gaping holes in this plan, but he was prepared to trust Buca's instincts. LeMaine had seen enough of the Buca's skills on Zeia. LeMaine would follow Buca's lead.

LeMaine stood up. "Let's move it on out, Hellhounds."

The Hellhounds picked up their weapons, checked them, and put on their backpacks. Kellogg pointed his medical scanner at Monk, caught LeMaine looking at him, and nodded.

That was good enough for LeMaine and he followed the Iumians to the exit.

Erias and Thaki came up him at the threshold. "We're leading the first fighter group, Captain," Erias told him. "We're prepared to defend you during the repairs, even if it means landing with you."

"I appreciate that, son, but I wouldn't ask you to do that. You fall back with your people. We'll handle the *Renown*."

Erias shook his head. "No, Sir. We'll stick with you until the *Renown* gets off the ground."

Thaki shot a peek behind LeMaine's shoulder. "Your corporal sounds pretty confident, but there's always a chance you'll find something he overlooked. We're prepared for you to take parts from our fighters if you need them."

LeMaine raised his eyebrows. "You don't want to do that, son. Your people need every ship on deck."

"Not as much as we need the *Renown*, Sir. We're also prepared to abandon our fighters and crew the *Renown* if you need additional hands."

"We were cannoneers at Soclitese, but we've done our share of fighting on transports, too," Erias added. "We can handle ourselves on the *Renown*."

LeMaine crushed the young man's shoulder. "I'm sure you can, but let's not let it come to that. Let's get out there. If the *Renown* can fly again without cannibalizing your fighters, we'll do it."

The two brothers exchanged glances and then Erias nodded. "Yes, Sir."

"Good. Let's go."

The Iumians and the Hellhounds assembled at the big doors opening into Saevis's tangled neighborhoods. Axichis fighters tumbled and rolled in the air over the city dropping bombs everywhere.

More rockets plummeted from the atmosphere. They concentrated on the city's most heavily constructed center, but that wouldn't last. As soon as the defenders showed themselves, the Axichis would target them instead, but there was no way around it.

LeMaine didn't have a second to wait. Aaglik gave the order, "Go!" and all the Iumians charged into the street. The Hellhounds took off after them and the whole crew veered through explosions and imploding buildings on a dead run for the airfield.

LeMaine swept his carbine into every alley searching for Axichis ground troops, but he didn't see any. Iumian fighter craft whistled out of nowhere to occupy the Axichis, but the natives couldn't stop the rockets falling from the sky.

LeMaine ran closer to his Hellhounds. The squad stayed close in a tight group. The Iumians outstripped them and reached the airfield first, but everyone had to fall back when devastating rocket fire pounded the area.

"What happened to the distraction?" Polasek yelled.

"Aaglik already deployed the decoy squad!" Erias hollered back. "This is the patrol."

"Some patrol!" Heckler boomed.

"The Axichis must have reinforced it," Peterman remarked.

LeMaine squinted toward the airfield. He couldn't even see the ships the Hellhounds were supposed to take.

"We'll go first," Erias yelled in LeMaine's ear. "We'll take it on the chin."

"Don't do anything stupid!" LeMaine called back.

Erias grinned at him. "Stupid is my middle name."

"I hope you kicked your parents' asses for that."

Erias laughed and grabbed his brother by the shirt. "See you on the other side. Let's go."

The Iumian pilots broke cover, made a mad dash onto the airfield, and vanished into the smoke.

"How long do we wait?" Nunn asked.

LeMaine didn't answer. The Axichis attackers swarmed more thickly than ever. If this bombardment did its work, the first fighter group might not even get off the ground.

Booms and crashes echoed from all sides. An Axichis rocket hit the building behind the Hellhounds' hiding place. Blocks and debris rained on their heads.

LeMaine ducked under his arms and O'Hara put his backpack over his head to shield himself.

"Don't let them hit your scope, Sergeant," Polasek yelled at him.

O'Hara started to answer when LeMaine saw it. "There! The first group is away!"

Fifteen Iumian fighters blasted out of the smoke gunning their engines to the west. They broke away from the main battle, but the Axichis didn't give them a minute of breathing space.

The Iumian pilots already in the air added their guns to the ruse. They pursued the Axichis and pounded the enemy from behind to make it look like they wanted to stop the Axichis from hunting down the decoy squad.

The Axichis drove the Iumians for miles out of the city before the rear pursuit caught up. The Axichis rounded on their attackers a few miles from the city's edge. The first group hurtled many miles into the countryside with no Axichis following them.

The first group came limping back, and when they saw what was going on, they dove in and closed the Axichis between both flanks.

"This isn't going according to plan," Peterman remarked.

"You can say that again," Heckler growled. "This could take all day."

"I have an idea," LeMaine told them. "Let's go."

"Are you sure, Sir?" O'Hara asked. "That wasn't the plan."

"What plan?" LeMaine stood up. "Let's go. Get to your ships and launch."

He took off running into the smoke. The Hellhounds hesitated for one second and then bolted after him. Nunn grinned when she caught up to him. "Setting yourself up for another insubordination charge, Sir?"

"You better believe it."

He couldn't see his assigned ship until Nunn dodged hard to the right. She charged out of sight and LeMaine didn't see her, either, not until he covered another hundred yards.

He barely spotted her darting into an open hatch. She already had the engines running by the time LeMaine got on board.

"Tell me if you're going to do something like that!" LeMaine yelled at her.

"You said get to the ship and launch."

LeMaine dove into his cannon placement as four other fighters launched nearby. LeMaine didn't even get his safety harness on before Nunn yanked the ship into the air.

"Hey!" LeMaine bellowed.

"What?" Nunn yelled back.

LeMaine growled under his breath. She didn't give him a chance to say anything else. She slammed the throttle to the wall and plunged the fighter on a collision course for the air battle.

The first group got all mixed up with the Iumian patrol. The combined Iumian forces matched the Axichis in numbers, but the Iumians still couldn't drive the Axichis any farther out of town.

Nunn drove the fighter to its fastest speed. She didn't brake for an instant before she plowed nose first into the swarm.

LeMaine had all he could handle just keeping up with her. He slammed his cannon to port and opened fire just as Nunn skidded between two parallel flanks of Axichis. LeMaine barely had to aim at all. She raced past the enemy and LeMaine's shots sliced the flank in half.

"How many was that, Sir?" O'Hara chirped in his ear.

"Buca, one," Buca added.

"Make that your last one, asshole," Lemon called from across the battle.

"Hard to starboard, Sergeant," Peterman ordered.

"On it, Sir," O'Hara replied.

Shots erupted on all sides. Buca no longer had any advantage over the other Hellhounds. The kill count mounted from every direction.

The Hellhounds turned the tide and the Iumian defenders started to get the upper hand. "Drive them into the countryside!" Erias ordered.

"Not so fast, son," LeMaine replied. "We can take them here. We can finish them off so they don't see where we went."

"What about the atmospheric blockade?" Polasek asked. "They'll see us either way."

"Then we have no reason to spare them. The more we finish off now, the fewer enemy fighters we'll have to worry about later."

"You heard the man." Erias pulled his fighter around for another pass. "Finish them off."

"Circle to port, Monk," LeMaine ordered. "Polasek, you take starboard. Peterman, you and Kellogg come with me."

"Not fair, Sir!" Lemon argued. "You're taking all the glory."

"Hey, what about us pilots?" Nunn interjected. "We don't get to shoot at all so count your blessings."

"We can share our gunners' kill count," Heckler suggested. "That's only fair, right?"

"Good," Nunn replied. "That's twenty for me and twenty for the captain."

"Now you're fixing your numbers," O'Hara protested, but LeMaine didn't hear any more.

Monk and Polasek cut a wide path around the Axichis with Buca and Lemon firing into the swarm. The enemy bunched together for protection and fired outward at the Iumians who kept tightening their net.

Nunn, Peterman, and Kellogg joined in for a few revolutions and the Iumians closed the trap.

LeMaine added his fire to the mix. He didn't keep track of his kill count, but Nunn did it for him. He didn't hear the other Hellhounds' numbers. He held his breath measuring his timing down to the micron.

On Nunn's third pass, he saw what he was looking for. All the Axichis fighters rotated their noses back toward Saevis. They concentrated their fire that way to cut a path for themselves.

LeMaine stopped shooting and locked his gaze on the enemy craft. The Axichis wavered for a second until, in one sudden assault, they all lunged at once and leapt forward to break through.

"Now!" LeMaine ordered.

Nunn slammed the fighter hard to port and buried the ship in the Axichis flank. Kellogg and Peterman did exactly the same thing.

LeMaine opened fire sweeping his cannon every which way. He targeted anything moving across his view and explosions blocked him from seeing anything.

Vertigo made his head spin, but he only swung his gun faster and more wildly. More cannon fire erupted on all sides until the deafening boom of exploding craft blocked out all else.

Nunn blasted out of the swarm. "Your turn, boys! They're all yours."

Peterman and Kellogg skimmed out of the debris cloud and Monk, Polasek, and the Iumians took over. They converged on what remained of the Axichis and finished them off down the last ship.

"And stay gone!" O'Hara called to no one in particular. "If you ever try to invade our system again, you'll get more of the same."

"Can you boys handle things from here?" LeMaine asked Erias.

"Don't worry about us. Just get out to the forest. Call us if you need parts or help."

"You got it, son. Take us out of here, Nunn."

Chapter 25

LeMaine squinted through the canopy below his cannon pod. "There she is. Monk, you and Buca get down on the ground pronto. The rest of us will stay airborne and give you cover."

"Yes, Sir."

Monk angled his fighter downward and landed among the trees. Buca darted out and vanished inside the *Renown*.

"I hope to hell he knows what he's doing," Lemon muttered.

"Are you seriously telling me that Buca doesn't know what he's doing?" Heckler growled in LeMaine's other ear. "I trust him with that ship even more than Monk. The guy's a damn genius."

"Let's not get carried away with ourselves," Peterman interjected. "Buca's good, but he isn't perfect. He can make mistakes."

"Are you kidding me?" Monk asked from the grounded fighter. "Did you see what he did with that racer on Ziea? He modified it to make it ten times faster. He caught that scumbag Macon because Buca's racer left Macon's in the dust....and don't even get me started on what he did to the weapon's system."

"Cut the chit-chat, Hellhounds," LeMaine interrupted. "We got company."

Nunn spun their craft around and a groan went through the Hellhounds. A flock of massive Axichis warships descended through the atmosphere. Eight of them hovered over Saevis while a dozen more landed on the ground.

"Christ Almighty!" Heckler snarled.

"So now you're getting religious?" O'Hara teased. "I never knew you had it in you, Corporal."

"How many of those cocksuckers are there?" Lemon asked.

"Scans reading fifty with another hundred on standby in the atmosphere," Peterman replied.

LeMaine thought fast. "Patch me through to Erias."

Erias's face appeared on LeMaine's controls. "We got a serious problem here, Captain."

"I can see that, son. We're aborting the mission."

"No!" Erias yelled back. "We need the *Renown*. We have to get her off the ground. She's our only chance at fighting these warships."

"The *Renown* won't do us any good against them, son. Besides, we would have to ground these fighters to send our crew over to the *Renown*. We only have one person on board at the moment and he'd be flying the ship. There would be no one available to man her cannons."

Erias glanced away from the screen and his expression pinched. "Yes, Sir. You're right."

"Listen to me, son. We can't even bring out any Iumians to take over these fighters and we need every available craft. Get your people to safety and don't look back. Saevis isn't safe for anyone anymore. I can see ground troops deploying from here. We'll find another way to regroup."

Erias sighed. "Yes, Sir."

Just then, another display blinked to life on LeMaine's controls. "The *Renown's* power supply is back online, Sir," Buca reported. "I'm rerouting to the engines...."

"Forget the *Renown*. Abandon ship."

Buca froze staring at LeMaine through the feed. "Sir?"

"I said abandon ship. Shut down all power to the *Renown* and get back to the fighter now. You and Monk get off the ground ASAP. Get as far away from the *Renown* as you can."

"Uh.... yes, Sir," Buca replied and started scrambling over his controls.

"How do you want to play this, Sir?" Polasek asked.

LeMaine made one more survey of the scene on the ground. Rockets from the atmosphere still pounded Saevis, but the Axichis somehow managed to hit the city without putting their own warships in danger.

More warships glided over the city patrolling for anything that moved. The Iumian fighters who helped the Hellhounds reach the *Renown* couldn't get back to the city with so many enemy vessels blocking the way.

The Iumians made a few futile attempts to whiz past their enemies, but anyone could see it was hopeless. A scattered collection of Iumian craft launched from the airfield, but they immediately met their deaths as three warships converged to gun the Iumians down.

LeMaine glanced down at his controls. Dozens of life signs spread across the ground radiating outward from the Iumian bunker. The Iumians were abandoning Saevis. What choice did they have?

"Let's go, Nunn," he ordered.

"Where are we going, Sir?"

LeMaine took his eyes away from the Axichis warships for a fraction of a second. "Incoming!" Monk roared.

LeMaine didn't have time to turn around before a crushing smash knocked his craft hard to port. The impact hurled him against his harness and his head kept going. His skull nailed the sidewall before Nunn yanked the ship upright.

The ship went spinning off somewhere else. Dozens of voices shrieked in LeMaine's ears. He struggled to pull himself back to consciousness, but he couldn't separate one voice from the next.

Stars exploded in his eyes before he realized that other Iumian fighters were blowing right in front of him. He couldn't tell if any of them belonged to the Hellhounds.

"Sir!" Nunn bellowed. "Captain! Talk to me!"

"Pull back!" Polasek ordered. "Retreat to the hills!"

"Captain LeMaine is hit!" Nunn called back. "He isn't answering."

"I'm.... I'm okay, Corporal," LeMaine husked.

"All Iumian forces—fall back!" Polasek snapped. "Erias! Do you read? Fall back to the hills!"

LeMaine dragged his vision into focus and almost lost his lunch. Fourteen warships advanced out of the city. They targeted the Iumian fighters hovering over the forest. The Axichis fired, but the Axichis could hit the defenders from beyond the Iumians' range. No one could fight these invaders.

The Axichis crawled over the landscape picking off the Iumians one after another. Four more exploded right in front of LeMaine's eyes. Were Erias and Thaki dead already?

LeMaine grabbed his cannon and swept it up. More shots spat from the Hellhounds' fighters, but all their shots fell short. Nothing could stop the Axichis.

The next instant, Nunn pulled the fighter backward and broke for the mountains. LeMaine had no idea where to go, but a second later, one of the Iumians raced past his pod.

"Follow me, Hellhounds," Erias called. "We have an emergency rendezvous location behind those peaks."

"You heard the man," LeMaine ordered. "Follow Erias."

LeMaine turned his attention to the controls in front of him. He collapsed in relief when he read all the Hellhounds alive and on track. Monk and Buca had gotten away and no power signature came from the *Renown*. Another brilliant plan had just bitten the dust.

"You okay, Sir?" Nunn asked.

"What's wrong with him?" Polasek asked.

"Nothing," LeMaine grumbled. "I hit my head. That's all."

"How's your vision?" Kellogg asked. "Can you focus all right?"

"I...uh...." LeMaine struggled to look at something on the ground. "It's hard. I can see all right. It's just hard to focus."

"We'll reach the base in a sec." Erias and the other Iumians raced up the mountains. The forest ended on the slopes and left the peaks bare.

"Where's your rendezvous?" LeMaine asked.

"There's a canyon...." Erias barely got the words out when an Axichis laser sizzled across the forest. It came from a warship suspended over Saevis. The laser scorched the treetops, zinged past LeMaine's pod, and smashed into one of the Iumians.

"Thaki!" Erias shrieked. "Thaki! NO!"

Three more lasers cut him off and three more Iumians detonated right on Erias's tail. "Gun it!" LeMaine ordered. "Get over those mountains and step on it!"

The remaining pilots blasted up the mountain, but the Axichis kept bombing the slopes with impossible shots. They fired from hundreds of miles away and still hit their targets with pinpoint accuracy.

"Let's go, Erias!" LeMaine called. "We have to go. Move it out, Hellhounds."

Nunn hit the throttle and the Hellhounds streaked up the peaks with the Iumians. Erias hesitated a second longer and then dogged the defenders up and over the mountaintop.

"Where are we going?" LeMaine asked.

"Down here." Erias dropped behind the tallest mountain and vanished into a bottomless canyon. His voice sounded shaky, but he flew as well as ever.

He sprinted ahead of the others and led the way into winding caverns buried in the trackless wilderness. LeMaine relaxed as they got farther away from Saevis. The Axichis wouldn't be able to follow the Iumians here. It was the perfect escape route.

Erias finally whirled in midair over a base tucked between two sheer cliffs. The Iumians spiraled around a small, short landing zone and each one set down one after the other.

The Hellhounds stayed aloft and landed last. LeMaine felt sick when he unbuckled his harness and tried to climb out of his pod.

He had to sit down and cradled his spinning head. Nunn looked in on him. "You okay, Sir?"

"I don't feel good."

"Kellogg!" Nunn yelled outside. "The captain needs you."

LeMaine hated this feeling, but he stayed where he was until Kellogg came over. Kellogg shoved himself into the pod and scanned LeMaine's head. "You lost consciousness, didn't you?"

"Yeah...uh...it only seemed like a few seconds, but I could be wrong."

"Look at me."

LeMaine hauled his pounding head up and did his best to make eye contact with Kellogg, but it wasn't easy.

Kellogg turned to Nunn who, along with Heckler and Polasek, stood outside the pod watching and listening. "Go inside and see what kind of medical facilities they have here."

Nunn bolted and Polasek squatted down. "How's it hanging, Captain?"

LeMaine waved toward the open hatch where Nunn had disappeared. "Take over for me, Lieutenant."

"Don't worry," Kellogg interrupted. "I can fix this in a few minutes, but you better come with me. We shouldn't do it here."

Kellogg helped LeMaine to his feet. LeMaine swayed and had to support himself against the pod wall. "What's the problem, Sergeant?"

"You have a subarachnoid bleed. I'll relieve the pressure and you'll feel better, but you better take it easy for a few hours afterward."

"There's a war on in case you hadn't noticed, Sergeant. This isn't the time or the place for me to take it easy for a few hours."

Kellogg patted him on the back while LeMaine hobbled out of the ship. "Sorry, Sir, but orders are orders. Go sit down for a while and then I'll clear you for active duty."

"You better," LeMaine growled.

Kellogg laughed, but Nunn came back before he could say anymore. "They have an infirmary that looks like a closet and it's full of injured Iumians."

"I don't care," Kellogg replied. "Just find me a place where the captain can sit down for a while."

Just then, Lulara came toward them leading a tall Andaath female. "Captain Owen LeMaine, this is Alruna. She's in command of this base."

The Andaath stuck out her hand. "It's a pleasure to meet you, Captain. Aaglik has been telling me about the help you gave our people in Saevis."

LeMaine shook her hand and started to speak, but Kellogg cut him off. "Excuse me, Ma'am, but Captain LeMaine is injured. Do you have some place where he can sit down while I work on him?"

"Of course." Alruna shot LeMaine a questioning glance, but he was rapidly losing the ability to think or see straight.

Kellogg took hold of LeMaine's elbow and LeMaine followed Kellogg's direction gratefully. By the time they reached some sort of structure in the distance, LeMaine's vision had gone completely fuzzy.

"Sit down, Sir," Kellogg ordered.

LeMaine had to let Kellogg push him down into a chair. LeMaine strained his eyes, but he couldn't see anything.

He felt Kellogg touching his head and doing something. Polasek's voice came from a massive distance. "What's the problem?"

No one answered him. LeMaine couldn't get his voice to work. All at once, something hot and wet gushed down the side of his face and all his confusion vanished. His eyes snapped into laser focus. His ears popped and his brain switched back on.

He was in another command center like the Saevis bunker. Iumians of all species worked on electronic equipment monitoring the situation all over the planet. A few monitored the war farther afield on other Elian planets.

Kellogg mopped the wet stuff off LeMaine's forehead. Kellogg moved his own face in front of LeMaine's eyes. "Your pupils are back to normal. Can you see all right now, Sir?"

"Yes. Thank you, Sergeant."

Polasek and Peterman stood behind Kellogg. Polasek kept scowling at LeMaine. "Are you sure he's all right?"

"He's fine," Kellogg replied. "I've just relieved the pressure."

"How are you going to clear him for active duty with a big hole in the side of his head?"

Kellogg rolled his eyes to Heaven and shot a grin at LeMaine. "I'm going to electrolyze it as soon as you stop pestering me."

Polasek made a face at LeMaine, too, and LeMaine found himself chuckling. He was back.

"If you're feeling better, Captain," Alruna cut in from a few feet away, "we could use your consultation on the warship situation."

Kellogg pressed down on LeMaine's shoulder to make him stay in his chair.

"I don't know how much use I'll be to you," LeMaine told her. "There are only ten of us and we don't even have a ship. We've been using borrowed Iumian fighter craft and they won't be much good against those warships. We just had to flee from them."

Kellogg moved in front of LeMaine's face again. "I'm attaching the bone electrolyzer to your skull. This is going to hurt."

"What are you doing?" Alruna asked.

"I'm sealing the hole I drilled in his skull."

"Don't you have a gouger?" Alruna asked.

"A what?" Kellogg asked. "I never even heard of it."

"It's a device that seals bone. It uses Nablium to fuse the fracture through the skin. It doesn't require electrolyzation."

"We saw it at the bunker, but Kellogg wasn't there," LeMaine told her.

"I won't be using anything I haven't used before or at least seen used," Kellogg replied. "If you're ready, Sir, you can lie down on the floor."

LeMaine stretched out on the floor. "This is barbaric," Alruna muttered.

"At least it works." Kellogg punched the trigger on the electrolyzer and a scorching bolt of lightning shot straight to LeMaine's brain.

He blacked out, and a second later, his eyelids fluttered. He blinked up at Kellogg. "It's over, Sir. You can get up." Kellogg grasped LeMaine's wrist and hauled him to his feet. "How do you feel?"

"I feel fine...except that I have a headache."

"I can give you something for that. Tell me if your condition changes."

"Thank you, Sergeant."

Kellogg shot LeMaine one of his crazy grins. "Now we're even for you zapping me on Ziea."

"Count your lucky stars Lemon wasn't around to see this," Peterman added. "Or Nunn."

"Where is everyone?" LeMaine asked.

"They're out there checking their fighter craft. The Iumians are rearming us in case we need to fight again.... though I don't know what we're going to do if the warships come *here*."

"They won't come here," Alruna told him. "They can't get into these canyons."

"I'm sorry, but you're misinformed," Peterman replied. "The Axichis warships can target Iumian fighters from hundreds of miles away. They can hit us from orbit. They don't have to enter this canyon or any other. We'd be sitting ducks if they decided to come after us."

Alruna looked around at LeMaine. "That's impossible."

"It's true," LeMaine replied. "We need to come up with a contingency plan as soon as possible."

Just then, one of the technicians called out, "Incoming transmission from Aaglik. It's for you, Alruna."

Alruna went over there and LeMaine listened over her shoulder. "What's the situation, Aaglik?" she asked.

"About as bad as you can imagine. We're under steady bombardment and the Axichis are all over the planet. We can't get out. We're trapped here and we expect the Axichis ground troops to overrun the bunker any second now."

"There has to be a way to get the rest of our people out."

Aaglik's eyes darted sideways. "Captain LeMaine, I need you to do something for me."

"Name it. I'm at your service."

"I need you to find Erias and bring him here. I need to talk to him."

LeMaine looked around and caught Peterman's eye. Peterman nodded and took off somewhere.

"What resources do you still have left in the bunker?" Alruna asked. "Can't we salvage anything?"

"There's nothing left. Most of our equipment has been destroyed and the airfield is a moonscape. There's nothing to salvage and there won't be anyone else to evacuate pretty soon. Forget the bunker and Saevis in general."

"We can't do that!" Alruna exclaimed. "We'll get you out."

Aaglik grinned showing all his horrible teeth, but just then, Peterman returned with Erias. LeMaine and Alruna moved out of the way and Erias took their place in front of the screen. "What's up?"

Aaglik's grin vanished. "I'm sorry to tell you this, son, but Kaex is gone. We lost him about half an hour ago. I'm sorry. The medics did all they could, but the damage to his central nervous system was too great. I wish I could do something. I wish I was there with you."

A horrible silence fell over the command center. Erias staggered away from the screen and collapsed into the chair that LeMaine had just vacated.

LeMaine stepped up to the screen and placed his hand on Erias's shoulder. "Do what you can, Aaglik. If you can get out or if there's anything we can do, just tell us. I wish we could say the *Renown* would get you out, but that's out of the question as of now."

"There's nothing you can do, Captain. Just keep fighting the good fight for us. Do what you can to help our people."

"They're our people now, my friend."

Aaglik grinned again. "I know. I'll see you on the other side."

Aaglik cut the line. LeMaine stared at the empty screen. That was another good man gone. There would be no winners in this war. There never were.

He straightened up and looked down at Erias. The young man sat bowed and unmoving in his chair. LeMaine didn't say anything to comfort him. There were no words for this. Erias lost both his brothers in the space of half an hour. Now he was alone.

LeMaine took a deep breath and turned to Alruna. "What resources do you have at this base?"

"Fighter craft, mostly. We do have communications with Elia, but we haven't been able to raise anyone since the bombardment started."

"When was the last time you tried?"

"About four hours ago."

"Try again. I need to call in a favor."

Chapter 26

L eMaine sat in a quiet room with a giant communications array in front of him. Polasek kept zipping back and forth across LeMaine's line of sight. "How long is this likely to take, Lieutenant?"

"Almost there." Polasek went back to whispering to himself and adjusting this and that. "There. It's done."

"You're sure now? You don't need another few hours at it?"

"No, Sir. I'm sure."

"All right. Open it up."

Polasek did something to the array. Nothing happened at first, but after a minute or two, the line blinked to life and LeMaine found himself looking at Commander Russel Lodge.

The commander's uniform was ripped and covered in grime. His hair looked scorched on one side of his face and part of his mustache was gone.

LeMaine frowned at him. "Are you on Oalia, Commander?"

"God, no!" Commander Lodge gasped. "Are you insane? Oalia is a hive of Axichis. We pulled out of there hours ago."

"Where are you, then?"

"We're on Brov. It's serving as our temporary Command base." Commander Lodge furrowed his brow. "Are you okay, Captain? You're covered in blood."

"I'm okay. Listen. We've rigged up an encrypted channel. We need you to bring the Military to Iumia."

Commander Lodge rolled his eyes to Heaven. "What do you think we've been trying to do?"

"You have?"

"Of course. If the Axichis get a foothold on Iumia, the whole damn system is finished."

"So.... you know about the warships?"

"Of course we know about them."

"Is there any way you can mount an assault?"

"It's underway...or at least en route."

"When will it happen?"

Commander Lodge groaned. "How long is a piece of rope? It will happen when we get there."

"That isn't soon enough. The Iumian defense has collapsed. If you don't bring in the assault now, you can kiss Iumia goodbye. That's the plain truth, Russell."

"Okay, okay." Commander Lodge did something on the desk in front of him. "I'll try to step it up."

"Where's Colonel Nicholson?"

Commander Lodge pursed his lips. "We have fourteen attack cruisers...."

"Don't you have any bombers?" LeMaine interrupted.

"All the bombers are tied up in other parts of the system. We can't spare them."

"You just said Iumia was the most important priority. You just said that, if we lose Iumia, the rest of the system is finished. Don't you think you should pull the bombers back here?"

"I don't make the decisions on that."

LeMaine fought his annoyance under control. "Maybe you should put me in touch with someone higher up the chain of command. It sounds like they don't understand the situation on the ground."

"All right, all right. I'll try to send the bombers."

"When?" LeMaine demanded.

"I'll.... have to work on that. I'll get back to you when I know."

LeMaine gritted his teeth. This was getting nowhere. "All right, Russell. Thank you. I'll talk to you later."

"I'll do my best to send the bombers, Owen. I just...it's complicated."

"I can see that, Sir. Thank you again."

LeMaine nodded to Polasek who cut the channel. LeMaine stood up. "That was a total waste of time."

"What are we going to do?" Peterman asked.

"God only knows."

LeMaine led the way out of the room. Alruna, Erias, all the Hellhounds, and most of the Iumian pilots and technicians waited for him to give them the good news.

"Well?" Alruna asked. "What did he say?"

"We're on our own."

A groan went through the assembled defenders. "This is nuts," Heckler growled. "How are we supposed to fight all those warships?"

"We're too far away from the *Renown* to retrieve her," Nunn pointed out.

"The *Renown* wouldn't do anything against those bastard warships anyway," Lemon countered. "The *Renown* might as well not even be on the same planet as we are for all the good she can do us."

"Not necessarily." LeMaine turned to Buca. "Do you think you could recreate the masking technology the colonists used on Ziea?"

"Polasek has the frequencies in his communications array, doesn't he?" Buca asked. "I could patch the frequencies to our remotes. That should mask us."

"What does masking our signals do for us?" Peterman asked. "We would have to use it on our fighters to get anywhere near the warships. Even then, we don't have the firepower to destroy them. They're too big."

"It's more important that we draw them away from the Iumians," LeMaine replied. "At this point, I'm more concerned with making sure the maximum number of Iumians survive this invasion. If the warships find this base, no one will survive."

"Excuse me for interrupting, Captain." All eyes turned to Lulara. She stood in the back of the group and hadn't spoken since the Hellhounds first arrived. "I think I have a solution to our problem."

"Let's hear it."

"You want to use Polasek's array to feed masking frequencies through your remotes to hide yourselves, but we might use Polasek's array to feed a different frequency back to the Axichis."

"How do you figure?" Polasek asked.

"Every ship uses some energy source to power its engines and weapons systems. The Axichis are obviously using a power source we don't know about if they can generate laser shots that travel so far."

"We don't even know what that power source is," Nunn countered. "How would we counteract it?"

"By using a reverse frequency signal. We can check the frequencies on the Iumian fighters that survived the Axichis' last attack. We can calibrate another array—maybe not

Polasek's if it isn't strong enough. We can feed a counter-frequency back to the Axichis to disrupt their systems."

Monk frowned and rubbed his chin. "I don't know if that will work."

"What choice do we have?" Peterman asked. "We can't fight them with weapons, but we might be able to do it this way."

"My array won't be big enough or strong enough," Polasek replied, "and I wouldn't like to suggest we send the frequency from here. If it doesn't work, the signal could lead the Axichis straight to this base."

"As it happens, I have another idea," Lulara told him.

"Well, lay it all on us," LeMaine replied. "We have absolutely nothing to lose at this point."

"I suggest we use the *Renown*," Lulara went on. "The ship's communications system is probably the strongest on the planet, now that the bunker has been destroyed. We can also assume that getting the signal as close as possible to the warships will have the best chance of success."

"How did I know she was going to suggest that?" Heckler snarled.

"Because you have a death wish," Kellogg replied.

"What's to stop the Axichis from blowing the *Renown* out of the sky the instant we power up the engines?" O'Hara asked.

"We'll be masked all the way there," Lulara replied. "If the frequency works, it will protect the *Renown* from Axichis fire."

"Famous last words," Peterman interjected.

"We could even use the Axichis shots to transmit the signal to the warships," Lulara went on. "Every shot they make against us will feed back to destroy them."

"Um.... Sorry to burst your bubble, lady.... but this is all hypothetical," Lemon cut in. "You don't actually know that this mythical frequency of yours will do jack shit. You're blowing smoke out of your ass.... or in this case, your mouth."

Lulara bristled, but LeMaine only laughed. "She's right, Lulara. None of this means squat if the frequency doesn't actually disrupt the Axichis. We wouldn't know any of that unless and until we get to the *Renown*, power up her engines, launch, and get all in the Axichis' faces in a ship we don't know will even fly. It's a pipe dream."

"Do you have a better idea?" Lulara asked.

LeMaine threw up his hands and puffed out his cheeks. "No. I don't. I guess we're doing it."

"You don't have to do this, Captain," Alruna interrupted. "We can fall back deeper into the mountains. You can ride out the war here instead of throwing your lives away."

"Isn't that what Colonel Nicholson told you to do anyway?" Polasek asked.

"If any of you wants reassignment to the Iumians, you can stay and fulfill your duties here," LeMaine replied. "I won't hold it against you, but I'm going out there. I don't plan to ride out the war in safety. In any case, we don't know the Axichis won't come a-knocking out here anyway. If there's a chance this could work, I'm doing it."

"Captain!" Erias got to his feet. "I'm staying behind. I'm sorry, but I'm not coming with you. You can call me a coward, but my place is here...with my people."

"I understand, son, and no one on this squad thinks you're a coward. Your people need you." LeMaine walked up to him and, without giving himself a moment to think twice, he put his arms around the young man and hugged him. "You did great work out there. I'm proud of you. Your people are lucky to have you."

Erias hugged him back and the two men clapped each other on the back. LeMaine stood back and Erias wiped away tears, but he was also smiling.

LeMaine broke away. "All right, Hellhounds. Let's get to work."

Chapter 27

Monk glanced down at the remote panel on his sleeve. "Are you sure this will work?"

Kellogg slapped him on the back. "There isn't a force in creation that could hide *you* from the enemy, big guy."

"I'll hide *you* from the enemy under my heel if you don't shut up," Monk countered. "If you're stupid enough to stick your head in front of a gun, you deserve what you get."

"Don't be so jumpy, Monk," O'Hara told him. "If the Axichis spot you, you won't ever see them coming. One minute, you'll be walking along looking at your remote. The next minute, you'll be sitting on a cloud strumming your golden harp."

"And trying to flap the wings that are too small to lift your giant body," Nunn chimed in.

LeMaine made one last check of his weapon, adjusted his backpack, glanced down at his remote, and stepped out into the open. "Let's go."

The sun peeked above the forest as dawn crept over the landscape. The Hellhounds had traveled a long way to get back to the *Renown* and now the ship was in sight.

LeMaine had been glad to leave the Iumian base. After forty-eight hours of intense preparation, Lulara had finally figured out what she thought was the right frequency and programmed into Polasek's communications array. They just needed the *Renown's* systems to deploy the frequency against the Axichis.

LeMaine couldn't stop checking his remote all the way here. He tried not to see the rest of the Hellhounds doing the same thing, but the Axichis warships didn't come near them. If the Axichis could detect the Hellhounds approaching the *Renown*, they would have done it by now.

The warships clustered the most thickly over Saevis. They'd already destroyed the last Iumian holdouts that might resist their invasion. The city smoked in the distance as the

Hellhounds got nearer, but the Axichis bombardment dwindled with every passing day until it ended altogether.

Fewer warships patrolled the countryside. With no Iumian insurgence, the Axichis didn't need to attack anyone anymore. There was no one left to attack.

The Axichis also didn't go near the mountains. If the Axichis suspected Iumian resistors were hiding there, the invaders didn't act on it.

The Hellhounds wound their way through the forest and LeMaine hunkered down behind a fallen tree. His remote showed him the *Renown* just twenty yards away.

He raised his head just enough to spot the ship and ducked again. "There she is. Buca, you'll go on board and get the power system up and running. Fire up the engines and bring the weapons system online as fast as you can."

"Yes, Sir."

"Lulara, you and Polasek get to the cockpit. Patch Polasek's array to the communications system. The Axichis will come after us the instant Buca switches on the power."

"It's gonna be tight in the cockpit with all three of us trying to work at the same time," Polasek pointed out.

"You can sit on Lulara's lap, lover boy," Nunn told him.

Polasek blushed and squinted over the log toward the *Renown*. "I don't think that will be necessary."

"The rest of you get to your cannons on the double," LeMaine ordered. "The minute Buca brings them online, stand by to fire with everything we've got."

"What about ammunition?" Peterman asked. "We still don't know what reserves we have."

"It doesn't really matter," LeMaine replied. "We'll fire with whatever we have and hope for the best."

"Hope for the best," Heckler growled. "I like them odds."

"What about Monk?" Buca asked. "If you want to get off the ground as quickly as possible, he should be in the cockpit, too. He should be ready to fly as soon as the engines build up power."

"That's gonna make it really tight," Kellogg remarked. "You and Polasek might not make it out without serious tissue damage."

The others laughed. "Monk can man the cannons," LeMaine told Buca. "You pilot the ship."

"Sir!" Monk wailed. "You can't do this to me!"

"How exactly do you think you're gonna reach the cockpit with three other people in there?" O'Hara asked. "Either you can fit in there or they can. You'd crush them to death."

"Stop fooling around," LeMaine interrupted. "Buca's flying the ship. Monk, you're manning a cannon, so get used to it. If there was another way, we would do it."

Heckler punched Monk's shoulder. "Look on the bright side, son. You'll actually be able to get you some kill count for once, now that Buca won't be shooting at anybody."

"What about me?" Lulara asked. "Do you want me on a cannon, too?"

"Yeah—the cockpit cannon. I want you up front with Buca so you can adjust the frequency if we need it."

Buca and Lulara exchanged glances. They hadn't had much to do with each other since the Hellhounds landed on Iumia and Lulara apologized for treating him so badly.

Now they would be together in the *Renown's* cockpit. They would be working side by side to defeat the Axichis. If they came together or turned against each other, it would happen now.

LeMaine pretended not to see that glance. He had bigger fish to fry. "Right. Let's do this."

He stood up and all the Hellhounds got to their feet. They swept their weapons from one side to the other, but LeMaine could already see on his remote that they were completely alone. The warships remained airborne over Saevis. None of them came any nearer.

His pulse quickened as he got closer to the *Renown*. The ship looked as bad as she did when the Hellhounds left her behind. No one would ever suspect she might fly again.

Doubts nagged him as he got nearer to the ship. He didn't know she would fly now. Buca could be wrong about the *Renown*. She might be damaged beyond repair.

He pushed those thoughts away. The ship definitely had power—just enough power to get the Axichis' attention. When that happened....

The Hellhounds closed tighter around him as they neared the branches blocking the hatch. The whole squad picked up the pace walking faster. Breathless tension gripped the Hellhounds until they stood right outside the branches. "Go!" LeMaine ordered.

The squad plunged through the underbrush. Buca, Lulara, and Polasek bolted for the cockpit. The rest of the Hellhounds dropped their weapons and their packs on their seats and dove into their cannon placements.

LeMaine took Polasek's placement next to Peterman. Monk got stuck trying to climb into the spare placement where Buca usually sat. A second later, Monk dropped into the seat on LeMaine's other side.

LeMaine grabbed his cannon just as the power switched on. The engines shrieked to life and power flickered to the cannon controls.

LeMaine searched everywhere and his heart stood still when he saw his worst nightmare coming true. Axichis warships were already leaving Saevis and streaking across the landscape heading straight for the *Renown*.

"I sure hope you're using the right frequency!" he yelled.

"So do I!" Lulara replied.

"Hold onto your lunches!" Kellogg roared as the first smash blasted into the forest.

Axichis lasers sheared treetops from their trunks. Branches snapped and crackled all over the place. Debris peppered the *Renown's* hull.

"Hold on!" Buca bellowed and the *Renown* erupted through the canopy. LeMaine fought to keep his cannon steady as the ship lifted over the branches and the Axichis came in fast and furious.

The enemy opened fire from miles across the countryside. Devastating smashes rocked the *Renown*.

"Get those frequencies up and running!" LeMaine called.

"Working on it!" Lulara replied.

"Work on it faster before we all die!"

LeMaine swung his cannon upward as a massive warship loomed directly over the *Renown*. The Axichis vessel blocked out the sky and the *Renown* buzzed around it like a fly.

Lasers erupted from the warship's sides. Blasts screeched across the hull and then hit the forest. Matchsticks and twirling branches showered the *Renown*.

Buca plunged into the mix veering from one warship and another. He flew at breakneck speed in lunatic figure-eights and reckless contortions. He somersaulted past the Axichis weapons ports and dodged their lasers with expert precision.

"What the hell are you doing?" Monk shrieked. "That's my ship you're messing with!"

"What was that you were saying about kill count being everything?" Buca called into the rear compartment. "I don't hear any numbers back there."

"Oh, hell no!" Lemon muttered. "No, he didn't. I swear to God I'll cut his goddamn balls off!"

Buca laughed. The sound set LeMaine's hair on end. He'd never heard Buca laugh so joyously before, but LeMaine didn't have time to think about that right now.

Buca made another pass under one of the warships' bellies and all the cannon on the port side exploded. The Hellhounds hammered the enemy hulls with cannon fire, but they couldn't even scratch the surface.

Buca cut it dangerously close and skimmed within inches of the enemy's side. Screams went up from the placements across the compartment, but Buca only peeled off and skated even closer to the next warship.

His maneuver worked. The warships couldn't hit the *Renown* at this range. Buca rolled the ship away from the nearest ship and plunged straight down toward the top of the next one.

Monk doubled over and groaned. "Don't ever let him fly the ship again, Sir.... please.... I can't take it."

"I got it!" Lulara yelled. "The frequency is deploying! Target the Axichis! Don't hold back!"

"What the hell do you think we've been doing—picking their damn teeth?" Nunn roared.

Lulara didn't answer. Buca went through one of his gut-turning rolls and cannon fire blasted from the *Renown's* front cannon.

Lulara targeted the Axichis laser ports and hit one of them. The thing detonated with a boom that rocked the *Renown* off her course. Buca had to fight the controls to bring the ship back into position.

"Open it up!" Lulara bellowed. "Target their weapons! The frequency is working."

Buca dragged the *Renown* in a tight arc to breeze past another warship. He steered directly under its belly and brought the *Renown* within spitting distance of the Axichis guns.

LeMaine's heart stood still when he looked right into the laser aperture. It would blow the *Renown* to smithereens with all the Hellhounds on board.

Nunn, O'Hara, Kellogg, and Heckler all unloaded on that side. They pounded the aperture with every ounce of their firepower, but it still wasn't enough.

The *Renown's* speed carried her past the aperture. Another ten Axichis laser ports dotted the hull. LeMaine brought his cannon around to lock on his target. Monk, Peterman, and Lemon all did the same thing, but at that moment, the first aperture opened fire.

The shot smacked the *Renown* hard on the port side. LeMaine heard Heckler roaring and Nunn screaming. All the other laser apertures erupted at the same time. LeMaine lost sight of the battle in a catastrophic supernova of gunshots hitting his placement.

A crushing impact struck the *Renown* and she hurtled sideways as the warship exploded a few feet from the *Renown*. The blow sent the *Renown* reeling.

Voices yelled and screamed on all sides. LeMaine couldn't see anything for a minute until the *Renown* came to a standstill hundreds of yards from the battle.

A billowing plume of smoke, fire, and floating scrap metal whirled and rotated where the warship had been moments before. Lightning crackled inside the hurricane.

"Woo-hoo!" Kellogg cheered. "Hellhounds: one. Axichis: zero."

"We can give Lulara that one," LeMaine cut in.

"Damn straight!" Heckler rumbled. "Lulara: one. Hellhounds: zero. You know what this means, Hellhounds."

"It's all on." Lemon brought her cannon up and narrowed her eyes at the remaining warships.

"Get us in there, Buca," LeMaine ordered. "It's time to kick some Axichis ass."

Chapter 28

Buca slammed the throttle down and the *Renown* sprinted back into the battle. All the enemy warships rounded on the *Renown* at once, but LeMaine no longer cared about any of that.

Buca plunged into an even more insane flight path that bore no resemblance to any kind of course LeMaine that could recognize. He no longer believed Buca wasn't steering at all, but the Maczhi pilot never once put the *Renown* in danger of crashing.

He squeaked between two enormous warships that dwarfed the *Renown* by a mile. All the Hellhounds opened fire on both sides, but their shots only made the Axichis mad.

Both warships wheeled to follow the *Renown* with their guns. Both warships pounded the *Renown* as she barely squeezed between their massive hulls. All those shots crushed the *Renown* in a massive blast that ricocheted back on the enemy.

All the *Renown's* cannons swung in reverse as Buca rocketed out the other side of the explosion. LeMaine slammed his cannon backward aiming for any Axichis ship that might follow the *Renown*.

Instead, he stared into the *Renown's* wake where a tower of smoke, ash, and trash rose to the atmosphere itself. Both warships were gone.

"Whoo!" Heckler hooted. "Give that man a cigar!"

"Who's next, Buca?" Nunn called.

"What's my kill count now?" Buca asked.

"More warships coming in hot!" Lulara announced. "We're going straight to the source, folks."

LeMaine swung his cannon back to the front. Fourteen more warships advanced out of Saevis. Patrol ships returned from all over Iumia to hunt down the *Renown*.

"All right," LeMaine muttered. "Let's give 'em all a little taste of this."

"You hear that, Kellogg?" Nunn asked. "Give 'em a little taste of this."

"I'll give 'em more than they bargained for."

"Hold onto your shorts," Buca told them. "This is gonna get messy."

O'Hara cackled. "He's talking like us now!"

Buca gunned the engines and hurtled toward Saevis to meet the incoming Axichis. "Arm up, Hellhounds!" LeMaine ordered. "Open fire as soon as we get within range. Hit as many of them as you can. We want them bent on destroying us so we can blow as many of them as possible."

"Bring it on," Monk growled from LeMaine's other side.

"Don't wreck the ship after we just got her back, Buca," Peterman chimed in.

"You don't worry about me. Just work your guns."

"We can definitely do that," Lemon replied. "Guns are our favorite."

"Here we go!" Lulara called.

LeMaine, Monk, and Peterman all wheeled to aim to the front. The *Renown* zoomed across the landscape and the Axichis closed into a tight rank just the way LeMaine hoped they would.

"You Hellhounds ready?" Buca asked.

"We were born ready," O'Hara replied. "I was, anyway."

"Now!" Buca bellowed and hit the throttle.

He pulled the helm hard to starboard and the *Renown* skated over on one side. She listed all the way onto her starboard wing and the G force nearly towed LeMaine out of his seat.

He followed the Axichis warships with his cannon and all the Hellhounds opened fire shooting downward past the *Renown's* belly. Buca raced the whole length of the Axichis line while the Hellhounds pounded every warship in sight.

Lulara slammed her cannon down and all the *Renown's* guns stuttered in a deadly slice. The Axichis tracked the *Renown's* every move and their weapons enveloped the *Renown* in a deafening concussion of noise.

LeMaine hunched low in his seat. He didn't have to target. He crammed down the firing mechanism and concentrated everything on hitting the Axichis anywhere and everywhere.

An ear-splitting impact slammed the *Renown* even harder. She pirouetted off her attitude and cartwheeled away from Saevis, but Buca recovered much more quickly this time.

The instant the ship stopped soaring out of control, he brought her around, gunned it for the remaining warships, and slalomed around them. LeMaine concentrated everything on shooting as many enemy craft as possible. He didn't have to blow them up. He only had to draw their fire.

The *Renown* left a trail of destruction that covered the skies over Saevis. LeMaine couldn't see beyond his cannon placement anymore.

Exploding fuel, torn ship parts, and flying scrap peppered his view. He couldn't tell if the hulls outside his placement belonged to intact ships or were just part of the general mayhem.

He heard yelling in the background and he became aware of Monk hollering on LeMaine's right, but he couldn't make out any words over the din.

Out of nowhere, a cataclysmic explosion caught the *Renown* in a death grip. The ship jostled up and down and in every direction before she slammed down hard on the ground.

LeMaine floundered out of a daze and looked around. He couldn't hear the battle anymore and the engines were dead. Everything sounded way too quiet.

Monk, Lemon, and Peterman all blinked at him from their placements on either side of him. "You folks okay?" he asked.

"What happened?" Peterman asked.

"Buca happened." LeMaine unbuckled his harness and went over to Monk. "Remind me never to let that guy fly the *Renown* ever again, Corporal." Monk nodded weakly while LeMaine unbuckled him. "Come on. Get your guns and suit up."

LeMaine went into the rear compartment and found Polasek and Lulara crawling out of the cockpit. "Are we still alive?" Polasek asked.

"*We* are. How's Buca?"

Polasek had to check. "He's all right, but he's bleeding. Where's Kellogg?"

LeMaine stuck his head into the port cannon placements. "Everyone still alive, Hellhounds?"

Kellogg, Nunn, Heckler, and O'Hara nodded up at him in a trance.

LeMaine bumped Kellogg's shoulder. "Get your kit, Sergeant. Buca is injured."

"Injured!" O'Hara squeaked. "Is that all?"

"He should be dead after the shit he pulled," Heckler growled.

"Arm up to deploy," LeMaine ordered. "We don't know the situation outside."

He went up to the cockpit and dropped into the seat next to Buca. He expected Buca to be semi-conscious or at least partially incapacitated. No such luck.

Buca frowned at the controls and worked furiously to do something on Polasek's communications array. The array had become disconnected from the dashboard during the crash.

Buca ran his hand across his forehead to wipe blood out of his eyes before he went back to scrambling to reconnect the array.

"What's the situation, Corporal?" LeMaine asked. "Did she lose power again?"

"She didn't lose power, Sir." Buca hissed the words through gritted teeth and shot one flinty glance toward the cockpit window.

That one look gave LeMaine a sinking feeling in the pit of his stomach. He didn't want to follow that glance, but he had to.

He glanced through the window and shot out of his seat when he saw another twenty warships moving in on the *Renown*. He understood in a heartbeat. The *Renown* was totally defenseless without the array feeding the right frequency to the ship's systems.

LeMaine grabbed Buca's arm. "Deploy!" he roared. "Get off the ship! Get outside—now!"

No one answered him. He made it out of the cockpit in time to see the rest of the Hellhounds lunge for the hatch. Peterman released it and the Hellhounds fell over themselves tumbling outside.

Buca hesitated a fraction of a second too long. He kept trying to reconnect the array to the dashboard and he slowed LeMaine down.

"Leave it!" LeMaine bellowed. "I said leave it! Come on!"

He gave Buca one last yank and dragged him out of the cockpit. Both men landed hard on the floor.

LeMaine looked around in desperation. He couldn't reach his carbine or his pack. None of that mattered right now.

He vaulted to his feet, seized Buca by the collar, and dove for the hatch just as the first Axichis shot crashed into the *Renown's* nose.

The ship thumped under LeMaine's stomach and slapped him back down. Buca slammed down next to him. LeMaine didn't have time to make sure Buca was still conscious or even alive.

LeMaine whipped onto his side, flung his arms around Buca, rolled the other way, pitched through the hatch, and Buca landed on top of him on the ground.

Heckler and Kellogg grabbed LeMaine and Buca. They started to pull when another punishing boom struck the *Renown*. The ship exploded and all four men hurtled backward.

They crashed into something painfully solid. Kellogg shoved his face in front of LeMaine and yelled over the pounding bombardment. "Can you walk?"

LeMaine didn't have time to nod. Monk wrestled LeMaine to his feet and shook him. The next thing LeMaine knew, he was running—running for his life through non-stop concussions. They ripped up the ground on all sides and dirt and shrapnel struck him in the face.

Half the Hellhounds ran in front of him. He couldn't turn around to see where the rest were. He kept telling himself to check on them, but Monk wouldn't let him.

Kellogg ran at LeMaine's side and aimed his scanner at LeMaine, but a second later, Kellogg vanished. "Where's Buca?" LeMaine called to nobody.

"Get down!" Monk bellowed and tackled LeMaine hard on the ground.

LeMaine scrambled onto his hands and knees trying to see where he was and bumped into Monk's giant body.

That moment gave him a clear view of the Hellhounds huddled behind a fallen Iumian fighter craft. Most of its hull had been blasted to a hollow wreck. It wouldn't provide much cover, but it was better than nothing.

Axichis warships covered every inch of sky that LeMaine could see. Their monstrous hulls blended into each other so he couldn't tell one from another.

Their bombardment enveloped Saevis and blanketed Iumia in explosions. More warships headed into the mountains destroying everything in sight.

Kellogg knelt in front of Buca. "How is he?" LeMaine croaked.

"He's all right. He has a small laceration to his scalp. I'm sealing it now. You saved his life, Sir."

LeMaine shot another glance at the Axichis invasion force. He only saved Buca's life so Buca could die in this apocalypse with the rest of the Hellhounds. Any second now, the Axichis would hit the Iumian fighter where the Hellhounds were hiding. The enemy would blow the Hellhounds away and that would be the end.

LeMaine tried to adjust his weapon before he remembered that he didn't have one. He felt naked and vulnerable without it, but a carbine wouldn't do any good in this battle. Buca didn't have a carbine, either—not that it mattered.

Monk squinted into the distance. "We could try to make it back to the city."

No one answered. Nunn and Heckler both stole peeks over the fighter's ripped hull, but they sat down a second later without offering any suggestions. There were no suggestions to make.

LeMaine forced himself to think. He was in charge here. He was responsible for these people's lives. He had to find a way to get them out of here, but he couldn't think of anything.

Every direction offered another hideous way for them to meet their deaths. Escape was impossible.

LeMaine looked toward Saevis. Monk must be right. The city wasn't much more than a ruin now, but it was better than waiting out here in the open to get blasted to pieces.

More warships floated over the city decimating any building left standing. If LeMaine ordered the Hellhounds to go in there, they would be running straight into another bombardment. Nowhere was safe.

He had no options left. He opened his mouth to give the order, but at that moment, without warning, a comet dropped through the atmosphere. It whistled in a howling shriek, smashed into an Axichis warship, and the enemy craft imploded with a hollow boom.

A withering shockwave woofed over the landscape. The concussion flattened two more of the remaining buildings in its path.

LeMaine ducked and pulled Monk and Kellogg down with him, but not before ten more rockets streaked down from the high atmosphere. LeMaine didn't see where they were coming from.

LeMaine covered Kellogg's head with his own arm. All the Hellhounds hunkered down as the shockwave rippled over their heads. Debris and shrapnel whistled past the Iumian fighter.

LeMaine waited for the blast to pass before he looked out. When he did, he could almost believe he'd died in the *Renown* and he was having a nice dream of the afterlife.

Fifty gigantic ships descended through the atmosphere over Saevis, but they weren't Axichis warships. They were bombers and they pelted into the warships with every gun blazing.

Dozens of attack cruisers zoomed down between the bomber's sides. They scattered gunfire all over the place and sent the Axichis staggering. Elian troop and armament ships landed on the ground.

They deployed remote artillery posts and hundreds of soldiers started scrambling to man the posts. The Elian Military had arrived.

Chapter 29

"**G**o!" LeMaine yelled. "Move!"

He sprang out of his hiding place, but the other Hellhounds didn't move for a second. They took a minute to realize what he was doing before they realized he was running away from them.

"Follow me!" he called. "Come on!"

The whole squad charged into the open. Deafening booms rocked the landscape, but no more rockets blasted the countryside to rubble.

The Axichis warships wheeled away and laid into the Elian bombers. The Military attacked in such force that the Axichis had to fight their hardest just to stay alive.

LeMaine headed for the nearest artillery post. He didn't care about anything but getting his people to shelter. He had never been so relieved in his life.

He slowed just enough to make sure all the Hellhounds caught up. The gunners manning the posts spotted the squad and flew into a frenzy.

They called to each other and pointed at the Hellhounds. Some of the gunners swiveled their weapons toward the squad before the gunners realized who it was. Then they went back to shooting upward at the Axichis.

LeMaine reached the post first. He stood on the parapet waving all his people under cover of the big guns. They pounded every few seconds and unleashed epic rocket volleys at the Axichis ships' undersides, but the artillery didn't do any damage.

In fact, none of the Elian guns seemed to be damaging the Axichis at all. The Elian bombers destroyed a bunch of Axichis warships in the battle's early stages, but now the Elian cannons didn't seem to be harming the Axichis at all. Did the Axichis have a way to deflect Elian gunfire?

LeMaine raced to the nearest gun and yelled at the sergeant in charge. "We can help! Give us some guns!"

The sergeant cupped his hand to his ear and then waved LeMaine away. LeMaine looked around for some way to aid the Elian assault.

More equipment transports landed all over the field around the wreckage of the *Renown*. The Elian Military set up more artillery posts as far as the eye could see and more troops deployed to man them. The Military didn't need the Hellhounds.

LeMaine turned the other way when Lulara rushed toward him. Her mouth moved and she gesticulated wildly trying to communicate with him, but he couldn't hear her over the noise.

He moved his ear right next to her mouth and she pointed up at the Elian bombers. He could hear from her tone that this was important, but he still couldn't understand her.

He glanced up to the bomber she was pointing at when one of the Axichis warships opened fire on the artillery post. The warship stopped shooting at the bombers, pivoted its lasers downward, and smashed the post to smithereens.

The shot hit the big gun right behind LeMaine. The impact flung him against Lulara and he blacked out. He came to and took a second to realize that Buca was dragging him across open country toward Saevis.

Buca dumped him next to a wall and paused only long enough to meet LeMaine's eye. "Stay here, Captain."

Buca bolted back onto the field under intense enemy fire. LeMaine struggled to pull his head together. The Axichis turned their guns on the artillery posts and eruptions of blowing rockets erupted all over the field.

Buca had deposited LeMaine near one of the last remaining walls still standing at the city's very farthest edge. LeMaine couldn't even tell what the building used to be, but at least he was out of danger here.

He couldn't say the same for the gunners and equipment still stranded on the field. The Hellhounds dashed from one post to another trying to reach safety. In the very farthest rear behind the last stragglers, Buca bent over Lulara who had fallen unconscious on the ground.

LeMaine vaulted out of his hiding place and sprinted to Monk and Kellogg. They were the nearest to him and Kellogg floundered under Monk's weight.

LeMaine dove under Monk's other arm and staggered to the wall. Kellogg went down on his knees in front of Monk and LeMaine left them there.

He raced back for Lemon, O'Hara, and Heckler. Heckler dragged O'Hara by one arm and carried Lemon over one shoulder. LeMaine grabbed O'Hara. "Go! Get over there! Get to Kellogg!"

LeMaine left O'Hara next to Monk, and when LeMainee looked back out, he saw Nunn, Peterman, and Polasek running well. That left Buca and Lulara.

Buca started to pick up Lulara, but when LeMaine ran toward them, a brutal rocket strike hit right in front of him. He heard the whistle a fraction of a second before it blew up in his face and he dove sideways just in time.

The blast trembled the ground beneath his chest and stomach. He squinted through a rain of dirt, but he didn't see Buca and Lulara at all anymore. Did they get hit?

He couldn't stay here, but when he thought about retreating, he saw something that made him think twice.

One of the big artillery pieces had fallen not far from where he lay. It wasn't attached to its support pedestal anymore, but the gun itself was still intact. It just didn't have any ammunition with it.

He didn't know what the hell he would do with it, but if he *could* do anything with it—anything at all—he couldn't leave it lying out here. He was nearer to it than any of the Hellhounds. He might never get another chance like this.

He pushed himself up. His whole body ached and his head pounded, but he had to do this. This was the only weapon on the whole field that would do any good against the enemy.

He sprang toward the gun, skidded in the dirt next to it, and checked it. It was undamaged except for the pedestal mount that connected it to its post.

He grabbed the butt and heaved. He bent every ounce of his strength to move it an inch. He nearly broke his back hauling it another six inches before he had to stop and rest.

The Axichis bombardment built to a bone-shaking pitch. LeMaine didn't dare to look up. He didn't want to see what was going on up there—not until the last possible moment.

He forced himself to stand up and took hold of the piece to make another attempt when Heckler appeared at his side followed by Polasek.

Heckler shot LeMaine a ferocious glance, stooped over the gun's muzzle, strapped his muscular arms around it, and heaved it off the ground.

Polasek joined LeMaine and together they hefted the gun out of the dirt. They staggered one painstaking step after another toward the wall where the other Hellhounds waited for them.

LeMaine collapsed next to Lemon and wheezed to catch his breath. "Where's.... where's Buca?"

Kellogg met LeMaine's eye once and went back to working on O'Hara's injured leg. "He's......" Nunn faltered. "He's over there."

LeMaine pivoted onto his knees. His arms and legs trembled from exhaustion. He spent his last shred of energy bringing that artillery piece to safety. He still didn't even know if he could use it. He didn't have a single rocket that would fit it.

He looked in the direction Nunn indicated and he didn't see anything at first. Axichis warships swept back and forth overhead with Elian attack cruisers wheeling between them.

Elian bombers blasted the warships with hundreds more shots than they took. The Elian assault didn't stop the Axichis from laying waste to the ground forces who were still trying to set up more artillery posts on the field.

The Axichis stalked one post after another systematically blasting them to kingdom come. They smashed one post to rubble before they migrated to the next.

The bombers targeted the warships targeting the artillery posts, but the Axichis still defended themselves well enough to do plenty of damage.

One post remained between Saevis and the Hellhounds' hiding place. Dark shapes swarmed all over the big guns. The Elians loaded the guns as fast as they could and unloaded on the enemy.

The Elians landed rockets on at least one warship and it staggered forward to crash into its sister ship, but the artillery still couldn't destroy these giant vessels.

The Axichis completely ignored this post. They concentrated their attack on the field where more posts sat closer to each other. The Axichis would have to leave all these easier targets to eliminate the one post annoying them.

LeMaine didn't see any other place Buca could have taken Lulara. The bodies moving around the big gun looked human, not Maczhi or Cezian, but LeMaine couldn't be sure from this distance.

He started to pull his head down to examine the artillery piece when a sound set his hair on end. One warship broke away from the others and headed for the lone post.

Two Elian bombers moved in to block the warship's path. They guarded the post and bombarded the warship to hold it off, but out of nowhere, the Axichis vessel opened fire. Its lasers zipped straight past the bombers and hit the post.

The gunners scattered at that first shot and two people broke cover running for the Hellhounds' wall.

"Get it up!" LeMaine sprang to his feet and grabbed the piece. "Hurry! Get it in position!"

He never understood where he found the strength to lug the piece onto the wall. Heckler, Kellogg, Nunn, and Polasek helped him. They balanced the piece on the crumbling wall to aim at the Axichis warship.

Buca and Lulara sprinted across the field making for the wall, but Axichis blasts kept erupting all around them. Buca veered hard to his right and toppled under another cruel assault. Lulara staggered the other way, corrected, and ended up crawling over to Buca.

She tried to pick him up and then dove on top of him to protect him from more Axichis shots.

LeMaine looked around for anything he could use against the enemy. "Give me your Crossfire cartridges."

The Hellhounds stared up at him in dumb shock. A second later, Heckler pounced on his carbine and started stripping out the magazine. He crammed the cartridge into LeMaine's hand.

One after another, the Hellhounds unloaded their carbines and passed their ammunition cartridges to LeMaine. He jammed them one after another into the Crossfire port on the artillery piece. This wouldn't be enough to shoot the gun more than once. He would have to make it count.

Polasek, Nunn, and Heckler steadied the piece while LeMaine swiveled it upward to aim at the Axichis ship hammering the artillery post. A few gunners remained behind firing again and again, but they still couldn't damage the enemy. Only the bombers could do anything against the Axichis.

Lulara heaved Buca into a sitting position. She turned her blood-streaked face toward the wall and her countenance turned to a mask of hideous determination.

She hauled him to his feet. Lemon and Peterman both stood up and stepped out from behind the wall to help Lulara bring Buca in. At that moment, an Axichis laser veered dangerously close to the wall.

All the Hellhounds ducked and LeMaine fired the artillery piece. It struck the warship, but the shot only bounced off.

That moment gave the bombers a split second to rush the warship, but the fight attracted more attention from the rest of the enemy force.

More warships gathered from all over. The battle raged directly over the Hellhounds' hiding place. Lemon and Peterman tried one more time to go out to help Lulara, but their comrades pulled them back down.

LeMaine laid the piece aside. It was useless to him without more ammunition and he had no idea where he could get any more.

He straightened up to go out for Lulara and Buca when he saw her charging him across the field. Buca's knees buckled with every step and gore covered his face.

LeMaine leapt out of hiding when another Axichis laser blasted into the ground on the other side of the wall. He stumbled, caught his balance, and bolted onto the field just as a second shot splintered right in front of him.

He staggered under the blow and fell hard against the wall. Peterman pulled him down, but LeMaine kept searching the area for any sight of Lulara and Buca.

They both lay on the ground ten feet from safety—or whatever safety this wall could give them. LeMaine crawled out to help them, but Peterman stopped him before Peterman advanced himself.

He prepared to run out into the enemy's teeth when Buca lurched into a sitting position. He crawled, flopped, and crawled again to where Lulara lay.

Buca took hold of her jacket and yanked her one excruciating inch at a time toward the wall. Peterman, LeMaine, and Polasek caught him and pulled them both in.

Lulara lay where she fell. Blood covered her face and saturated her jacket in a slick, damp puddle. Her face looked different somehow—as if someone had molded it differently from just a few minutes before.

Kellogg swiveled over to her and started working rapidly to find the source of the bleeding. He stripped open her jacket to reveal a landscape of destroyed tissue.

Lulara's bleary eyes rotated one way and then another and she flailed her arms blindly. "Buca.... Buca...."

He grabbed her hand. ""I'm here. I'm here."

"Buca...." She choked and blood bubbled between her lips.

Buca pressed her hand between both of his. He gazed down at her ruined face with curious expression.

Lulara turned her head. "Try to keep still," Kellogg panted, but she didn't hear him.

She tore her hand out of Buca's grasp and extended it to LeMaine. "Captain...."

LeMaine glanced up at Kellogg, but Kellogg only gave him a very subtle shake of his head. LeMaine knew that gesture only too well. He wished he didn't.

LeMaine took her hand and cradled it. "I'm right here. You're safe. You did real good. You can rest now."

"Captain...." She gulped down the blood in her mouth.

"I'm here. We're all here. You're with the Hellhounds."

"Captain...." She dragged her hand out of his grasp and he felt something hard against his palm. He looked down at a tiny computer chip. Where did it come from?

"The frequencies...." she husked.

LeMaine looked up and his ears rang. The frequencies.... Of course! The frequencies were the only way to defeat the Axichis.

Lulara met his gaze in one last moment of clarity before she turned away. She looked straight up at Buca. "Buca.... thank you...."

She extended her hand to him, but her arm flopped to the ground before he could take it. Her eyes lost focus and Kellogg sank back on his ankles. He didn't even try to work on her. It was too late. That last Axichis blast did too much damage and now she was gone.

Chapter 30

L eMaine looked down at the chip in his hand. Lulara died to give him this chip. This must have been what she was trying to tell him at the artillery post.

This was the key to winning not just the battle for Iumia but the whole damn war. This chip was the key to driving the Axichis out of the Elian system forever. He just had to figure out how to deploy it.

He scanned the battle. The *Renown* was gone. The Elian attack cruisers and bombers were too high up for him to reach them.

He thought through what little resources he had left. Polasek's communications array was gone, too. LeMaine had no way to contact the Elian Military Command. Now all the Hellhounds were unarmed thanks to him.

The battle on this field drew more Axichis warships from the city. The whole invasion force assembled directly overhead with bombers, attack cruisers, and other Elian craft mixed up in the fight.

LeMaine's brain fixated on one thing only. He needed some communications equipment to transmit these frequencies to the Elian fleet. Nothing else mattered, but where could he get communications equipment now?

Another Axichis rocket slammed hard into the dirt not far from the wall. All the Hellhounds ducked for cover and LeMaine made up his mind. He couldn't stay here.

"Follow me!" he told the Hellhounds. "And stay together."

"Where are we going?" Peterman asked.

"The bunker. If you get separated, meet us there."

"The bunker?" Polasek asked. "That's...."

LeMaine didn't wait for him to finish. He pushed off the wall and started running. He no longer checked the surroundings for potential threats. He wouldn't be able to do anything about them and deploying these frequencies overrode everything else.

He only broke stride long enough to make sure the Hellhounds stayed with him, but in a minute, he no longer even did that. They ran in a tight bunch helping their comrades and pulling each other closer if anyone fell behind.

None of the familiar landmarks survived the Axichis bombardment. LeMaine couldn't use them to guide himself back to the bunker. He almost ran past it before Polasek corrected him.

Mountains of rubble blocked their original entrance. LeMaine went around the building to the tunnel. Another pile of broken masonry partially obstructed the threshold. The Hellhounds had to scramble inside, but once they did, they were safe.

The squad hesitated there and LeMaine listened. "The Axichis are gone. We should be all right here for now."

"You don't think we'll be able to find anything in here, do you?" Polasek asked. "Aaglik said all their equipment was destroyed in the bombardment."

O'Hara thumped Polasek on the shoulder. "That's what you're here for, Lieutenant. You can scrounge up an array from spare parts, can't you?"

LeMaine turned away. "Let's go downstairs and see what we can find."

The squad headed down the tunnel to the underground command center. "Everything looks relatively intact," Kellogg remarked. "That's strange. Aaglik said it had all been destroyed."

"And where is everyone?" Heckler added. "They didn't die here. They must have evacuated somewhere."

Polasek went over to one of the stations and started fiddling with everything. "The power is still on."

LeMaine held out the chip. "Can you transmit this to the Elian fleet?"

"Give me a second." Polasek sat down in the technician's empty chair.

Lemon went back to the stairs. "Maybe they have some ammo in this place."

"Go check it out," LeMaine told her. "Take Heckler and Buca with you."

"I got something, Captain," Polasek interrupted. "Everything is working except the transmission dish. It was in the hills with the cannon placements, but it isn't anymore."

"So.... you can't raise the fleet?"

"I can raise them, but I can't transmit—not from here."

"What do you mean? Is there somewhere else you can raise them?"

"Yeah—there."

Polasek pointed to a chart of Saevis on his display. It tracked the movements of every ship in the Iumian atmosphere. The majority assembled on the field outside of town.

Polasek's finger rested on a spot LeMaine recognized. It was the airfield. Ten Iumian fighter craft sat there, but none of them was moving.

"This makes no sense," Peterman argued. "Aaglik said the airfield was a moonscape. The Axichis destroyed every fighter that could stand against them."

"You see this?" Polasek indicated some readings on the side of the screen. "This shows the elevation of each signature. These fighters are underground. It looks like the Iumians kept them in reserve in case of emergencies."

"Why didn't Aaglik and the rest take them to escape?" Peterman asked. "They threw their lives away for nothing."

"Not necessarily," LeMaine cut in. "Aaglik knew no fighters could get out of the city with so many warships around. He left these fighters in place for someone else to use."

"Are you seriously suggesting......?" Peterman began.

LeMaine handed Polasek the chip. "I want you to take this, son. As soon as we get those fighters powered up, transmit the frequencies to every Elian ship—no exceptions. The rest of us will cover you until you get close enough."

"I won't need to," Polasek replied. "Those fighters will all have onboard communications systems powerful enough to deploy the frequencies against the Axichis."

"Even better." LeMaine turned back to the squad. "Let's get going. We don't have much time."

Just then, Lemon returned. Heckler and Buca hauled a giant crate between them and they dropped it on the floor with a thump. "Lock and load, Hellhounds!" she called. "We're back in business."

The squad gathered around and tore open the crate. They stuffed their pockets with gel cartridges and armed every weapon. LeMaine still didn't have a carbine until Heckler handed him one.

LeMaine took it gratefully. "Thank you, Corporal."

Heckler dipped his chin. "A man isn't a man without his weapon."

"It's too bad we can't arm *these* with the frequencies," Kellogg remarked.

"They're too small anyway, dumbass," Lemon snapped. "If you shot an enemy warship with one of these, the warship would explode and fall on your wrinkled little head."

"Call me a dumbass the next time you break something and need me to save your tired ass," Kellogg muttered.

"Lemon's right," LeMaine added. "We need to be able to fly away once we blow them up."

O'Hara cracked one of his crazy grins. "Are you saying we have your blanket permission to fly like Buca does? Hee-hee! I can't wait."

"You don't have my blanket permission to kill yourself," LeMaine told him. "Just do the job and skedaddle."

Heckler elbowed Buca. "You hear that, son? You don't have the captain's permission to kill yourself."

"Or the rest of us," Peterman interjected.

"I never killed anyone," Buca pointed out.

"Except the enemy, right?" Nunn asked.

"Of course them," Buca corrected, "but unless I'm mistaken, I did have the captain's blanket permission to do that."

"You're damn straight," LeMaine replied.

"And by 'skedaddle', he doesn't mean zipping and zooming around and making your squad mates sick to their stomachs," Polasek added.

"In my language, that is what 'skedaddle' means," Buca told him and everyone laughed.

"If we're done analyzing the semantic meanings of Elian linguistic cultural differences," LeMaine cut in, "we have a war to fight."

"Stop it, Captain," O'Hara teased. "You'll make Lemon feel bad."

"Go fuck yourself, shithead," Lemon spat and everyone laughed.

LeMaine climbed back upstairs and into the tunnel. "How do we get to the ships?"

"There's a shaft under a building on the airfield's northeast corner." Polasek squinted toward the battle. "It doesn't look like we'll face much resistance, though."

"Let's hope not." LeMaine moved closer to his second-in-command and lowered his voice to a murmur. "I meant what I said. Get those frequencies away no matter what, even if it means leaving the rest of us behind."

Polasek nodded up at him and his bright eyes told LeMaine he understood perfectly. "You got it, Sir."

LeMaine checked the squad. The others adjusted their gear and their weapons until they turned their eyes to face front. It was time.

LeMaine didn't have to give the word. The whole squad took off at a run through the city. The Axichis didn't come after them. The battle still boomed and pounded out of sight, but it was a good thing the Hellhounds were already moving at top speed.

Out of nowhere, an Axichis rocket blasted into a nearby building. The explosion didn't threaten the Hellhounds. It was still too far away, but it got the message across loud and clear.

LeMaine grabbed Polasek and pushed him forward. "Go! Get to the field!"

The other Hellhounds moved in behind Polasek. LeMaine looked everywhere for the attacker, but the shots were coming from the field hundreds of yards away.

That left only one option: keep moving. He picked up speed and followed Polasek in a breakneck course between ruins. Polasek was already so far ahead that none of the Hellhounds could catch him.... except Buca.

Buca overtook LeMaine and inched up alongside Polasek. The two comrades vanished into the warren of streets that weren't streets anymore.

LeMaine moved closer to the other Hellhounds and dodged piles of rock, twisted unrecognizable wreckage, and plenty of bodies. He just hoped the Axichis would target him and leave Polasek alone.

He stumbled around another mountain of debris and blundered into a devastated landscape of craters. Only the absence of any buildings told him that this used to be the airfield.

"The northeast corner!" Nunn veered aside and started to circle the airfield.

The squad had to scramble over more rubble to find the entrance. It took them down a narrow flight of stairs to an underground hangar nearly as big as the airfield on the surface.

Ten fighters remained of what appeared to be a sizable reserve air force. LeMaine couldn't see any way to get these ships out of the underground hangar. The stairwell from the surface was barely wide enough for three people to walk abreast. The ceiling seemed to be constructed of solid rock.

Buca and Polasek worked over a control station to one side. They must be trying to find the exit.

"Uh...." Kellogg began when the squad entered the cavern.

"Get to your fighters!" LeMaine ordered. "You, too, Polasek. Leave it alone, Buca. Load up."

LeMaine clambered into his fighter and all the other ships powered up around him. He checked that Polasek and Buca were ready, too. Everything looked hunky-dory except that they had no way out of this hangar.

"Standing by to launch on your order, Sir," Heckler called.

"Yeah, I got that, son," LeMaine replied. "Working on it."

"You better come up with something pretty quick," Peterman told him. "Check your long-range readouts."

LeMaine widened the readouts of Iumia and his blood ran cold. More Axichis warships were invading from their own system. They crossed the border into Elia and converged on Iumia.

The Elian bombers on the field were holding their own for now, but they wouldn't be looking so good as soon as the new Axichis reinforcements showed up.

LeMaine made a wide sweep of the Elian system. All the remaining Elian bombers were tied up in other areas fighting off more hordes of Axichis invasion craft.

The bulk of the Elian fleet was totally outgunned defending Elia itself. They wouldn't be coming to the rescue anytime soon.

"Get those frequencies away, Lieutenant," LeMaine ordered.

"I can't, Sir!" Polasek replied. "The roof is blocking transmission. The system is working just fine, but without a working transmission dish, I would have to be on the surface or in the atmosphere to reach the rest of the fleet."

"Arm all cannons!" LeMaine ordered.

"Sir?" Peterman asked.

"Shoot the roof out!" LeMaine explained. "Destroy the roof and launch as soon as it comes down."

"Hell, yeah!" Heckler rumbled. "This is my kind of launch."

"Cycle up your engines to full power!" LeMaine ordered. "Open fire!"

He smashed his firing mechanism to the limit, unloaded on the roof, and the rest of the Hellhounds joined in. Cannon fire bombarded the ceiling and the impact ricocheted back on the fighters.

LeMaine lifted off the floor and inched upward. He kept his cannons belching while he scanned the ceiling for any sign of weakness.

"Over here!" O'Hara yelled. "It's starting to buckle"

At his word, the rock caved in almost on top of O'Hara's fighter, but he wasn't there anymore. He pounded that one spot with crushing force and blasted through as the whole roof imploded.

LeMaine gunned his engines, raced to the spot, and swerved falling boulders to rocket into the sky. The nine Hellhounds swooped over Saevis leaving the hangar behind.

"Frequencies patched in and deployed to all fighters!" Polasek reported.

"Just what I want to hear, Lieutenant," LeMaine replied. "Let's rock and roll, Hell-hounds."

"Rocking and rolling," Heckler confirmed and the squad rocketed it back to the field.

Chapter 31

LeMaine raced in sight of the battle. It kept raging as hot as ever. Elian bombers and Axichis warships stood head to head smashing each other with punishing fire. They occupied each other so fully that both sides completely ignored the attack cruisers zipping and diving in and out of the fight.

LeMaine saw at a glance that the Elian fleet had exactly the same problem as before. Their weapons didn't damage the Axichis armor while the Axichis pounded the Elians to scrap.

LeMaine drove his fighter to the limit to get there in time. He streaked onto the field just as the bomber *Talon* detonated off his port wing.

The bomber exploded in a torrent of noise and fire. The shockwave jostled LeMaine's fighter for a second before he corrected.

He checked his surroundings to make sure he was in the right place and then throttled straight into the heart of the battle. He hurdled attack cruisers and aimed for the warships.

He zeroed in on their weapons ports and zoomed his fighter straight into the path of their lasers. He took hundreds of shots and continuous concussions rocked his hull.

He hauled his helm hard to starboard and screamed within inches of the nearest warship. Explosions followed him as each Axichis shot rebounded back on the warship that fired it. A blistering supernova of power and energy caught his fighter.

He lost helm control and the fighter tossed out of the fireball. His ship pitched end over end until LeMaine couldn't tell where he was.

"Stand aside, folks!" Kellogg crowed in his ear. "LeMaine: one. Axichis: nil."

"Did you see that, Hellhounds?" O'Hara joined in. "That's showing how it's done."

LeMaine had to chuckle while he turned his fighter around to regroup. "I think we can forget about the kill count for today."

"No damn way, Sir!" Heckler called. "We're just getting started."

"We have to catch up with that jackass Buca," Lemon cut in.

"You better pack a lunch if you want to do that," Peterman added.

"I'm hearing a whole lot of chit-chat and not a lot of shooting, Hellhounds," LeMaine told them. "Let's see you put some numbers on the board before you talk about catching up with anybody."

"You heard the man." Nunn gunned her fighter back into the battle and vanished in a cloud of gunfire.

"Transmit the frequencies to the rest of the fleet, Polasek," LeMaine ordered.

"I already did, Sir, but they aren't using them. It looks like they don't understand the transmission."

LeMaine scrambled with his communications. "I don't see Colonel Nicholson on the Command roster."

A chill ran up LeMaine's spine when he realized what that meant. Commander Lodge wouldn't tell LeMaine where Colonel Nicholson was. Was the colonel already dead?

LeMaine started to search for Commander Lodge's vessel when another smash of shots hit his fighter. He recovered and spotted four Elian attack cruisers coming after him.

"Cocksuckers!" Lemon yelled. "We're on the same side, you dimwits!"

"Forget them!" LeMaine tightened his grip on his throttle. "Let's get this job done. We'll work out the details later."

He plunged into the battle one more time, but with so many Hellhounds weaving in and out of the Axichis warships, LeMaine found it nearly impossible to target any enemy craft.

Deafening explosions and balls of erupting gas surrounded every ship on both sides of the line. LeMaine plunged into the chaos and nearly collided with Buca coming the other way.

"What's your kill count now, Corporal?" LeMaine asked.

"I have no idea," Buca replied. "I can't see anything."

"Get out of the cloud," LeMaine ordered. "Get behind the Axichis line. Do you hear me, Hellhounds? Get out of the cloud!"

No one answered him. LeMaine gave it up and ripped his fighter into reverse. He put on speed, streaked through another wall of smoke, and pulled up short when he saw a giant steel hull coming at him at top speed.

He slammed his controls away, barely scraped around the ship, and broke through into clear sky. Six of the other eight Hellhounds flew wild behind the battle.

"Come on, assholes!" Monk snarled. "Come and get some. You know you want it."

"Converge!" LeMaine ordered. "Sigma formation! Draw their fire away from the fleet."

Five Hellhounds obeyed him and dropped into formation on LeMaine's tail. Buca took a second longer and raced after them on a parallel course to the Axichis rear line.

The Hellhounds spat cannon fire on the Axichis from behind. The maneuver worked and four warships fired backward to return the Hellhounds' fire.

Each warship went up in flames as their assault ricocheted back on them. The Hellhounds sprinted free on the other end of the line.

LeMaine wheeled in search of his next target, but he couldn't see anything through the mayhem.

The Elian bombers retreated back to Saevis and watched the Axichis ships blowing one after another. The smoke cleared and two more Iumian fighters blasted out of the cloud.

"Peterman: ten," Peterman chirped.

"Heckler: eleven," Heckler countered.

LeMaine laughed. "Congratulations, Corporal. You finally beat Peterman."

"What about you, Buca?" O'Hara asked. "How many did you get?"

"Only five."

The squad exploded in cheers. They hooted and whooped so loudly that LeMaine had to move his head away from the communications system, but he couldn't stop laughing. They did it. It was over.

He turned back to his controls searching for Commander Lodge. LeMaine found him on the *Lucidity*, a bomber near the end of the Elian flank.

"Captain Owen LeMaine to *Lucidity*," he called. "Request immediate communication with Commander Russell Lodge of Elian Military Command. I repeat: this is Captain Owen LeMaine of the Elian Special Forces relaying from a commandeered Iumian fighter craft. I request emergency communications with Commander Russell Lodge of Elian Military Command."

"They better not start shooting at us again," Polasek muttered. "Someone needs some cosmogeography lessons if they don't even recognize an Iumian fighter."

"It was an honest mistake, Lieutenant," LeMaine replied. "They were bound to get confused about who we were."

Just then, his communications system crackled. "What in the holy hell did you just do, Owen?" Commander Lodge croaked. "That was.... that was.... incredible."

LeMaine laughed in relief when he saw his old friend. "We're transmitting frequencies to the whole fleet, Russell. My communications expert is sending instructions to patch these frequencies through your systems. The frequency will rebound on the Axichis. It's the only way to defeat them."

Commander Lodge frowned. "That shouldn't be theoretically possible."

"You've seen the evidence with your own eyes." Another muffled boom caught LeMaine's ear and he checked his long-range readouts. "Axichis reinforcements are moving in! Patch the frequencies through your systems now! Polasek...."

"All over it, Sir," Polasek replied. "Sending detailed instructions."

Another gunshot blasted LeMaine's hull, but when he looked around, he didn't see anything. "What was that?"

Five more concussions pounded in his ears. "We're under fire!" Monk called. "The enemy is firing from orbit."

LeMaine checked his readouts one last time. Monk was right. The Axichis reinforcements rained Iumia with rockets from beyond the atmosphere.

"They're out of range!" Peterman cried. "The frequencies won't work from here."

"Get aloft!" LeMaine ordered. "Get up there and draw their fire."

"The bombers are launching!" Polasek pointed out. "The whole fleet is responding....and they're running the frequencies through their shields."

"Gun it, Hellhounds!" LeMaine repeated.

He swiveled his fighter skyward and punched the throttle, but at that moment, a rocket zoomed past his ship and smashed nose first into Buca's craft. "NO!" Heckler bellowed.

LeMaine tried to tear his eyes away from the wreck of Buca's fighter pinwheeling in freefall toward Saevis. Just as fast, five more rockets whistled into the Hellhounds' grouping.

The first one tore Monk's wing off. "I'm going down!" he roared.

The second one punched a hole straight through Nunn's hull. She screamed once and then communications cut out.

She wheeled sideways with smoke billowing from the destroyed cockpit. LeMaine lost sight of her as the third rocket plunged straight for him.

He jerked his controls to port and the rocket plowed into his fighter's front flank. Fire ripped across the side of his face and a gut-wrenching screech tore the ship apart.

Howling shrieks and explosions shook him on all sides. He barely looked up to see where he was and saw the ruins of Saevis rushing at him. He floundered for the controls.

"Captain!" Polasek yelled in his ear. "Captain LeMaine, do you copy?"

LeMaine didn't have time to answer before his stricken fighter lurched under his hand. He struggled to wrestle the controls in line, but the ship only flopped and stuttered.

The starboard engine didn't respond at all, and when he looked to see why, he couldn't see anything through smoke and ash trailing off the hull.

He fought the helm and managed to tilt the nose up, but only an inch or two. He was no longer plummeting toward the ground. Instead, he was hurtling straight for a bombed-out building.

He leaned all the way over in his seat and strained his arms to the breaking point to avoid the building, but the ship still didn't obey him enough. His port wing clipped the building and the fighter spun away in a dizzy corkscrew to smash into a different building.

The ship crashed into the wall with a bone-shaking bang and then smashed into the ground. LeMaine sat still just long enough to read an alert blinking on his controls. *Port engine imminent overload: Emergency evacuation.*

An alarm should have accompanied that alert, but half the dashboard lay black and dead in front of him. LeMaine scrambled to unclip his safety harness, but when he tried to raise the cockpit cover, it wouldn't budge.

He stood up on his seat and jammed his shoulder against the glass. He heaved with all his might, but it still wouldn't unlock. Those words kept blinking in his face. *Port engine imminent overload: Emergency evacuation.* How long did he have before the fighter blew?

He looked around wildly for anything he could use to break the glass. He snatched the control stick and wrenched. He kicked at the bolt holding it to the floor. It wouldn't release.

He hopped back onto the seat, flexed his knees, and drove his shoulder upward into the cockpit cover again and again. He roared in pain and desperation, but this fighter had been too well constructed.

He spun right and left....and then he remembered. He dove under his seat, pulled out his carbine, hunkered down on the floor, shut his eyes, and fired upward. The glass shattered, but it didn't fall.

He vaulted onto the seat again, and this time, the whole splintered cover folded out of the way. He tossed it aside, snatched his gear, and dove onto the pavement just as the port engine housing detonated with an ear-splitting boom.

LeMaine rolled as far as he could and covered his head until the blast subsided. He peeked out. The fighter was nothing but a blackened hulk now.

He picked himself up and dusted himself off. The battle no longer raged west of town. Flashes of light blinked in the high atmosphere, but he couldn't see or hear anything from the ground.

He was completely alone on this planet. He had no way to know if any of his squad survived the last Axichis assault nor did he have any other way to get off this planet.

He could only think of one thing. The Iumians still had their base in the mountains. Erias and Alruna were still there with the last of their people. They were LeMaine's only allies left.

He heaved a sigh and started walking. The mountains were a long way off, but at least the Iumians had communications equipment there. LeMaine would be able to contact Commander Lodge again, even if LeMaine couldn't do anything else to help fight the war.

The war was out of his hands now. He did his duty. He got the frequencies to the fleet. Now it was their job to deploy them.

He walked for a mile. He kept his carbine hanging in front of him with his finger on the trigger, but he didn't take too much trouble to check the surroundings. This city was completely destroyed. He must be the only person left alive for miles in any direction.

The sensation of having no one to talk to and no one to look out for became more surreal with every passing moment. He couldn't remember the last time he'd been completely alone like this.

He spent all his time around the Hellhounds or around Command personnel when the squad wasn't deployed somewhere. On those rare occasions when he made it back to Elia, he spent every spare moment with his family.

He was just about to walk around another corner not thinking about anything in particular. His thoughts wandered far away when a withering blast shook the air just a few blocks ahead.

He jolted to high alert, rushed to the nearest corner, and hid while he pulled his carbine up. He snuck forward holding his breath. He peeked around the corner tensed for the slightest threat.

A shimmering ball of smoke and fire coiled and plumed from a wrecked ship that lay smashed and destroyed at the base of a nearby building. So much smoke concealed the wreck that he diddn't recognize it, but he definitely recognized the lone figure squatting on the ground.

Buca paid no attention to the wreck. He worked over a carbine and a backpack spread out on the pavement in front of him.

The instant LeMaine recognized Buca, Buca's head snapped up. His eyes narrowed at LeMaine's hiding place and Buca's nostrils flared.

LeMaine stepped into the open and lowered his weapon. "I thought you were dead."

"What made you think that?"

"Only the way your ship exploded in midair and plunged to crash on the ground." LeMaine squinted into the smoke. "How did you survive, anyway?"

"I could ask you the same thing." Buca looked up at the sky. "How do we get back up there?"

"We don't. I was just on my way back to the mountains to rendezvous with the Iumians. I don't see any other option. Do you?"

"No. I hadn't gotten that far in planning my next move. I was just determining what resource I had before I made a decision."

LeMaine clapped Buca on the shoulder and laughed. "You're a born Hellhound. Do you know that?"

"I'm not such a Hellhound that I could save Lulara."

LeMaine winced. "You're a Hellhound because you tried....and because you're still talking about it now. Come on. Get your gear and let's get out of here."

Buca put on his backpack and he and LeMaine continued westward. The explosion of Buca's fighter brought LeMaine back to the present. He paid much more attention to the surroundings now. He had at least one Hellhound to watch out for.

"Monk and Nunn went down right after you," he told Buca. "They might be out here, too."

"Let's hope not," Buca replied. "We wouldn't be much good to them without Kellogg."

"I'm not totally useless as a medic. I'm not Kellogg, but I'm okay."

"That's better than I am," Buca replied. "I never got any medical training, being alone all the time."

LeMaine stopped himself from asking about Buca's background. This was Buca's first mission with the Hellhounds. It was still too early to start asking personal questions.

Another crash startled both of them. Buca and LeMaine both brought their weapons up, but the noise came from high above their heads. It didn't sound like gunfire or even explosions. It sounded like glass breaking.

The two men tiptoed closer and tracked the noise to a building torn off several stories above the ground. LeMaine sidestepped around its pocked walls and lowered his weapon when he spotted Monk's enormous upper body hanging out of one of the highest floors.

"What the hell do you think you're doing, Corporal?" LeMaine called.

Monk's head shot up. Soot smudged his cheeks and his hair stuck out from his head in a crown of static. "Sir? Is that you?"

"It's me. Now do you mind telling me what the hell is going on?"

"Uh…" Monk looked behind him. "My fighter is….in here…. somewhere…."

LeMaine and Buca exchanged glances. "Is he crazy?" Buca asked.

"Why is your fighter up there, Corporal?" LeMaine called up.

"I…. uh…. think it crashed here, Sir…. but I can't be sure."

"Get your gear and get down here, Corporal…. unless you're injured."

"I'm not injured, Sir. I can't say the same for the fighter, though."

"Leave it. Do you have any way to get down?"

"I…uh…." Monk looked around stupidly.

"He could have a head injury and not know it," Buca muttered.

Monk pulled his head inside and more crashes and bangs echoed through the building. A moment later, the sound died.

Buca and LeMaine waited, but in the silence that followed, LeMaine heard another sound. He discounted it at first, but after another minute, he couldn't deny it anymore.

It sounded like rats scurrying in the basements, but it couldn't be that. Rats didn't exist on this planet.

LeMaine trained his ears behind him. The sound was barely loud enough to hear, but it was definitely there.

He nudged Buca. "Go get Monk, will you? This is taking too long."

Buca set off for the building. LeMaine turned away and followed the sound. It led him a block away, but he still couldn't make out what it was.

He stopped in front of a mountain of debris and rubble blocking the way. He had to go around it and then climb another mound into a different street. More heaps of gravel had narrowed it to a few feet.

He advanced around another pile and yelled. "Nunn!"

She didn't hear him or maybe she couldn't. She lay flat on her stomach pulling herself one painstaking yard after another by her arms. Dust and dirt covered her fatigues and caked her hair.

LeMaine knelt down next to her. "Nunn! Corporal!" He touched her shoulder, but she didn't respond.

LeMaine dropped his carbine, ripped open his backpack, and pulled out his medical scanner, but she wouldn't stop crawling across the ground. She didn't use her legs. This could get bad.

LeMaine put down the scanner and took hold of her by the shoulders. "Easy, Corporal. You can stop now. Molly! It's me. It's Captain LeMaine."

He eased her over onto her back. Her dull eyes swept the sky and buildings behind his head. "Captain?"

"I'm here," he choked. "I'm here. Just lie still. I'm with you."

"Captain? I can't see you."

"Easy, girl. Just lie quietly for a second while I...."

He grabbed his scanner and aimed it at her head. Buca appeared at his side. "What's wrong with her?"

"Find her fighter." LeMaine glanced behind him. "She must have crashed near here."

"I tried......to land.... Captain...." Nunn babbled.

"You did great, Corporal. You did perfect."

"Captain?" she asked. "Are you still there?"

He didn't answer and his heart sank when he saw most of her left brain concussed and swollen. The scanner detected vastly reduced brain activity on that side. He couldn't do jack shit about that.

He scanned down her body. Her torso and internal organs were okay, but her spinal cord had been severed just above the pelvis.

Buca came back with Monk. "She crashed a few blocks from here," Buca told LeMaine. "She must have crawled all the way here."

LeMaine looked around wildly. He couldn't leave Nunn here and he didn't dare to carry her all the way to the mountains.

"Captain?" she croaked again. "Don't leave me here."

LeMaine grabbed her hand. "No one is leaving you, Molly. We're right here. We'll get you out of here."

"Captain?" She looked around everywhere but at him. "Where are you?"

"Damn it!" Monk whispered.

"How do you want to do this, Sir?" Buca asked.

LeMaine surveyed the area fighting down the urge to panic. He would give anything for Kellogg right now...or a ship.

He bent over Nunn again, but at that moment, the scream of engines echoed across Saevis. Buca and Monk yanked up their carbines. LeMaine scrambled to retrieve his weapon.

He and the other two raced to the nearest corner and aimed their guns at the sky as a squadron of Iumians zoomed overhead.

LeMaine slumped. "Thank God!"

"They're coming around again," Buca remarked.

The Iumians cut a wide arc through the city skies and howled over the Hellhounds' position. LeMaine, Buca, and Monk retreated and protected their eyes as the fighters descended to land in the broad street.

LeMaine stepped out into view as the fighter pilots opened their cockpits. Erias hopped down and strode toward LeMaine with his arms out. "We've been looking for you. We got word from Command that you and some of your people went down out here."

"We did more than that." LeMaine jerked his thumb toward Nunn. "One of ours is injured. We need to evacuate her immediately."

Erias grinned at him. "That's why we're here. We brought these fighters for you."

"For us? What do you mean?"

"You take 'em. Take them to rejoin the fleet."

"We couldn't do that," LeMaine insisted. "How would you make it back to the base?"

"We'll double up." Erias glanced behind LeMaine. "Where's your man?"

"She's over here."

Five Iumians unloaded from the rest of the fighters. They followed LeMaine back to Nunn and carried her to Erais's ship.

Erias pulled down a folding berth behind the pilot's station and his people strapped Nunn to it. She kept looking around everywhere. "Captain!" she yelled in panic. "Captain LeMaine!"

"What's wrong with her?" Erias asked.

"She can't hear or see." LeMaine pressed her hand and patted her shoulder, but that only made her more agitated and desperate. She kept trying to fight her way out of the restraints. "We need to get her to a medic on the double."

"Go!" Erias signaled his people and they started to leave. "Monk and Buca can take two other fighters. The fleet is waiting for you in orbit. They've driven the Axichis off and the rest of the Hellhounds are on board the bomber *Lucidity*."

"Are you sure you want me to do this?" Monk asked. "I don't like taking one of your ships. You should keep it."

Erias laughed at him. "You Hellhounds are too noble for your own good. We brought them here for you." Erias shoved Monk and Buca toward the hatch. "Go! Command needs you."

Monk and Buca both glanced at LeMaine and he nodded. Erais came forward and gave LeMaine a hug. "I don't know how to thank you," LeMaine husked.

"Then don't. Just get out of here. You've done enough damage for one day."

He retreated and went to one of the other fighters. He and the two spare pilots loaded into different ships and launched. They hovered over Saevis until LeMaine, Monk, and Buca got airborne.

"Captain!" Nunn shrieked behind him. "Captain!"

"Don't you worry, darling," LeMaine told her even though he knew she couldn't hear him. "Just lie quiet. We're taking you home."

He launched and Erias's face appeared on his communications system. "You've got a clear shot to the *Lucidity*, Captain. Ride easy and give my regards to the rest of the squad."

"Thank you, son. I won't forget this."

Erais signed off as the Iumians blasted away across the landscape heading for the mountains.

"How's Nunn, Sir?" Buca asked.

"She needs Kellogg."

"Don't we all?" Monk muttered.

"You heard the man," LeMaine ordered. "Make tracks for the *Lucidity*."

"I'm picking up a homing beacon coming from Commander Lodge," Monk announced. "He's ordering us directly to the *Lucidity*."

"I'm reading it, Corporal. Oh, look at this. I'm getting orders to report to his ready room on the double."

Monk laughed. "No rest for the wicked, Sir."

"Does he plan to reprimand you for saving the whole system?" Buca asked.

"I guess I'll find out. I'm sending an emergency alert to the *Lucidity's* medical team. You Hellhounds stay with Nunn and make sure she gets to the medical bay ASAP."

"Yes, Sir," Monk replied. "She'll be in good hands with us."

LeMaine followed the homing beacon to the *Lucidity's* open flight deck. All three fighters landed and medics mobbed LeMaine's ship. They swarmed inside as soon as he opened the hatch and they surrounded Nunn all firing questions and orders at once.

Monk and Buca stood off to one side watching. They didn't have to do anything.

LeMaine fought his way outside. "See if you can find the rest of the Hellhounds. Tell them...." He trailed off.

"We'll tell them you're on your way to the firing squad," Monk replied.

LeMaine laughed. "It's been nice knowing you, Corporal."

Buca raised his eyebrows. "Will it really be that bad?"

"I don't know, but I better go see what Commander Lodge wants. See you boys later."

LeMaine headed off the flight deck and rode the *Lucidity's* internal elevator. The trip took long enough. He got a good look at the flurry of activity on every deck. The *Lucidity* crew scrambled to rearm, repair, and relaunch attack cruisers after engaging the Axichis in battle.

He passed the medical bay. Nearly every bed was already full. He would have liked to stick around and watch Nunn being brought in, but duty called.

He finally rode all the way to the top and exited on the Command deck. Officers went in and out of the bridge, conference rooms, and all the other Command posts all over the deck.

LeMaine made his way to the ready room and exploded in relieved laughter when Colonel Nicholson came toward him. The two men embraced and LeMaine had to fight his emotions under control. "You're alive, Sir! I was so worried."

"Not as worried as we were about you, Owen. Welcome back. You're a hero."

"Lulara was the hero. We're alive right now because of her."

Commander Lodge stepped forward and didn't even try to hide the tears in his eyes. "You made it! I knew you would."

LeMaine hugged his friend and then held him at arm's length. "Thank you, Russel. Thank you for my squad's lives."

"I told you I would bring the bombers as soon as possible."

"I shouldn't have doubted you. I'm sorry. You can demote me if you want to."

Colonel Nicholson burst out laughing. "You'd like that, wouldn't you? You'd like us to bust you down to private so someone else could run the Hellhounds. Then maybe you could retire to a desert island and get away from all this."

"No, Sir. I wouldn't want to leave the Hellhounds even if I was a private."

Colonel Nicholson's smile evaporated. "I'm glad you said that. We need you. We need you real bad."

"What's going on?" LeMaine glanced back and forth between his two superior officers. "What was so important that you needed me to report so soon?"

"We have another mission for you—a critical mission," Commander Lodge replied, "a mission we can't trust to anyone but the Hellhounds."

"What is it?" LeMaine asked.

Colonel Nicholson drew himself up to his full height and his expression turned deadly serious. "We're sending you and the Hellhounds behind enemy lines."

End of Book 1.

Keep Reading

H ellhounds Series: Book 2: Behind Enemy Lines

There's only one thing to do with the evil alien Axichis invasion taking over the Elian solar system—send in the Hellhounds. Going inside Axichis enemy lines puts the Hellhounds in position to hit the invaders where it counts, but the Hellhounds' best efforts might not make a difference in the overall invasion.

The invasion takes a turn for the worse when another neighboring alien population invades the Elian solar system. The Imoliv have always acted hostilely toward Elia. Could these new enemies be planning to cut Elia off at the knees now that the Axichis are weakening the defenders?

Everyone thought the Axichis were the Elians' allies, but they turned out to be enemies planning to stab Elia in the back. The Imoliv might appear to be Elia's enemies, but they might be Elia's greatest allies—especially now when the Imolive and the Elians have a common enemy.

You can find it at your favorite book retailer.

Sign Up Once--Get all Theo Mann's free books including brand new releases

S ign Up Once--Get all Theo Mann's free books including brand new releases

Humanity on the brink of annihilation.

A mysterious package, a corrupt officer, and a conspiracy that goes all the way to the top? What could possibly go wrong?

When a routine mission goes horribly wrong, Warrant Officer Ewing Archer and a handful of faithful friends get trapped in a battle to save the last survivors of Earth.

The human race has abandoned the ecological disaster of Earth. Now all that remains is a network of interconnected ships, stations, and satellites surrounding the planet.

But when war breaks out, Archer becomes a firebrand that could destroy it all....or save it.

Sign up at www.theomann.com to read it for free

About Theo Mann

I write 70 books per year—and yes, before you ask, all these books are my original creative work. Nothing written under my name is AI-generated or ghostwritten because I write better than AI and any ghostwriter out there.

People don't read fiction for entertainment or to escape from reality. People read fiction to see their humanity reflected in another person's character and story.

This is my promise to you. When you read my books, you'll see your own humanity reflected in the characters and stories. I take this commitment to my readers very seriously. My books are an intimate form of communication between us. I would never disrespect my readers by turning that over to a machine or another writer. This is my bond between me and you as my reader.

I write 20,000 words per day as my daily work output. If anyone with a public platform would like to challenge me to prove this in a controlled environment, feel free to contact me on this website's contact page.

I worked as a professional ghostwriter for fifteen years. Now I'm on a mission to set a Guinness World Record by writing 700 books over the next ten years and 1400 books over the next twenty years, all originally written by me. See my website for the full book list.

I'm also the author of *Proof for the Existence of God* and the *Crimes Against Fiction* blog. You can find all my nonfiction work at www.crimes-against-fiction.com.

If you have a story idea, or if you would like me to explore a series in more depth, or if you'd like me to explore a character by writing a spinoff series about that character or world, leave me a message on my website's contact page. I answer all reader emails, so ask me anything, tell me what you liked and didn't like, and let me know where you'd like your favorite series to go. I would love to hear your ideas and find out what you'd like to read next.

Find out more at www.theomann.com.

Also by Theo Mann (so far)